The Eyes of the Woods

A Story of the Ancient Wilderness

Joseph A. Altsheler

The Eyes of the Woods: A Story of the Ancient Wilderness

The present edition is a reproduction of previous publication of this classic work. Minor typographical errors may have been corrected without note, however, for an authentic reading experience the spelling, punctuation, and capitalization have been retained from the original text.

ISBN: 978-1-61895-785-6

FOREWORD

"The Eyes of the Woods" is an independent story, telling of certain remarkable events in the life of Henry Ware, Paul Cotter, Shif'less Sol Hyde, Silent Tom Ross and Long Jim Hart. But it is also a part of the series dealing with these characters, and is the fourth in point of time, coming just after "The Keepers of the Trail."

CONTENTS

CHAPTER I
THE FLIGHT

A strong wind swept over the great forest, sending green leaves and twigs in showers before it, and bringing clouds in battalions from the west. The air presently grew cold, and then heavy drops of rain came, pattering at first like shot, but soon settling into a hard and steady fall that made the day dark and chill, tingeing the whole wilderness with gloom and desolation.

The deer sought its covert, a buffalo, grazing in a little prairie, thrust its huge form into a thicket, the squirrel lay snug in its nest in the hollow of a tree, and the bird in the shelter of the foliage ceased to sing. The only sounds were those of the elements, and the world seemed to have returned to the primeval state that had endured for ages. It was the kingdom of fur, fin and feather, and, so far as the casual eye could have seen, man had not yet come.

But in the deep cleft of the cliff, from which coign of vantage they had fought off Shawnee and Miami, Henry Ware, Paul Cotter and Long Jim Hart sat snug, warm and dry, and looked out at the bitter storm. Near them a small fire burned, the smoke passing out at the entrance, and at the far end of the hollow much more wood was heaped. There were five beds of dry leaves with the blankets lying upon them, useful articles were stored in the niches of the stone, and jerked meat lay upon the natural shelves. It was a secret, but cheerful spot in that vast, wet and cold wilderness. Long Jim felt its comfort and security, as he rose, put another stick of wood on the fire, and then resumed his seat near the others.

"I'm sorry the storm came up so soon," said Henry. "Of course, Sol and Tom are hardened to all kinds of weather, but it's not pleasant to be caught in the woods at such a time."

"And our ammunition," said Paul. "It wouldn't hurt the lead, of course, but it would be a disaster for the powder to be soaked through and through. They'd have to go back to the settlements, and that would mean a long journey and a lot of lost time."

"I don't think we need be afraid about the powder," said Henry. "Whatever happens, Sol and Tom will protect it, even if their own bodies suffer."

"Then I'm thinkin' they'll have to do a lot of protectin'," said Long Jim. "The wind is blowin' plum' horizontal, an' the rain is sweepin' 'long in sheets."

Henry, despite his consoling words, was very anxious. Since their great battle with the invading Indian force and the destruction of the cannon, their supply of ammunition had run very low, and without powder and bullets they were lost in the wilderness. He walked to the narrow entrance of the cave, and, standing just where the rain could not reach him, looked out upon the cold and dripping forest, a splendid figure clothed in deerskin, specially adapted in both body and mind to wilderness life.

He saw nothing but the foliage bending before the wind and the chill sheets sent down by the clouds. The somber sky and the desolation would not have made him feel lonely, even had he been without his comrades. He had faced primeval nature too often and he knew it too well to be overcome or to be depressed by any of its dangers. Yet his heart would have leaped had he beheld the shiftless and the silent ones, making their way among the trees, the needed packs on their backs.

"Any sign, Henry?" asked Paul.

"None," replied the tall youth, "but they said they'd be here today."

Paul, who was lying on a great buffalo robe with his feet to the fire, shifted himself into an easier position. His face expressed content and he felt no anxiety about the traveling two.

"If Shif'less Sol promised to be here he'll keep his word," he said, "and Silent Tom will come without making any promises."

"You do talk won'erful well sometimes, Paul," said Long Jim, "an' I reckon you've put the facts jest right. I ain't goin' to be troubled in my mind a-tall, a-tall 'bout them fellers. They'll be here. Tom loves nice tender buffler steak best, an' I'm goin' to have it ready fur him, while Sol dotes most on fat juicy wild turkey, an' that'll be waitin' fur him, too."

He turned to his stores, and producing the delicacies his comrades loved began to fry them over the coals. The pleasant odors filled their rocky home.

"I give them two a half hour more," he said. "I ain't got any gift uv second sight. I don't look into the future—nobody does—but I jest figger on what they are an' what they kin do, an' then I feel shore that a half hour more is enough."

"Henry," asked Paul, "do you think the Miamis and the Shawnees will come back after us?"

"I reckon upon it," replied Henry, still watching the wet forest. "Red Eagle and Yellow Panther are shrewd and thoughtful chiefs, and Braxton Wyatt and Blackstaffe are full of cunning. They are all able to put two and two together, and they know that it was we who destroyed their cannon when they attempted the big attack on the settlements. They'll look upon us as the scouts and sentinels who see everything they do."

"The eyes of the woods," said Paul.

"Yes, that expresses it, and they'll feel that they're bound to destroy us. As soon as the warriors get over their panic they'll come back to put out the eyes that see too much of their deeds. They know, of course, that we hold this hollow and that we've made a home here for a while."

"But as they won't return for some time I mean to take my comfort while I can," said Paul sleepily. "I wouldn't exchange this buffalo robe, the leaves under it, the fire before my feet and the roof of rock over my head for the finest house in all the provinces. The power of contrast makes my present situation one of great luxury."

"Power uv contrast! You do use a heap uv big words, Paul," said Long Jim, "but I 'spose they're all right. Leastways I don't know they ain't. Now, I'm holdin' back this buffler steak an' wild turkey, 'cause I want 'em to be jest right, when Sol an' Tom set down afore the fire. See anythin' comin' through the woods, Henry?"

"No, Jim, nothing stirs there."

"It don't bother me. They'll 'pear in good time. They've a full ten minutes yet, an' thar dinners will be jest right fur 'em. I hate to brag on myself, but I shorely kin cook. Ain't we lucky fellers, Paul? It seems to me sometimes that Providence has done picked us out ez speshul favorites. Good fortune is plum' showered on us. We've got a snug holler like this, one uv the finest homes a man could live in, an' round us is a wilderness runnin' thousands uv miles, chock full uv game, waitin' to be hunted by us. Ev'ry time the savages think they've got us, an' it looks too ez ef they wuz right, we slip right out uv thar hands an' the scalps are still growin' full an' free, squar'ly on top uv our heads. We shorely do git away always, an' it 'pears to me, Paul, that we are 'bout the happiest an' most fort'nate people in the world."

Paul raised his head and looked at Jim, but it was evident to the lad that his long comrade was in dead earnest, and perhaps he was right. The lad shifted himself again and the light of the blaze flickered over his finely-chiseled, scholarly face. Long Jim glanced at him with understanding.

"Ef you had a book or two, Paul," he said, "you could stay here waitin' an' be happy. Sometimes I wish that I liked to read. What's in it, Paul, that kin chain you to one place an' make you content to be thar?"

3

"Because in the wink of an eye, Jim, it transports you to another world. You are in new lands, and with new people, seeing what they do and doing it with them. It gives your mind change, though your body may lie still. Do you see anything yet, Henry, besides the forest and the rain?"

"A black dot among the trees, Paul, but it's very small and very far, and it may be a bear that's wandered out in the wet. Besides, it's two dots that we want to see, not one, and—as sure as I live there are two, moving this way, though they're yet too distant for me to tell what they are."

"But since they're two, and they're coming towards us, they ought to be those whom we're expecting."

"Now they've moved into a space free of undergrowth and I see them more clearly. They're not bears, nor yet deer. They're living human beings like ourselves."

"Keep looking, Henry, and tell us whether you recognize 'em."

"The first is a tall man, young, with light hair. He is bent over a little because of the heavy pack on his back, and the long distance he has come, but he walks with a swing that I've seen before."

"I reckon," said Long Jim, "that he's close kin to that lazy critter, Shif'less Sol."

"Closer even than a twin brother," continued Henry. "I'd know him anywhere. The other just behind him, and bent also a little with his heavy pack, is amazingly like a friend of ours, an old comrade who talks little, but who does much."

"None other than Silent Tom," said Paul joyfully, as he rose and joined Henry at the door. "Yes, there they are, two men, staunch and true, and they bring the powder and lead. Of course they'd come on time! Nothing could stop 'em. The whole Shawnee and Miami nations might be in between, but they'd find a way through."

"An' the buffler steak an' the wild turkey are jest right," called Long Jim. "Tell 'em to come straight in an' set down to the table."

Henry, putting his fingers to his lips, uttered a long and cheerful whistle. The shiftless one and the silent one, raising their heads, made glad reply. They were soaked and tired, but success and journey's end lay just before them, and they advanced with brisker steps, to be greeted with strong clasps of the hand and a warm welcome. They entered the rocky home, put aside the big packs with sighs of relief and spread out their fingers to the grateful heat.

"That's the last work I mean to do fur a year," said Shif'less

4

Sol. "'Twuz a big job, a mighty big job fur me, a lazy man, an' now I'm goin' to rest fur months an' months, while Long Jim waits on me an' feeds me."

"Jest now I'm glad to do it, Sol," said Jim. "Take off your clothes, you an' Tom, hang 'em on the shelf thar to dry, an' now set to. The steaks an' the turkey are the finest I ever cooked, an' they're all fur you two. An' I kin tell you fellers that the sight uv you is good fur weak eyes."

Shif'less Sol and Silent Tom ate like epicures, while, denuded of their wet deerskins but wrapped in dry blankets, they basked in the heat.

"Not a drop of rain got at the powder," said the shiftless one presently, "an' even ef we don't capture any from the Injuns we ought to hev enough thar to last us many months."

"Did you see anything of the warriors?" asked Henry.

"We hit one trail 'bout fifty miles south uv here, but we didn't have time to foller it. Still, it's 'nough to show that they're in between us an' the settlements."

"We expected it. We discovered sufficient while you were gone to be sure they're going to make a great effort to end us. They look upon us as the eyes of the woods, and they've concluded that their first business is with us before they make another attack on our villages."

Shif'less Sol helped himself to a fresh piece of the wild turkey, and made another fold of the blanket about his athletic body.

"Paul hez talked so much 'bout them old Romans wrapped in their togys that I feel like one now," he said, "an' I kin tell you I feel pow'ful fine, too. That wuz a cold rain an' a wet rain, an' the fire an' the food are mighty good, but it tickles me even more to know how them renegades an' warriors rage ag'inst us. I've a heap o' respeck fur Red Eagle an' Yellow Panther, who are great chiefs an' who are fightin' fur thar rights ez they see 'em, but the madder Blackstaffe an' Wyatt git the better I like it."

"Me, too," said Silent Tom with emphasis, relapsing then into silence and his preoccupation with the buffalo steak. The shiftless one regarded him with a measuring gaze.

"Tom," he said, "why can't you let a feller finish his dinner without chatterin' furever? I see the day comin' when you'll talk us all plum' to death."

Silent Tom shook his head in dissent. He had exhausted speech.

Paul, who had remained at the door, watching, announced an

5

increase of rain and wind. Both were driving so hard that leaves and twigs were falling, and darkness as of twilight spread over the skies. The cold, although but temporary, was like that of early winter.

"We needn't expect any attack now," said Henry. "Join us, Paul, around the fire, and we'll have a grand council, because we must decide how we're going to meet the great man hunt they're organizing for us."

Paul left the cleft, and sat down on a doubled blanket with his back against the wall. He felt the full gravity of the crisis, knowing that hundreds of warriors would be put upon their trail, resolved never to leave the search until the five were destroyed, but he had full confidence in his comrades. In all the world there were not five others so fit to overcome the dangers of the woods, and so able to endure their hardships.

"I suppose, Henry," said Paul, with his mind full of ancient lore, "now that the Roman Senate, or its successor, is in session you are its presiding officer."

"If that's the wish of the rest of you," said Henry.

"It is!" they said all together.

Henry, like Paul, was sitting on his doubled blanket with his back against the stony wall. Jim Hart, his long legs crossed, occupied a similar position, and, by the flickering light of the fire, Shif'less Sol and Silent Tom, wrapped in their blankets, looked in truth like Roman senators.

"Will you tell us, Henry, what you found out while we wuz away?" asked the shiftless one. Henry had made a scouting expedition while the two were gone for the powder and lead.

"I made one journey across the Ohio," replied their chief, "and at night I went near a Shawnee village. Red Eagle was there, and so were Blackstaffe and Wyatt. Lying in the bushes near the fire by which they sat, I could catch enough of their talk to learn that the Shawnee and Miami nations are going to bend all their energies and powers to our destruction. That is settled."

"I feel a heap flattered," said Shif'less Sol, "that so many warriors should be sent ag'inst us, who are only five. What wuz it that old feller was always sayin', Paul, every time he held up a bunch o' fresh figs before the noses o' the Roman senators?"

"Delenda est Carthago, which is Latin, Sol, and it means just now, when I give it a liberal translation, that we five must be wiped clean off the face of the earth."

"I've heard you say often, Paul, that Latin was a dead language, an' so all them old dead sayin's won't hev any meanin' fur

6

us. I kin live long on the threats o' Braxton Wyatt an' Blackstaffe, an' so kin all o' us. But go on, Henry. I 'pologize fur interruptin' the presidin' officer."

"I learned all I could there," continued Henry, "but I was able to gather only their general intention, that is their resolve to crush us, a plan that both Wyatt and Blackstaffe urged. However, when I trailed a large band two days later, and crept near their camp, I discovered more."

"What wuz it?" exclaimed the shiftless one, leaning forward a little, his face showing tense and eager in the glow of the flames.

"They're going to spread a net for us. Not one body of warriors will seek us, but many. Red Eagle will lead a band, Yellow Panther will be at the head of another, Braxton Wyatt will be in charge of a third, Blackstaffe will take a fourth, and there will be at least seven or eight more, though some of them may unite later. Shif'less Sol has put it right. We'll be honored as men were never honored before in this wilderness. At least a thousand warriors, brave and skillful men, all, will be hunting us, two hundred to one and maybe more."

"And while they're hunting us," said Paul, his eyes glistening, "we'll draw 'em off from the settlements, and we'll be serving our people just as much as we did when we were destroying the big guns, and filling the warriors with superstitious alarm."

"True in every word," said Henry, his soul rising for the contest. "Let 'em come on and we'll lead 'em such a chase that their feet will be worn to the bone, and their minds will be full of despair!"

"You put it right," said the shiftless one. "I think I'll enjoy bein' a fox fur awhile. The forest is full o' holes an' dens, an' when they dig me out o' one I'll be off fur another."

"We know the wilderness as well as they do," said Henry, "and we can use as many tricks as they can. Now, since they're spreading a great net, we must take the proper steps to evade it. Having besieged our refuge here once, they'll naturally look again for us in this place. If they catch us inside they'll sit outside until they starve us to death."

"Which means," said Paul regretfully, "that we must leave our nice dry home."

"So it does, but not, I think, before tomorrow morning, and we'll use the hours meanwhile to good advantage. We must begin at once molding into bullets the lead that Sol and Tom brought."

Every one of the five carried with him that necessary implement in the wilderness, a bullet mold, and they began the task

7

immediately, all save Henry, who went outside, despite the fierce rain, and scouted a bit among the bushes and trees. The four made bullets fast, melting the lead in a ladle that Jim carried, pouring it into the molds, and then dropping the shining and deadly pellets one by one into their pouches. Three of them talked as they worked, but Silent Tom did not speak for a full hour. Then he said:

"We'll have five hundred apiece."

Shif'less Sol looked at him reprovingly.

"Tom," he said, "I predicted a while ago that the time wuz soon comin' when you'd talk us to death. You used five words then, when you know your 'lowance is only one an hour."

Tom Ross flushed under his tan. He hated, above all things, to be garrulous. "Sorry," he muttered, and continued his work with renewed energy and speed. The bullets seemed to drop in a shining stream from his mold into his pouch. But Shif'less Sol talked without ceasing, his pleasant chatter encouraging them, as music cheers troops for battle.

"It ain't right fur me to hev to work this way," he said, "me sich a lazy man. I ought to lay over thar on a blanket, an' go to sleep while Jim does my share ez well ez his own."

"When I'm doin' your share, Sol Hyde," said Long Jim, "you'll be dead. Not till then will I ever tech a finger to your work. You are a lazy man, ez you say, an' fur sev'ral years now I've been tryin' to cure you uv it, but I ain't made no progress that I kin see."

"I don't want you to make progress, Jim. I like to be lazy, an' jest now I feel pow'ful fine, fed well, an' layin' here, wrapped in a blanket before a good warm fire."

Henry went back to the cleft, and took another long look. The conditions had not changed, save that night was coming and the wilderness was chill and hostile. The wind blew with a steady shrieking sound, and the driving rain struck like sleet. Leaves fell before it, and in every depression of the earth the water stood in pools. Over this desolate scene the faint sun was sinking and the twilight, colder and more solemn than the day, was creeping. He looked at the wet forest and the coming dusk, and then back at the dry hollow and the warm fire behind him. The contrast was powerful, but only one choice was left to them.

"Boys," he said, "we'll have to make the most of tonight."

"Because we must leave our home in the morning?" said Paul.

"Yes, that's it. We'll have to take to the woods, no matter how hard it is. Chance doesn't favor us this time. I fancy the band led by Braxton Wyatt will make straight for our house here."

"Since it's the last dry bed I'll have fur some time I'm goin' to sleep," said Shif'less Sol plaintively. "Everybody pesters a lazy man, an' I mean to use the little time I hev."

"You've a right to it, Sol," said Henry, "because you've walked long and far, and you've brought what we needed most. The sooner you and Tom go to sleep the better. Paul, you join 'em and Jim and I will watch."

The shiftless one and the silent one turned on their sides, rested their heads on their arms and in a minute or two were off to the land of slumber. Paul was slower, but in a quarter of an hour or so he followed them to the same happy region. Long Jim put out the fire, lest the gleam of the coals through the cleft should betray their presence to a creeping enemy—although neither he nor Henry expected any danger at present—and took his place beside his watchful comrade.

The two did not talk, but in the long hours of rain and darkness they guarded the entrance. Their eyes became so used to the dusk that they could see far, but they saw nothing alive save, late in the night, a lumbering black bear, driven abroad and in the storm by some restless spirit. Long Jim watched the ungainly form, as it shambled out of sight into a thicket.

"A bad conscience, I reckon," he said. "That b'ar would be layin' snug in his den ef he didn't hev somethin' on his mind. He's ramblin' 'roun' in the rain an' cold, cause's he's done a wrong deed, an' can't sleep fur thinkin' uv it. Stole his pardner's berries an' roots, mebbe."

"Perhaps you're right, Jim," Henry said, "and animals may have consciences. We human beings are so conceited that we think we alone feel the difference between right and wrong."

"I know one thing, Henry, I know that b'ars an' panthers wouldn't leave thar own kind an' fight ag'inst thar own race, as Braxton Wyatt an' Blackstaffe do. That black b'ar we jest saw may feel sore an' bad, but he ain't goin' to lead no expedition uv strange animals ag'inst the other black b'ars."

"You're right, Jim."

"An' fur that reason, Henry, I respeck a decent honest black b'ar, even ef he is mad at hisself fur some leetle mistake, an' even ef he can't read an' write an' don't know a knife from a fork more than I do a renegade man who's huntin' the scalps uv them he ought to help."

"Well spoken, Jim. Your sense of right and wrong is correct nearly always. Like you, I've a lot of respect for the black bear, and

9

also for the deer and the buffalo and the panther and the other people of the woods. Do you think the rain is dying somewhat?"

"'Pears so to me. It may stop by day an' give us a chance to leave without a soakin'."

They relapsed again into a long silence, but they saw that their hope was coming true. The wind was sinking, its shriek shrinking to a whisper and then to a sigh. The rain ceased to beat so hard, coming by and by only in fitful showers, while rays of moonlight, faint at first, began to appear in the western sky. In another half hour the last shower came and passed, but the forest was still heavy with dripping waters. Henry, nevertheless, knew that it was time to go, and he awakened the sleepers.

"We must make up our packs," he said.

The five worked with speed and skill. All the lead, newly brought, had been molded into bullets, and the powder, save that in their horns, was carried in bags. This, with the blankets and portions of food, constituted most of their packs. Some furs and skins they left to those who might come, and then they slipped from the warm hollow, which had furnished such a grateful shelter to them.

"It's just as well," said Henry, "that we should let 'em think we're still in there. Then they may waste a day or two in approaching, so hide your footprints."

The earth was soft from the rain, but the stony outcrop ran a long distance, and they walked on it cautiously so far as it went, after which they continued on the fallen trunks and brush, with which the forest had been littered by the winds of countless years. They were able, without once touching foot to ground, to reach a brook, into which they stepped, following its course at least two miles. When they emerged at last they sat down on stones and let the water run from their moccasins and leggings.

"I don't like getting wet, this way," said Henry, "but there was no choice. At least, we know we've come a great distance and have left no trail. There'll be no chance to surprise us now. How long would you say it is till day, Sol?"

"'Bout two hours," replied the shiftless one, "an' I 'spose we might ez well stay here a while. We're south o' the hollow an' Wyatt an' his band are purty shore to come out o' the north. The woods are mighty wet, but the day is goin' to be without rain, an' a good sun will dry things fast. What we want is to git a new home fur a day or two, in some deep thicket."

They began to search and presently found a dense tangle, with several large trees growing near the center of it, the trunk of one of them hollowed out by time. In the opening they put their bags of powder, part of their bullets and other supplies, and then, wrapped in their blankets, sat down in the brush before it.

"Now, Henry," said Shif'less Sol, "it's shore that we ain't goin' to be besieged, though our empty holler may be, an' that bein' the case, an' the trouble bein' passed fur the moment, you an' Jim, who watched most o' the night, go to sleep, an' Tom an' Paul too might take up thar naps whar they left 'em off. I'll do the watchin', an' I'll take a kind o' pride in doin' it all by myself."

The others made no protest, but, leaning their backs against the tree trunks, soon fell asleep, while the shiftless one, rifle under his arm, went to the edge of the canebrake, and began his patrol. He bore little resemblance to a lazy man now. He was, next to Henry, the greatest forest runner of the five, a marvel of skill, endurance and perception, with a mighty heart beating beneath his deerskins, and an intellect of wonderful native power, reasoning and drawing deductions under his thatch of blonde hair.

Shif'less Sol listened to the drip, drip of water from the wet boughs and leaves, and he watched a great sun, red and warm, creep slowly over the eastern hills. He was not uncomfortable, nor was he afraid of anything, but he was angry. He remembered with regret the pleasant hollow, so dry and snug. It belonged, by right of discovery and improvement, to his comrades and himself, but it might soon be defiled by the presence of Indians, led by the hated renegade, Braxton Wyatt. They would sleep on his favorite bed of leaves, they would cook where Long Jim Hart had cooked so well, though they could never equal him, and they would certainly take as their own the furs and skins they had been compelled to leave behind.

The more he thought of it the stronger his wrath grew. Had it not been for his fear of leaving a betraying trail he would have gone back to see if the warriors were already approaching the hollow; but his sense of duty and obvious necessity kept him at the edge of the brake in which his comrades lay, deep in happy slumber.

Morning advanced, warm and beautiful, sprinkling the world at first with silver and then with gold, the sky gradually turning to a deep velvety blue, as intense as any that the shiftless one had ever seen. The myriads of raindrops stood out at first like silver beads on grass and leaves, and then dried up rapidly under the brilliant rays of the sun. A light breeze blew through the foliage, and sang a pleasant song as it blew.

Shif'less Sol felt a wonderful uplift of the spirits. In the

11

darkness and rain of the night before he might have been depressed somewhat at leaving their good shelter for the wet wilderness, but in the splendid dawn he was all buoyancy and confidence.

"Let 'em come," he said to himself. "Let Braxton Wyatt an' Blackstaffe an' all the Miamis an' Shawnees hunt us fur a year, but they won't get us, no, not one of us."

Then he sank silently in the deep grass and slid cautiously away, not toward the dense brake, but to a point well to one side. His acute ear had heard a sound which was not a part of the morning, and while it might be made by a wild animal, then again it might be caused by wilder man. He thanked his wary soul, when, looking above the tops of the grass, he saw two warriors, Shawnees by their paint, emerge from the woods and walk northward, to be followed presently by a full score more, Braxton Wyatt himself at their head.

And so the band had come out of the south, instead of the north! Doubtless they had circled about before approaching, in order to make the surprise complete, and the trigger drew the finger of the shiftless one like a magnet, as he looked at the renegade, the most ruthless hunter among those who hunted the five. Although the temptation to do so was strong, Shif'less Sol did not fire, knowing that his bullet would draw the attack of the band upon his comrades and himself. Instead, he followed them cautiously about half a mile.

He was confirmed in his opinion—in truth, little short of certainty in the first instance—that they were marching against the hollow, and its supposed inmates, as presently they began to advance with extreme care, kneeling down in the undergrowth and sending out flankers. Shif'less Sol laughed. It was a low laugh, but deep, and full of unction. He knew that the farther march of Wyatt and his warriors would be very slow, having in mind the deadly rifles of the five, the muzzles of which they would feel sure were projecting from the mouth of the rocky retreat. It was likely that the entire morning would be spent in an enveloping movement, dusky figures creeping forward inch by inch in a semi-circle, and then nothing would be inside the semi-circle.

Shif'less Sol laughed to himself again, and with the same deep and heartfelt unction. Then he turned and went back to his comrades, who yet slept soundly in the brake. The cane was so dense that they lay in the dimness of the shadows, and there was no disturbing light upon their eyes to awaken them. Shif'less Sol contemplated them with satisfaction, and then he sat down silently near them. He saw no reason to awaken them. Braxton Wyatt was now formally arranging the siege of the rocky refuge and its vanished defenders, and he would not interrupt him for worlds in that congenial task. For the third time he laughed to himself with depth and unction.

The sun rose higher in a sky that arched in its perfect blue over a day of dazzling beauty. The last drop of rain on leaf or grass dried up, and the forest was a deep green, suffused and tinted, though, with a luminous golden glow from the splendid sun. The shiftless one raised his head and inhaled its clear, sweet odors, the great heart under the deerskins and the great brain under the thatch of hair alike sending forth a challenge. Not all the Shawnees, not all the Miamis, not all the renegades could drive the five from this mighty, unoccupied wilderness of Kain-tuck-ee, which his comrades and he loved and in which they had as good a right as any Indian or renegade that ever lived.

It was so still in the canebrake that the birds over the head of the watcher began to sing. Another black bear lumbered toward them, and, catching the strange, human odor, lumbered away again. A deer, a tall buck, holding up his head, sniffed the air, and then ran. Wild turkeys in a distant tree gobbled, a bald eagle clove the air on swift wing, but the sleepers slept placidly on.

CHAPTER II
THE GREAT JOKE

Mid-morning and Henry awoke, yawning a little and stretching himself mightily. Then he looked questioningly at Shif'less Sol who sat in a position of great luxury with his doubled blanket between his back and a tree trunk, and his rifle across his knees. The look of satisfaction that had come there in the morning like a noon glow still overspread his tanned and benevolent countenance.

"Well, Sol?"

"Well, Henry?"

"What has happened while we slept?"

"Nothin', 'cept that Braxton Wyatt an' twenty Shawnee warriors passed, takin' no more notice o' us than ef we wuz leaves o' the forest."

"Advancing on our old house?"

"Yes, they've set the siege by now."

"And we're not there. I'll wake the others. They must share in the joke."

Paul, Long Jim and Silent Tom wiped the last wisp of sleep from their eyes, and, when they heard the tale of a night and a morning, they too laughed to themselves with keen enjoyment.

"What will we do, Henry?" Paul asked.

"First, we'll eat breakfast, though it's late. Then we'll besiege the besiegers. While they're drawing the net which doesn't enclose us we might as well do 'em all the harm we can. We're going to be dangerous fugitives."

The five laughed in unison.

"We'll make Braxton Wyatt and the Shawnees think the forest is full of enemies," said Paul.

Meanwhile they took their ease, and ate breakfast of wild turkey, buffalo steak and a little corn bread that they hoarded jealously. The sun continued its slow climb toward the zenith and Paul, looking up through the canes, thought he had never seen a finer day. Then he remembered something.

"I suggest that we don't move today," he said. "They won't approach the hollow until night anyway, and it wouldn't hurt for us to lie here in the shelter of the brake and rest until dark."

14

Henry looked at him in surprise.

"Your idea is sudden and I don't understand it," he said.

"So it is, Henry, but it never occurred to me until a moment ago that this was Sunday. We haven't observed Sunday in a long time, and now is our chance. We can't wholly forget our training."

He spoke almost with apology, but the leader did not upbraid him. Instead, he looked at the others and found agreement in their eyes.

"Paul talks in a cur'ous manner an' has cur'ous notions sometimes," said Shif'less Sol, "but I don't say they ain't good. It's a long time since we've paid any 'tention to Sunday, but the idee sticks in my mind. Mebbe it would be a good way fur us to start our big fight ag'inst the tribes an' the renegades."

"When Cromwell and his Ironsides advanced against the Royalists," said Paul, "they knelt down and prayed first on the very field of battle. Then they advanced with their pikes in a solid line, and nothing was ever able to stand before them."

"Then we'll keep Sunday," said Henry decisively.

Paul, feeling a thrill of satisfaction, lay back on his blanket. The idea that they should observe Sunday, that it would be a good omen and beginning, had taken hold of him with singular power. His character was devout and a life in the wilderness among its mighty manifestations deepened its quality. Like the Indian he wanted the spirits of earth and air on his side.

The five had acquired the power of silence and to rest intensely when nothing was to be done. Their food finished, they lay back against their doubled blankets in a calm and peace that was deep and enduring. It was not necessary to go to the edge of the canebrake, as in the brilliant light of the day they might be noticed there, and, where they lay, they could see anyone who came long before he arrived.

Paul, as he breathed, absorbed belief and confidence in their success. Surely so bright a sky bending over them was a good omen! and the tall canes themselves, as they bent before the wind, whispered to him that all would be well. Henry in his own way was no less imaginative than his young comrade. He let his eyelids droop, not to sleep, but to listen. Then as no one of the five stirred, he too heard the voice of the wind, but it sang to him a song far more clear than any Paul heard. It told of triumphs achieved and others yet to come, and, as the great youth lifted his lazy lids and looked around at the others, he felt that they were equal to any task.

The afternoon, keeping all its promise of brilliant beauty,

waxed and waned. The great sun dipped behind the forest. The twilight came, at first a silver veil, then a robe of dusk, and after it a night luminous with a clear moon and myriads of stars wrapped the earth, touching every leaf and blade of grass with a white glow.

Still the five did not stir. For a long time they had seemed a part of the forest itself, and the wild animals and birds, rejoicing in the dry and beautiful night after the stormy one that had passed, took them to be such, growing uncommonly brave. The restless black bear came back, looked at them, and then sniffing disdainfully went away to hunt for roots. The great wings of the eagle almost brushed the cane that hung over Henry's head, but the little red eyes were satisfied that what they saw was not living, and the dark body flashed on in search of its prey.

"Three hours more at least, Paul," said Henry at last, "until Sunday is over."

"And I suggest that we wait the full three hours before we make any movement. I know it looks foolish in me to say it, but the feeling is very strong on me that it will be a good thing to do."

"Not foolish at all, Paul. I look at it just as you do, and since we've begun the observance we ought to carry it through to the finish. You agree with me, don't you, boys?"

"I shorely do," said the shiftless one.

"Ef Paul thinks it's right it's right," said Long Jim.

"Can't hurt anythin'; it may help," said Silent Tom.

They resumed their silence and waiting, and meanwhile they listened attentively for any sound that might come from those who were stalking their old home. But the deep stillness continued, save for the light song of the wind that sang continually among the leaves. Henry, in his heart, was truly glad of Paul's idea, and that they had concluded to observe it. A spiritual atmosphere clothed them all. They had come of religious parents, and the borderer, moreover, always personified the great forces of nature, before which he was reverential. The five now were like the Romans and the Greeks, who were anxious to propitiate the gods ere going into action.

Henry gazed at the moon, a silver globe in the heavens, and he distinctly saw the man upon its surface, who returned his looks with benevolence, while the countless stars about it quivered and glittered and shed a propitious light. Then he gazed at his comrades, resting against the trunks of the trees, and unreal in the silver mist. They were yet so still that the wild animals might well take them to be lifeless, and the power to sit there so long without stirring a muscle was one acquired only by warriors and scouts.

16

A faint whining cry came out of the silver dark, a sound that had traveled a great distance on waves of air, and every one of the five understood it, on the instant. It was one of the most ominous sounds of the forest, a sound full of ferocity and menace, the howl of the wolf, but they knew it came from human lips, that, in truth, it was a signal ordered by the leader of the besieging band. Presently the reply, a similar cry, came from another point of the compass, traveling like the first on waves of air, until it died away in a savage undernote.

"They've probably set their lines all the way around our hollow, and they're sure now they'll hold us fast," said Henry, with grim irony.

"That's 'bout it, I take it," said Shif'less Sol, "an' it 'pears to me that this is the time for us to laugh, purvidin' it won't be in any way breakin' uv our agreement to keep the day till its very last minute."

He looked questioningly at Paul.

"To laugh is not against our compact," replied the lad, "since it has such good cause. When a net is cast for us, and those who cast it are so confident we're in it, we've a right to laugh as long as we're outside it."

"Then," said Shif'less Sol with conviction, "ez thar's so much to laugh at, an' we've all agreed to laugh, we'll laugh."

The five accordingly laughed, but the laughs were soundless. Their eyes twinkled, their lips twitched, but the canebrake, save for the ceaseless rustle of the singing wind, was as silent as ever. No one five feet away would have known that anybody was laughing.

"Thar, I feel better," said Shif'less Sol, when his face quit moving, "but though they're a long distance off I kin see with my mind's eyes Braxton Wyatt an' his band stalkin' us in our home in the rock, an' claspin' us in a grip that can't be shook off."

"Shettin' down on us," said Silent Tom.

The shiftless one bent upon him a reproving look.

"Thar you are, Tom!" he said, "talkin' 'us to death ag'in. Can't you ever give your tongue no rest?"

Silent Tom blushed once more under his tan, but said nothing, abashed by his comrade's stern rebuke.

"Yes, I kin see Braxton Wyatt an' his band stalkin' us," resumed Shif'less Sol, having the floor, or rather the earth, again to himself. "Braxton's heart is full o' unholy glee. He is sayin' to hisself that we can't git away from him this time, that he's stretched 'bout us a ring, through which we'll never break. He's laughin' to hisself jest az we laugh to ourselves, though with less cause. He's sayin' that

17

he an' his warriors will set down at a safe distance from our rifles an' wait patiently till we starve to death or give up an' trust ourselves to his tender mercy. He's braggin' to hisself 'bout his patience, how he kin set thar fur a month, ef it's needed, an' I kin read his mind. He's thinkin' that even ef we give up it won't make no diff'unce. Our scalps will hang up to dry jest the same, an' he will take most joy in lookin' at yours, Henry, your ha'r is so fine an' so thick an' so yellow, an' he hez such a pizen hate o' you."

"Your fancy is surely alive tonight, Sol," said Henry, "and I believe the thought of Braxton Wyatt's disappointment later on is what has stirred it up so much."

"I 'low you're right, Henry, but I'm thinkin' 'bout the grief o' that villain, Blackstaffe, too. Oh, he'll be a terrible sorrowful man when the net's closed, an' he finds thar's nothin' in it. It will be the great big disappointment o' his life an' I 'low it will be some time afore Moses Blackstaffe kin recover from the blow."

The silent laugh again overspread the countenance of the shiftless one and lingered there. It was one of the happiest moments that he had ever known. There was no malice in his nature, but he knew the renegades were hunting for his life with a vindictiveness and cruelty surpassing that of the Indians themselves, and he would not have been true to human nature had he not obeyed the temptation to rejoice.

"A half hour more and Sunday will have passed," said Henry, who was again attentively surveying the man in the moon.

"An' then," said Long Jim, "we'll take a look at what them fellers are doin'."

"It will be a good move on our part, and if we can think of any device to make 'em sure we're still in the hollow it will help still more."

"Which means," said Paul, "that one of us must pass through their lines and fire upon them from the inside, that is, he must give concrete proof that he's in the net."

"Big words!" muttered Long Jim.

"I think you put it about right," said Henry.

"Mighty dang'rous," said Shif'less Sol.

"I expected to undertake it," said Henry.

"You speak too quick," said the shiftless one. "I said it wuz dang'rous 'cause I want it fur myself. It's got to be a cunnin' sort o' deed, jest the kind that will suit me."

"By agreement I'm the leader, and I've chosen this duty for myself," said Henry firmly.

"Thar are times when I don't like you a-tall, a-tall, Henry," said Shif'less Sol plaintively. "You're always pickin' out the good risky adventures fur yourse'f. Ef thar's any fine, lively thing that will make a feller's ha'r stan' up straight on end an' the chills chase one another up an' down his back, you're sure to grab it off, an' say it wuz jest intended fur you. That ain't the right way to treat the rest o' us nohow."

"No, it ain't," grumbled Silent Tom, but Shif'less Sol turned fiercely on him.

"Beginnin' to talk us to death ag'in, are you, Tom Ross?" he exclaimed. "Runnin' on forever with that garrylous tongue o' yourn! You jest let me have this out with Henry!"

Again Tom Ross blushed in the darkness and under the tan. A terrible fear seized him that he had indeed grown garrulous, a man of many and empty words. It was all right for Shif'less Sol to talk on forever, because the words flowed from his lips in a liquid stream, like water coursing down a smooth channel, but it did not become Tom Ross, from whom sentences were wrenched as one would extract a tooth. Paul laughed softly but with intense enjoyment.

"When I die, seventy or eighty years from now," he said, "and go to Heaven, I expect, when I pass through the golden gates, to hear a steady and loud but pleasant buzz. It will go on and on, without ceasing. Maybe it will be the droning of bees, but it won't be. Maybe it will be the roar of water over a fall, but it won't be. Maybe it will be a strong wind among the boughs, but it won't be. Oh, no, it will be none of those things. It will be one Solomon Hyde, formerly of Kentucky, and they'll tell me that his tongue has never stopped since he came to Heaven ten years before, and off in one corner there'll be a silent individual, Tom Ross, who entered Heaven at the same time. And they'll say that in all the ten years he has spoken only once and that was when he passed the gates, looked all around and said: 'Good, but not much better than the Ohio Country.'"

Both Shif'less Sol and Silent Tom grinned, but the discussion was not pursued, as Henry announced that he was about to leave them in order to enter the Indian ring, and make Wyatt and the warriors think the rocky hollow was defended.

"The rest of you would better stay in the canebrakes or the thickets," he said.

"We won't go so fur away that we can't hear any signal you may make," said Long Jim Hart. "Give us the cry uv the wolf. Thar are lots uv wolves in these woods, Injun an' other kinds, but we know yourn from the rest, Henry."

19

"And don't take too big risks," said Paul.

"I won't," said Henry, and he quickly vanished from their sight among the bushes. Two hundred yards away, and he stopped, but he could not hear them moving. Nor had he expected that any sound would come from them to him, knowing that they would lie wholly still for a long time, awaiting his passage through the Indian lines.

The heart of the great youth swelled within him. As truly a son of the wilderness as primitive man had been thousands of years ago, before civilization had begun, when he depended upon the acuteness of his senses to protect him from monstrous wild beasts, he was as much at home now as the ordinary man felt in city streets, and he faced his great task not only without apprehension, but with a certain delight. He had the Indian's cunning and the white man's intellect as well, and he was eager to match wits and cunning against those of the warriors.

He would have been glad had the night turned a little darker, but the full burnished moon and showers of stars gave no promise of it, and he must rely upon his own judgment to seek the shadows, and to pass where they lay thickest. The forest, spread about him, was magnificent with oak and beech and elm of great size, but the moonlight and the starshine shone between the trunks, and moving objects would have been almost as conspicuous there as in the day. Hence he sought the brushwood, and advancing swiftly in its shelter, he approached the place that had been such a comfortable home for the five, but which they had thought it wise to abandon. A whimsical fancy, a desire to repay them for the evil they were doing, seized him. He would not only draw the warriors on, but he would annoy and tantalize them. He would make them think the evil spirits were having sport with them.

A half mile, and he sank to the earth, lying so still that anyone a yard away could not have heard him breathe. Two warriors stood under the boughs of an oak and they were looking in the direction of the hollow. He had no doubt they were watchers, posted there to prevent the flight of the besieged in that direction, and he was shaken with silent laughter at this spectacle of men who stood guard that none might pass, when there was none to pass. He was already having his revenge upon them for the trouble they were causing and he felt that the task of repayment was beginning well.

The two Shawnees walked back and forth a little, searching everything with their questing eyes, but they did not speak. Presently they turned somewhat to one side, and Henry, still using the shelter of the brushwood, flitted silently past them. Three or four hundred yards farther and he lay down, laughing again to himself. It had been ridiculously easy. All his wild instincts were alive and leaping, and his senses became preternaturally acute. He heard some tiny animals of the cat tribe, alarmed by his presence, stealing away among the bushes, and the sound of an owl moving ever so slightly in the thick leaves on a bough came to his ears. But he was so still that the owl became still too, and did not know when he arose and moved on.

Henry believed that the two warriors were merely guards on the outer rim and that soon he would encounter more, a belief verified within ten minutes. Then he heard talking and saw Braxton Wyatt himself and three Shawnees, one a very large man who seemed to be second in command. Lying at his ease and in a good covert he watched them, laughing again and again to himself. For such as he this was, in truth, fine sport, and he enjoyed it to the utmost. Wyatt was looking toward the point where the cliffs that contained the rocky hollow showed dimly in the silver haze. His face expressed neither triumph nor confidence, and Henry, seeing that he was troubled, enjoyed it.

"I wish we knew how well they are provided with food and ammunition," he heard him say.

"They will have plenty," the big warrior said. "The mighty young chief, Ware, will see to it."

Henry felt a thrill at the words. The Shawnee was paying a tribute to him, and he could not keep from hearing it.

"They beat us off before," said Wyatt gloomily. "We had them trapped in the hollow, but we could not carry it."

"But this time," said the warrior, "we will sit down before it, and wait until they come out, trembling with weakness and begging us to give them food that they may keep the life in their bodies."

"It will be a sight to make my eyes and heart rejoice," said Braxton Wyatt.

The hammer and trigger of Henry's rifle were a powerful magnet for his hand. The young renegade's voice expressed so much revenge and malice, so much accumulated poison that the world would be a much better place without him. Then why not rid it of his presence? He stood there outlined sharp and clear in the silver dusk, and a marksman, such as Henry, could not miss. But his will restrained the eager fingers. It was not wise now, nor could he shoot even a renegade from ambush. Using the extremest caution, lest the moving of a leaf or a blade of grass betray his presence, he passed on, and now he was sure that he was well within the Indian ring.

Advancing more rapidly he ascended the slope, and came to the hollow, which he reached while yet under cover. He waited a long time to see whether Wyatt had posted any sentinels within eyeshot or earshot, as he had no desire to be trapped inside, and then, feeling sure that they were not near, he entered.

Their home was undisturbed. The dead ashes of their last fire lay untouched. Various articles that they could not take with them were undisturbed on the rocky shelves. But he gave the interior only a few rapid and questing looks, and then he went outside again, his mind set on a dense clump of bushes that grew near the entrance.

He buried himself in the heavy shade, but he did not seek it alone because of shelter. He saw that a good line of retreat led from it over the shoulder of the hill, and then down a slope that admitted good speed. Having made sure of his ground, he filled his lungs and sent forth the cry of the wolf, long and sinister and full of a power that carried far over the forest. He knew that the listening four would hear it, and he knew, too, that it would reach the ears of Braxton Wyatt and all the Shawnees. And hearing it, they would be absolutely sure that the five were now in the hollow where they might be held until they dropped dead of hunger or yielded themselves to the mercy of those who knew no mercy.

Fierce, triumphant yells came from all the points of the circle about him, and once more and with deep content Henry laughed. He would fool them, he would play with them, and meanwhile his comrades, to keep the sport going, might sting them on the flank. After the yells, the night resumed its usual silence, and Henry, lying in his covert, watched on all sides, while he laid his plans to vex and torment Braxton Wyatt and his band. He knew it was an easy matter for his comrades and himself to escape this particular expedition sent against them, but it was likely that they would encounter other and larger forces farther south, and he wished the battlefield, if it shifted at all, to shift northward. Hence he intended to hold Wyatt there as long as possible.

After a while, he was sure that he saw the tops of some bushes moving in a direction not with the wind, and he was equally sure that Shawnees were coming forward. Nearly half an hour passed and then a bead of fire appeared as a rifle was discharged, and the shot had an uncommonly loud sound in the clear, noiseless night. He heard, too, the click of the bullet as it struck against the stone near the mouth of the hollow, and once more he laughed. It was an amusing night for him. The warriors, now that they had crept within range, would be sure to sprinkle the stone around the cleft with bullets, and lead was too precious in the wilderness to be wasted.

He flattened himself upon the earth, merely keeping his rifle thrust forward for an emergency, and he blended so perfectly with grass and foliage that not even the keen eyes of Shawnees ten feet away could have detected him. A second shot was fired, and he heard the bullet clipping leaves not far away; a third followed and then a volley, all of the bullets striking at some point near the entrance. The volley was followed by a long and fierce war whoop and far down the valley Henry caught sight of a dusky form. Quick as lightning he raised his rifle, pulled the trigger and the figure disappeared. Then another war whoop, now expressing grief and rage, came, and he knew that the band would think the bullet had been sent from the mouth of the rock fortress. He crept a little farther away, lest a stalker should stumble upon him, and reloaded his rifle.

He lay quite still a long time, and the first sound he heard was of slow and cautious footsteps. He listened to them attentively and he wondered. A warrior surely would not come walking in a manner that soon became shambling. Putting his ear to the earth he heard a soft and uncertain crush, crush, and then, raising his head a little, he traced a dark, ambiguous figure. But he knew it, nevertheless, by the two red eyes blinking in doubt and dismay. It was a black bear, doubtless the same one they had already disturbed.

Here he was, like Henry himself, within the Shawnee ring, but, unlike him, not there of his own free will. The shots and the war whoops had terrified him to the utmost, and they had always driven him back toward the center of the circle. Henry, moved by a spirit that was as much friendliness as sport, uttered a low woof. The bear paused, raised his head a little higher, and inhaled the wind. At any other time he would have fled in dismay from the human odor, but he was a harried and frightened black bear and that woof was the first friendly sound he had heard in a day. So he remained where he was, his figure crouched, his red eyes quivering with curiosity. Henry smiled to himself. His feeling for the animal was one of pure friendship, allied with sympathy. He knew that if the bear tried to plunge through the Indian ring in his panic they would certainly kill him. Moreover, they would cook him and eat him the next day. The Indians liked fat young bear better than venison.

It was a whimsical impulse of his generous nature to try to save the bear, and he edged around until the puzzled animal was between him and the mouth of the cave. The bear once started to run to the west, but a rifle shot fired suddenly in that segment of the circle stopped him. He remained again undecided, his tongue lolling out and his red eyes full of dismay. Henry crept slowly toward him, uttering the low woof, woof, several times, and bruin, disturbed in his mind and unable to judge between friends and enemies, edged away as slowly, until his back was almost at the mouth of the hollow. Then, with all the possibilities against such a combination of chances, it occurred nevertheless. A louder woof than usual from him was followed almost instantly by a Shawnee rifle shot, and the frightened bear, giving back, almost fell into the crevice. Then whirling, and seeing a refuge before him, he darted inside.

Henry, retreating into the dense bushes, flattened himself in the grass, and laughed once more. He had laughed many times that night, but now his mirth had a fresh savor. The bear and not the Indians had become the new occupant of their old home, and, despite the fact that it had been so recently a human habitation, he felt quite sure the animal, owing to his terror and the confusion of his ideas, would remain there until morning at least. The Shawnees would exert all their patience and skill in the siege of one bear that lived chiefly on roots, the greatest crime of which was to rob bees of their stored honey.

He raised himself until he could see the mouth of the cave, but all was still and dark there. Evidently the bear was at home and was using all available comforts. He would not come out to face the terror of the shots and of human faces. Henry could imagine him with his head almost hidden in one of their beds of leaves, and gradually acquiring confidence because danger was no longer before his eyes.

His whimsical little impulse having met with complete success he lay in his shroud of bushes and intense enjoyment thrilled through every vein. He had not known a happier night. All his primitive instincts were gratified. The hunted was having sport with the hunters, and it was rare sport too.

The mournful howl of a wolf came faintly from the northern rim of the forest. It made Henry start and wonder a little. He thought at first the cry had been sent forth by Silent Tom or Shif'less Sol, but as it was inside the Indian circle he concluded it must have been made by one of the warriors. But he changed his mind again, when the long, whining cry was repeated. His hearing was not less acute than his sight, able to differentiate between the finest shades of sound, and he felt sure now that the howl of a wolf was made by a wolf itself, the real genuine article in howls, true to the wilderness. When several more of the uneasy whines came doubt was left no longer. The Indian ring that had enclosed the rocky hollow and the black bear had also enclosed an entire pack of wolves. It complicated the situation, but for Wyatt and his band, not for Henry, and once more the spontaneous laugh bubbled up from his throat.

He inferred now that he had not seen all of the Indian force. There were probably other detachments to the west and north that had been drawn in to complete the ring, but he did not care how many they might be. The more they were the greater their troubles. A soft pad, pad in the thicket roused him to the keenest attention. Some larger animal was approaching him, unaware of his presence, the wind blowing in the wrong direction. But the wind came right for Henry and soon he discovered a strong feline odor. He knew that it was a panther, and presently he saw it in the moonlight, yellowish and monstrous, the hugest beast of its kind that he had ever beheld.

But the panther, despite its size and strength, would run away from man, and Henry understood. The Indian ring had closed about it too, and, frightened, it was seeking refuge. Powerful, clawed and toothed for battle, it would not fight unless it was driven into a corner, and then it would fight with ferocity. Henry reflected philosophically that the net might miss the particular fish for which it was cast and yet catch others. If the Indians closed in they had the panther and the black bear and perhaps the pack of wolves too. What would they do with them? His irrepressible mirth bubbled up. It was their problem, not his.

Resolved not to intervene again in these delicate affairs, he crouched as closely as he could to the earth, wishing the panther neither to see nor to hear him, but curious himself to know what it would do. The beast stalked out into the open, and it was magnified greatly by the luminous quality of the moonlight. It looked like one of its primitive ancestors in the far dawn of time, when man fought for his life with the stone axe. But the panther was afraid. The howls of the wolf, both the real and the false, frightened him. His instinct too told him that he was walled around by beings that could slay at a distance, and, within a certain area, he was a prisoner. He was sorely troubled and his great body trembled with nervous quivers. The wolf pack howled again, and he must have found something more alarming than ever in it, as he sheered off to one side, and his tawny eyes caught a glimpse of a black opening that almost certainly led to a magnificent den and refuge.

But the panther was cautious. He lived a life in which the foresight that comes from experience was compelled to play a great part. He did not dive directly for the cleft, and he might not have gone in at all, had not a sudden shift in the wind brought to him the human odor that came from the body lying so near in the bushes. Driven by his impulse he turned away and then sprang straight into the hollow.

Henry had not expected this sudden movement on the part of the panther, and he rose to his knees to see what would happen. A terrible growling and snarling and the shuffling of heavy bodies came instantly from the dusky interior. A moment or two later the panther bounded out, a huge ball of yellowish fur, in which two frightened and angry red eyes glared. Henry saw several streaks of blood on him and he stared at the animal, amazed. He did not know that a black bear could make such a fight against a powerful feline brute, but evidently, wild with terror, he had used all his claws and teeth at once. The panther caught sight of Henry looking at him, and, uttering a scream or two, bounded into the bushes. In the cave, the bear remained silent and triumphant.

"What will happen next?" said Henry to himself.

The howl of the wolf pack came in reply.

CHAPTER III
A MERRY NIGHT

The long whine, a mingling of ferocity, fear and perhaps of hunger too, came from a point nearer than before, and Henry was confirmed in his opinion that Wyatt's main band had been joined by other and smaller ones, thus enabling them to form a circle practically continuous, through which the wolves had not dared to break. The pack, moreover, was steadily being driven in toward the center of the circle which was naturally the rocky hollow. He foresaw further complications.

Henry was very thoughtful. Affairs were not going as he had expected, and yet he was not disappointed. He had believed that he would have to show great activity himself, slipping here and there, and putting in a timely shot or two, but other factors had entered into the situation, and, with his normal flexibility of mind, he resolved at once to put them to the best use.

The wind was blowing from the pack toward him, and, if it shifted, he meant to shift with it, but meanwhile he made himself as inconspicuous as possible, finding a small depression in which he stretched his body, thus being hidden from any eye except the keenest. Although the night was far advanced, it retained its quality of silky or luminous brightness, the whole world still swimming in the silver haze which the full moon and the countless stars cast.

He wondered what had become of the scratched and angry panther. Endowed with strength, but only with a fitful courage, it too must be lying somewhere near in the forest, torn by wrath and perplexity. He was quite sure that like the wolves it was encircled by the Indian ring, and would not dare the attempt to break it. He was compelled to laugh once more to himself. It was, in truth, a merry night.

But as the laugh died in his throat his whole body gave a nervous quiver. A cry came from a point not ten yards distant, a long, melancholy, quavering sound, not without a hint of ferocity, in fact the complaining voice of an owl. The imitation of the owl was a favorite signal with the forest runners, both white and red, but Henry knew at once that this cry was real. Looking long and thoroughly, he saw at last the feathered and huddled shape on the bough of an oak. It was a huge owl, and the rays of the moon struck it at such an angle that they made it look ghostly and unsubstantial. Had Henry been superstitious, had he been steeped too much in Indian lore, he would have called it a phantom owl. Nay, it looked, in very truth, like such a phantom, taking the shape of an owl, and, despite all his mind and courage, a little shudder ran through him.

Again the great owl cried his loneliness and sorrows to the night. It was a tremendous note, mournful, uncanny and ferocious, and it seemed to Henry that it must go miles through the clear air, until it came back in a dying echo, more sinister than its full strength had been. The Indian cast was bringing into the net more than Wyatt or any of the warriors had anticipated, but the owl at least was hooting its defiance.

The singular combination of the night and circumstance affected Henry's own spirit. He was touched less by the present and reality than by his sense of another time and the primordial elements became strong within him. In effect he was transported far back into those dim ages, when man fought with the stone axe, and his five senses were so preternaturally acute to protect his life that he had a sixth and perhaps a seventh. A whiff came on the wind. It was faint, because it had traveled far, but he knew it to be the odor of the panther. The big cowardly beast was crouched in a little valley to his right, and he was trembling, trembling at the approaching warriors, trembling at the great youth who lay in the depression, trembling at the unknown and monstrous creature that had plunged its iron claws into him in the dark, and trembling at the cry of the owl which it had heard so often before, but which struck now with a new terror upon its small and frightened brain.

Henry's own feeling of the supernatural passed. It was merely the old, old world in which he must fight for his life and turn aside the bands from his comrades and himself. Although the warriors had not called again to one another he divined that they were closing in, and he thought rapidly and with all the intensity and clearness demanded by the situation.

The owl hooted once more, the tremendous note swelling far over the wilderness, and then returning in its melancholy whine. Instantly setting his lips and swelling all the muscles of his mighty throat he gave back the cry, long, full and a match in its loneliness and ferocity for the owl's own call. Then he crouched so close that he seemed fairly to press himself into the earth.

He saw the owl on the bough move a little and he knew that it was in a state of stupid amazement. Like the panther its brain was adapted only to its own affairs and environment, else it would have made some progress in all the ages, and the cry of an owl coming from the ground when owls usually cried from trees was more than it could understand. Nevertheless it soon gave forth its long complaining note once more, and Henry promptly matched it. He was thinking not so much of its effect upon the owl as upon the Indians. Delicate as their senses were, they were not as delicate as his, and they might think the two notes were those of challenge indicating that the whole five, reinforced perhaps by a half dozen stalwart hunters, were within the ring, ready and eager to give battle, setting in very truth a trap of their own.

He heard presently the cry of a wolf from a point at least a half mile away, and it was answered from another segment of the circle at an equal distance. The sounds, as he easily discerned, were made by warriors, and it was absolutely certain now that the voices of the owls had caused them to pause and think. Having thus started this train he felt that he could wait and see what would happen, but he was stirred by curiosity, and he pulled himself forward until the thicket ended, and the earth fell away into the deep ravine that ran before the stony hollow.

He kept himself hidden in the edge of the dense bushes, but he could see in various directions. The great owl on the bough was quivering a little, as if it were still amazed and terrified by the answer to its own calls, coming from the heart of the earth itself and surcharged with mystery. The moonlight turned it to a feathery mass of silver in which the cruel beak and claws showed like sharp pieces of steel. Yet the bird did not fly away, and Henry knew that it was held by fear as well as curiosity, the dangers near seeming less than those far.

He looked then down into the ravine, and he was startled by the sight of the wolf pack at full attention. The wolves of the Mississippi Valley were not as large as the great timber wolf of the mountains, but when driven by hunger they showed like their brethren elsewhere extreme ferocity, and were known to devour human beings. Now the wolves like the owl were magnified in the luminous moonlight, and one at their head seemed to be truly of gigantic size. He reminded Henry of the king wolf that had pursued Shif'less Sol and himself, and he had a singular fancy that he was the same great brute, reincarnated. He shivered at his own thought, and then chided himself fiercely. The king wolf had been killed, he was as dead as a stone, and he could not come back to earth to plague him.

But the beast, like the bird, was truly monstrous. He stood

29

upon a slight mound at the bottom of the ravine, and his figure bathed in the glow of the moon and the stars rose to twice its real height. Henry saw the foam upon the red mouth, the white fangs and the savage eyes, in which, his fancy still vivid, he read hunger, ferocity and terror too. Around him but on the lower plane were gathered the full score of the pack, gaunt and fierce. Suddenly, the leader raised his head and like a dog bayed the moon. The score took up the cry and the long whine was carried far on the light wind, to be followed by deep silence.

The voice of the wolf bore Henry even farther back than the voice of the owl, and his preternaturally acute senses took on an edge which the modern man never knows in his civilized state. He heard the fluff of the owl's feathers as it moved and the panting of the wolves in the valley below. Then he saw the leader walk from the low mound and take a slow and deliberate course along the slope, with the others following in single file like Indians. The king was leading them nearer to the rocky hollow, and Henry suspected they were changing their position because the ring of warriors was beginning to close in again. He heard a flapping of wings, and a huge bald-headed eagle settled on a bough near him, whence it looked with red eyes at the owl, while the owl, with eyes equally red, looked back again.

The suspicious, not to say jealous, manner with which the two birds regarded each other, when the forest was wide enough for both, and countless millions more like them, amused Henry. Both were alarmed, and it was easy enough for them to fly away, but they did not do so, drawn in a kind of fascination toward the danger they feared. Meanwhile the wolves were still coming up the slope, but the black bear in the snug hollow never stirred.

The warriors signaled once more to one another and now they were much nearer. Henry retreated a little farther into the thicket, and then his plan came to him. The Indians were bound to approach him from the east and he would meet them with a weapon they little expected. The forest was still in dense green, but the wood was dry from summer heats, the effect of the great rain having passed quickly, and the ground was littered as usual with the dead boughs and trunks fallen through arboreal ages.

He drew softly away toward the mouth of the hollow, and then passed behind it, where, stooping in the thicket, he produced his flint and steel, which he put upon the turf beside him. Then, he gathered together a little pile of dry brushwood, and again took notice of the wind, which was still blowing directly toward the east and down the ravine, the only point from which the Indian attack could come. It had been repulsed there once before, but then Henry's comrades were with him, and five good rifles and the tremendous voice of Long Jim had prevailed. Now he was alone, and he did not intend to rely upon bullets. The moonlight held, clear and amazingly bright, and he distinctly saw the troubled owl and the vexed eagle, apparently still staring at each other and wondering what was the matter with the night and the place. The Indian calls to one another sounded once more, their own natural voices now and not the imitation of bird or animal, and their nearness indicated that the circle was closing in fast.

Henry had built up his heap of tinder wood, somewhat behind the mouth of the hollow, and, kneeling down, he used flint and steel with amazing rapidity and power. The sparks leaped forth in a shower, the dry wood ignited, and up came little flames which swiftly grew into bigger ones. Then he fanned his bonfire with all his might, and the flames sprang high in the air, roaring as they set a fresh blaze to every dry thing they touched. In less than two minutes a forest fire was in full and great progress, sweeping eastward and down the ravine directly into the faces of Braxton Wyatt and his advancing warriors. A great sheet of fire in varying reds, pinks and yellows, and sometimes with a blue tint, rose above the tops of the trees, and, as it rushed forward, it sent forth showers of ashes and sparks in myriads from its crimson throat.

Henry sprang up behind the fire and uttered terrific shouts, leaping and dancing as that far dim ancestor of his must have leaped and danced when he was glowing with a sudden and mighty triumph. The spirit of the ages had descended upon him too and as he bounded back and forth in the light of the flames he roared forth bitter taunts in a voice worthy of Long Jim himself. He told the owl to be up and away, and, rising on heavy wings and uttering a dismal hoot, it obeyed. Its big body was outlined for a moment or two against the red, and then it flew away over the forest. The eagle uttered a hoarse cry, drawn from its frightened throat, and followed the owl.

Then came another shriek, singularly like that of a human being, and the huge panther, driven from its covert by the intense heat, leaped madly forth and raced down the ravine before the pillar of flame. That panther was in a sorely troubled state even before the fire began, and now the collapse of its small intellect was complete. It saw the advancing Indian warriors, but, in its madness, was reckless of them. It advanced with great bounds straight at the line, cannoned against Braxton Wyatt himself, knocking him senseless into a thicket, and, magnified to twice its usual size before the amazed eyes of the Indians, disappeared at last in a yellowish streak down the ravine.

Terror tore at the hearts of the Indians themselves, brave warriors though they were. The strange cries of the night, of such varying character and coming from so many points, had depressed their spirits and filled them with superstitious awe. There was more in this than the human mind could account for and the sudden upspringing of the fire, bringing on its front the monstrous panther, if, in truth, it was a panther and not some huge and legendary beast, sent them to the verge of panic.

Their white leader, who might have restored their courage, lay senseless in the bush, and as the second in command, the big warrior, seized him to drag him away from the fire, the wall of flame emitted something even more terrifying than the magnificent figure of the mad panther. Out of the red glare shot a huge gaunt figure with long white teeth and slavering jaws, the king wolf, to the warriors the demon wolf. After him came a full score or more of wolves, almost as large, and howling their terror to the moon. Behind them was the gigantic figure of a phantom black bear, rushing with all its might, and through the red wall itself came the sound of threatening and awful cries.

The Shawnees could stand no more. Uttering yells of fright they fled, and fortunate it was for Braxton Wyatt that the big warrior slung him over his shoulder and carried him away in the crush.

Henry heard the cries of the warriors and he knew from their nature that panic was in complete control of the band. All things had worked for him. The bear in its fright, and as he had expected, had rushed from the cave just in time to flee before the flames, and he knew very well that his own shouts would be interpreted by the Indians as the menace of the evil spirits.

He followed the flames about a mile down the ravine, and then returned slowly toward the hollow. He knew that the fire would soon reach a prairie somewhat farther on, where it would probably die out, but he knew also that his triumph was achieved. Circumstances and the presence of the animals and the birds had helped him greatly, but his own quick wit and infinity of resource had put the capstone on success. He began to feel now the effect of the immense exertions he had made with both body and mind, and, before he reached the hollow, he turned aside into the woods where the fire had not passed and sat down on a rock.

He saw two or three miles away the wall of flame still moving eastward, but the distance even did not keep him from knowing that it had diminished greatly in height and vigor. As he had surmised, it would die presently at the prairie and the night would return to its wonted silence, lighted now only by the moon and stars. He was weary, but he had an immense feeling of satisfaction and he sat a while, looking at the fire, which soon sank out of sight behind the horizon, although its pathway, the broad swath that it had cut, still glowed with coals and sparks.

He wondered just where his comrades were. He might have sent forth a call for them, but he decided that it would be wiser not to do so at present, since they could reunite easily in the morning, and he remained, sitting in an easy position, still looking at the luminous point under the horizon, where the last embers of the fire were fading. A long time passed, and the stillness was so peaceful that he sank into a doze, from which he was aroused by a flare of lightning in the west. The beauty of the night had been too intense to last. The moon and stars that he had admired so much were going away, and the silky blue robe, shot with silver that was the sky, was dimmed by a long row of somber clouds trailing up from the west. The wind that touched Henry's face was damp and he knew rain would soon come.

He had no mind to have a wetting through and through after his great strain and labors, and his thoughts turned at once to the rocky hollow. The bear had rushed out of it madly and there must have been much heat there for awhile, but it had probably cooled by this time, and would afford him a good shelter.

He found to his great delight and relief that the interior was free from smoke, and not damaged at all. Some articles they had left on the shelves were not even charred, and the leaves that made their beds had escaped ignition. He would not have asked for anything better, and, after eating some venison from his knapsack and drinking from the cold water of the rivulet, he lay down on the bed nearest the cleft, where he could see the ravine and the forest beyond.

A storm was gathering, but secure in his shelter it soothed and lulled his spirit. The lightning, now red and intense, flared from every horizon, and the wilderness was filled with the deep roll of incessant thunder. The wind ceased to blow, but he knew that soon it would spring up again, and then the rain would come with it, although he would remain dry and warm in the stony shelter that nature had provided. An enormous sense of comfort, even luxury, pervaded him, both body and mind. He was like his primordial ancestor who had escaped from the dangers of the monstrous beasts and who now rested at ease in his cave. The strain upon his nerves departed, and soon he felt fit and able to meet any new danger, whenever it should come. But he was so sure that no such danger would appear that he allowed himself to fall asleep, having first covered his body with the blanket that he always carried at his back, as the night, under the influence of the wind and rain, was growing cold.

When he awoke the day had not yet come and it was very dark. The rain was pouring heavily, but not a drop reached him where he lay on his easy bed of leaves with the warm blanket drawn around his body. Without rising he pulled himself forward a little and looked forth. The last ember from the forest fire had been blotted out long since, and he heard the wash of the water as it rushed down the slopes, and the sweep of the torrent in the ravine. The contrast heightened the splendor of his own situation, which was all that one who was wild for the time could ask. He thought of his comrades and of what a home the hollow would be to them too, but he was not troubled about them. Such forest runners as Shif'less Sol and the others would be sure to find protection from the storm.

He fell asleep again, and, when he awoke the second time, dawn had come more than an hour, the rain had stopped and the heavens were burnished silver. Foliage and grass were already drying fast under a warm western wind, and Henry, making a breakfast off what was left of his venison, prepared to go forth. But he was halted by a shambling, dark figure that appeared on the slope leading down into the ravine. It was the black bear, and apparently it had some idea of returning to the fine shelter it had abandoned in such fright the night before. Henry was surprised that it should have come back. It must have been beaten about much in the storm, and, either its memory was short, or it had sunk its terrors in the recollection of the finest den that ever a bear had entered in the northern part of Kain-tuck-ee.

Henry had a friendly feeling for the bear, which he regarded as an animal of a companionable disposition, and no enemy, unless driven in a corner. Since he had to leave the hollow and his comrades would have to go with him he preferred on the whole that the bear should have it, but when he stood up in the entrance the animal caught sight of his tall figure and scrambled away in the forest. His place was taken by the figure of a huge cat which glared at Henry with yellowish-green eyes, and then turned back among the trees, filled with rage that the terrible, strange creature was yet there.

"It seems that I'm still an object of terror," thought Henry, with amusement. "Now for the eagle and the owl."

A great bird came out of the blue, and sailed on slow wing over the hollow and ravine. He knew instinctively that it was the bald eagle of the night before, drawn back with a fascination it could not resist to the place where it had been frightened so badly. But it did not alight. Keeping at a good height, it circled about and about and then disappeared again and for the last time to the eastward.

Henry's eyes searched the opposite slope of the ravine, and at last he discovered a mournful figure perched on the high bough of an oak. Its feathers were drooping, its head was bent down until it was almost buried in the feathers below its neck, and its entire attitude showed despondency. The owl, too, had come back, but only a part of the way, and, blinded by the sun, it sat there on the bough, mourning and mourning.

Henry laughed. He had laughed many times the night before and he could not keep from laughing that morning. The owl was quite the saddest spectacle the woods could afford, and he had no mind to disturb it.

"Stay there and grieve, my solemn friend," he said. "Truly, with the sun on you, your eyes closed and your heart sunk you'll be silent, but tonight you'll give forth your melancholy hoot, although I won't be here to hear it."

He looked to his ammunition, and stepped forth into a new and refreshed world, filled with cool drying airs and the appealing odor of leaf and grass. He descended into the ravine, the water falling in beads from the leaves as he brushed by, and followed for a little distance in the bare trail left by the fire. A mile farther on and a pair of great red eyes peering at him from a thicket saw in him a terrible beast that even the master of the wolves should avoid.

The huge leader gave a yelp, and as Henry turned suddenly, he saw the great wolf flitting away up the ravine, followed by the twenty gaunt figures of his pack. He could have dropped the big wolf with a bullet, but there was no need to do so, and he merely watched them until they disappeared in the forest, concluding that his companions of the night were as much afraid of him in the day as in the dark. All of them, save one band, had come back in a frightened way, but he knew that the Indians would not return. He was sure that they were still on their terrified flight toward the Ohio, and he followed in the path of the fire, until he came to the prairie where it had burned itself out.

35

It was only a little prairie, about two miles across, no other kind having been found in Kentucky, and, on the far side, he picked up the trail of the Indian band. He did not see any footsteps that turned out, and he wondered at their absence. What had become of Braxton Wyatt? His body had not been found in the path of the flames, and certainly he had not perished. Henry, after some thought, came to the right conclusion, namely, that he was being carried. But his hurt could not be any wound received in battle, and probably he would recover soon, another correct surmise, as a short distance farther on the trail of toes that turned out appeared.

All the steps seemed to be long, and Henry judged hence that the band was going fast, terror still stabbing at their hearts, long after the night had passed. Braxton Wyatt would be the first to recover from it, and Henry smiled at the thought of his rage when he should not be able to persuade the Shawnees that evil spirits, sent by Manitou, had not driven them from the valley. Their second defeat at the same place, and this time by invisible forces, would persuade them they must never return to the attack on the hollow.

Henry dropped the pursuit for the present, knowing that it was time to reunite his own forces, and he sent forth the cry of the wolf that the five, in common with the Indians, used so much. No reply and he repeated it a second and yet a third time before the answer came. Then it was in the south and it was very faint, but he had no doubt it was the voice of Shif'less Sol. Call and reply went on for a little while, and then, after a long wait, he saw the figures of the four appearing among the trees, the shiftless one leading.

The greeting was not effusive, but joyful. Henry told them in rapid words, tense and brief, all that had occurred the night before, and the shoulders of the four shook with silent laughter.

"You certainly scared them good, Henry," said Paul.

"I was helped a lot by circumstances."

"But you used the chances when they came."

"Where did you four hide when the storm broke?"

"We took refuge under the matted trees and boughs of a huge old windrow. It wasn't like the hollow, and some water came through, but on the whole we did fairly well, and soon dried out thoroughly this morning. We were mighty glad to hear your call, but we hardly hoped you would achieve as much as you did."

"An' havin' routed the first band that came ag'inst us," said Long Jim, "what do you 'low we ought to do next?"

"We've broken only a piece of the iron ring they're forging about us, and they'll soon mend that piece. It's a good thing to hit

36

first at those you see are trying to hit at you, and so I think we ought to follow up the success fortune has given us."

"An' it 'pears we kin do that best by keepin' right on the trail o' Braxton Wyatt an' his band," said Shif'less Sol.

"That's the way I see it," said Henry. "How do you feel about it, Tom?"

"Right plan," replied Ross.

Shif'less Sol fixed upon him such a look of stern reproof that Silent Tom reddened once more under his tan.

"Here you go gettin' volyble ag'in," said the shiftless one. "You used two words then, Tom Ross, when, ef you'd thought an' hunted 'roun' a leetle you might hev found one that would hev done ez well."

"And you Paul?" said Harry.

"I'm glad to follow where you lead."

"And you, Jim?"

"I'm uv Paul's mind."

"Then it's settled. Now, we'll have something to eat, and talk it over."

They soon found a little valley in which a clear rivulet was flowing. One was never more than a mile from running water in that country—and Long Jim and Silent Tom produced food from their deerskin pouches.

"Here's some ven'son," said Jim. "It's cold an' it's tough, but I reckon it'll do."

"I'm thinkin'," said Shif'less Sol, "that after a night like the one Henry has had he'll be pow'ful hungry fur somethin' better than cold ven'son."

"Mebbe so," rejoined Long Jim, "an' mebbe it's true uv all uv us, but whar are we goin' to git it?"

"I'm an eddycated man, Jim Hart, eddycated in the ways o' the woods, an' one o' the fust things you do when you're gittin' that sort o' an eddication is to learn to use your eyes. I hev used mine, an' jest before we set down here I noticed the fresh trail o' buffler runnin' off to the right, 'bout a dozen, I'd say, an' jest ez shore ez I'm here they're not more'n a mile away. I kin see 'em now, grazin' in a little open, an' thar is a young cow among 'em, juicy an' tender. Now I don't want to kill a young cow buffler, but we must hev supplies before we go on this expedition."

"Sol is right," said Henry, "and since he is so it's his duty to go and kill the buffalo. Tom, you'll go with him, won't you?"

"O' course," replied Silent Tom.

37

Shif'less Sol rose and looked to his rifle.

"I knowed I would hev to do all the work, besides supplyin' the thinkin'," he said. "Here I tell what's to be done when the others ain't able to think it out, an' then they tell me to go an' do it. It ain't fair to a lazy man, one who furnishes the intelleck. The rest o' you ought to work fur him."

"Go on you, Sol Hyde," said Long Jim Hart, rebukingly, "an' kill that buffler. Don't you know that when you kill it I'll hev to cook it, an' I ain't complainin'?"

"Quit braggin' on yourse'f, Jim Hart. You ain't complainin', 'cause you ain't got sense 'nuff to complain. You're plum' sunk so deep in sloth an' ig'rance that you're jest satisfied with anythin', no matter how bad it is. It's men o' intelleck like me who complain and look fur better things, who make the world go forward."

"Your idea uv goin' forward, Sol Hyde, is to do it ridin' on my shoulders."

"O' course, Jim. Ain't that what you're made fur? You're a hind—ain't that the beast, Paul, that carries burdens?—an' I'm the knight with the shinin' lance that goes forth to slay dragons, an' I go ridin', too."

"You go ridin', too! I don't see no hoss! An' you ain't been astride no hoss in years, Sol Hyde!"

"You deserve to be what you are, a hind, a toter o' burdens, Jim Hart, 'cause your mind is so slow an' dull. You ain't got no light, no imagination, no bloom, a-tall, a-tall! Did I say I wuz ridin' a real hoss? No, sir, not fur a second! But in the fancy, in the sperrit, so to speak, I'm ridin' the finest hoss that ever pranced, an' I'm settin' in a silver saddle, holdin' reins o' blue silk, an' that proud hoss o' mine champs an' champs his jaws on a bit made o' solid gold. Come on, Tom, I ain't 'preciated here. We'll kill that buffler, ef you don't talk me to death on the way. Remember now to hold your volyble tongue. The last time you spoke, ez I told you, you used two words when one would hev done jest ez well. Don't let your gabblin' skeer the buffler plum' to the other side o' the Ohio."

He stalked haughtily away, his rifle in the hollow of his arm, and Silent Tom followed meekly. The admiring gaze of Jim Hart followed the shiftless one as long as he was in sight.

"Ain't he the most beautiful talker you ever heard?" he asked. "Me an' him hev our little spats, but it's a re'l pleasure to hear him fetch out reasons an' prove that the thing that ain't is, an' the thing that is ain't. That's what I call a mighty smart man. Ef the Injuns ever git him he'll talk to 'em so hard that they'll either make him thar head chief, or turn him loose to keep from bein' talked to death."

They heard the sound of a shot, and then a faint halloo from the shiftless one, and when Henry went to the spot he found that he had slain a young cow buffalo, just as he had predicted. Long Jim Hart cooked the tender steaks in his finest style and they spent the rest of the day preparing for the journey, which they believed would take them across the Ohio, and which they knew would be full of dangers.

They put out their fire and rested until dusk came. Then they took up again the trail of Wyatt's band and traveled until midnight, when they slept until morning, all save the watch. Henry reckoned that they would reach the river by the next night, and there was a chance that the warriors might recover sufficiently from their fright to rally at the stream. But he felt that in any event he and his comrades must strike. Blackstaffe, Yellow Panther and Red Eagle with their forces would soon be in pursuit, and to escape the net would test the skill and courage of the five to the utmost. Yet all of them believed attack to be the best plan, and, after their sleep, they resumed the trail with renewed strength and vigor, pressing northward at great speed through the deep green wilderness.

CHAPTER IV
THE CAPTURED CANOE

As the five advanced they read the trail with unfailing eye. Henry saw more than once the traces of footsteps with the toes turned out, that is those of Braxton Wyatt, and he noticed that they were wavering, not leading in a straight line like those of the Indians.

"Braxton must have had a nice crack of some kind or other on the head," he said, "and he still feels the effects of it, as now and then he reels."

"'Twould hev been a good thing," said Shif'less Sol, "ef the crack, whatever it may hev been, hed been a lot harder, hard enough to finish him. I ain't bloodthirsty, but it would help a lot if Braxton Wyatt wuz laid away. Paul, you're eddicated, an' you hev done a heap o' thinkin', enough, I guess, to last a feller like Long Jim fur a half dozen o' lives, now what makes a man turn renegade an' fight with strangers an' savages ag'inst his own people?"

"I think," replied Paul, "that it's disappointment, and fancied grievances. Some people want to be first, and when they can't win the place they're apt to say the world is against 'em, in a conspiracy, so to speak, to defraud 'em of what they consider their rights. Then their whole system gets poisoned through and through, and they're no longer reasoning human beings. I look upon Braxton Wyatt as in a way a madman, one poisoned permanently."

"I hev noticed them things, too," said Shif'less Sol. "Thar are diff'unt kinds o' naturs, the good an' the bad, an' the bad can't bear for other people to lead 'em. Then they jest natchelly hate an' hate. All through the day they hate, an' ef they ain't got nothin' to do, even ef the weather is fine 'nuff to make an old man laugh, they jest spend that time hatin'. An' ef they happen to wake up at night, do they lay thar an' think what a fine world it is an' what nice people thar are in it? No, sir, they jest spend all the time between naps hatin', an' they fall asleep ag'in, with a hate on thar lips an in' thar hearts."

"You're talkin' re'l po'try an' truth at the same time, Sol," said Long Jim. "It's cur'ous how people hate them that kin do things better than theirselves. Now, I've noticed when I'm cookin' buffler steaks an' deer meat an' wild turkey an' nice, juicy fish, an' cookin' mebbe better than anybody else in all Ameriky kin, how you,

Shif'less Sol Hyde, turn plum' green with envy an' begin makin' disrespeckful remarks 'bout me, Jim Hart, who hez too lofty an' noble a natur ever to try to pull you down, poor an' ornery scrub that you be."

Shif'less Sol drew himself up with haughty dignity.

"Jim Hart," he said, "I'm wrapped 'bout with the mantle o' my own merit so well from head to foot that them invig'ous remarks o' yours bounce right off me like hail off solid granite. To tell you the truth, Jim Hart, I feel like a big stone mountain, three miles high, with you throwin' harmless leetle pebbles at me."

"And yet," said Paul, "while you two are always pretending to quarrel, each would be eager to risk death for the other if need be."

"It's only my sense o' duty, an' o' what you call proportion," said Shif'less Sol. "Long Jim, ez you know, is six feet an' a half tall. Ef the Injuns wuz to take him an' burn him at the stake he'd burn a heap longer than the av'rage man. What a torch Jim would make! Knowin' that an' always b'arin' it in mind, I'm jest boun' to save Jim from sech a fate. It ain't Jim speshully that I'm thinkin' on, but I'd hate to know that a man six an' a half feet long wuz burnin' 'long his whole len'th."

"Another band has joined Wyatt," said Henry. "See, here comes the trail!"

The new force had arrived from the east, and it contained apparently twenty warriors, raising Braxton Wyatt's little army to about sixty men.

"But they still run," said Shif'less Sol. "The new ones hev ketched all the terror an' superstition that the old ones feel, an' the whole crowd is off fur the Ohio. Look how the trail widens!"

"And Braxton Wyatt is beginning to feel better," said Henry. "His own particular trail does not waver so much now. Ah, they've stopped here for a council. Braxton probably stood on that old fallen log and addressed them, because the traces of his footsteps lead directly to it. Yes, the bark here is rubbed a little, where he stood. They gathered in a half circle before him, as their footprints show very plainly, and they listened to him respectfully. He, being white, was recovering from the superstitious terror, but the Shawnees were still under its spell. After hearing him they continued their flight. Here goes their trail, all in a bunch, straight toward the north!"

"An' thar won't be no stop 'til they strike the Ohio," said Shif'less Sol with conviction.

"I agree with you," said Henry.

"And so do all of us," said Paul.

"And of course we follow on," said Henry, "right to the water's edge!"

41

"We do," said the others all together.

"The Ohio isn't very far now," said Henry.

"Ten or fifteen miles, p'raps," said Shif'less Sol.

"And it's likely that we'll find a big force gathered there."

"Looks that way to me, Henry. Mebbe the band o' Blackstaffe will be waitin' to join that o' Wyatt. Then, feelin' mighty strong, they'll come back after us."

"'Less we fill 'em full o' fear whar they stan'. Mebbe they'll stop at the river a day or two, an' then we kin git to work. Water which hides will help us."

They passed on through the forest, noting that the trail was growing wide and leisurely. At one point the Indians had stopped some time, and had eaten heavily of game brought in by the hunters. The bones of buffalo, deer and wild turkey were scattered all about.

"They're feeling better," said Henry. "I don't think now they'll cross the Ohio, but we must do so and attack from the other side. They're not looking for any enemy in the north, and we may be able to terrify 'em again."

It was not long before they came to the great yellow stream of the Ohio, and in an open space, not far from the shore, they saw the fires of the Indian encampment.

"I think we'll have work to do here," said Henry, "and we'll keep well into the deep woods until long after dark."

They did not light any fire, but lying close in the thicket, ate their supper of cold food. Three or four hours after sunset Henry, telling the others to await his return, crept near the Indian camp. As he had surmised, two formidable forces had joined, and nearly two hundred warriors sat around the fires. The new army, composed partly of Miamis and partly of Shawnees, with a small sprinkling of Wyandots, was led by Blackstaffe, who was now with Wyatt, the two talking together earnestly and looking now and then toward the south.

Henry had no doubt that the five were the subject of their conversation. Wyatt must have recovered by this time all his faculties and was telling Blackstaffe that their enemies were only mortal and could be taken, if the steel ring about them was recast promptly. Henry had no doubt that an attempt to forge it anew would speedily be made by the increased force, but his heart leaped at the thought that his comrades and he would be able to break it again.

As he crept a little nearer he saw to his surprise a fire blazing on the opposite shore, and he was able to discover the forms of warriors between him and the blaze. With the Indians bestride the stream the task of the five was complicated somewhat, but Henry was of the kind that meet fresh obstacles with fresh energy.

He returned to his comrades and reported what he had seen, but all agreed with him that they should cross the river, despite the encampment on the far shore, and make the attack from the north.

"We'll do like that old Roman, Hannybul," said Long Jim, "hit the enemy at his weakest part, an' jest when he ain't expectin' us."

"Hannibal was not a Roman, Jim," said Paul.

"Well, then, he was a Rooshian or a Prooshian."

"Nor was he either of those."

"Well, it don't make no diff'unce, nohow. He wuz a furriner, that's shore, an' he's dead, both uv which things is ag'inst him. It looks strange to me, Paul, that a furriner with the outlandish ways that furriners always hev should hev been sech a good gen'ral."

"He was probably the best the world has produced, Jim. He was able with small forces to defeat larger ones, and we must imitate his example."

"And to do that," said Henry, "we shall cross the Ohio tonight. I think we'd better drop down a mile or two, beyond their fires and their sentinels, and then make for the northern shore."

"The river must be 'bout a mile wide here," objected Shif'less Sol. "That's a big swim with all our weepuns, an' ef some o' the warriors in canoes should ketch us in the water then we'd be goners, shore."

"You're right, there, Sol," said Henry. "It would be foolish in us to attempt to swim the river, when the warriors are looking for us, as they probably are by now, since Blackstaffe and Wyatt have got them back to realities."

"Then ef we don't swim how do you expect us to git across, Henry? Ez fur me, I can't wade across a river a mile wide an' twenty feet deep."

"That's true, Sol. Even Long Jim isn't long enough for that. I'm planning for us to cross in state, untouched by water and entirely comfortable; in fact, in a large, strong canoe."

"Nice good plan, Henry, 'cept in one thing; we ain't got no canoe."

"I intend to borrow one from the Indians. You and I will slip along up the bank and take it from under their noses. You're a marvel at such deeds, Sol."

"It's 'cause he's stealin' somethin' from somebody," said Long Jim.

"Shut up, Jim," said Henry. "It's lawful to steal from an enemy to save your own life, and these Indians mean to hunt us down if they have to employ three thousand warriors and three months to do it. Suppose we go now."

The five turned toward the south and west, making a deep curve away from the camp, a precaution taken wisely, as they soon had evidence, hearing shots here and there, which they were quite sure were those of red hunters seeking game, wild turkeys on the bough, or deer drinking at the small streams. They were compelled to go very slowly, in order to avoid them, but the night, luckily, was dark enough to hide their trail from all eyes, save those that might be looking especially for it.

They spoke only in whispers, but the young leader himself said scarcely anything, his mind being occupied with deep and intense thought. He knew that the venture in search of an Indian canoe would be accompanied by most imminent risks, the vigilance and skill of Shif'less Sol and himself would be tested to the last degree, but a canoe they must have, and they would dare every peril to get it.

They had gone about a mile when Henry suddenly raised his hand, and the five sank silently in the bush. A dozen warriors, treading without noise, passed within twenty feet of them and their course led toward the south. They flitted by so swiftly that it seemed almost as if shadows had passed, but Henry, who saw their faces, knew that they were not mere hunters. These men were on the warpath. Perhaps they had seen the trail of the five somewhere, and were going south to close up the broken segment of the circle there.

"They've probably had a hint from Blackstaffe," said Henry. "Next to Simon Girty he's the shrewdest and most cunning of all the renegades. He has reasoning power, and knowing that we'll take the bolder method, he's probably concluded that we've followed Wyatt's band."

"An' so he hez sent that other band south to shut us in," said Shif'less Sol.

"An' we might hev fled south ourselves from the fust," said Long Jim, "but I cal'late we ain't that kind uv people."

"No," said Henry. "We can't lead 'em in this chase back on the settlements. So long as they're trying to spread a net around us we'll draw 'em in the other direction. Now, boys, fall in behind me, and the first one that causes a blade of grass to rustle will have to make a present of his rifle to the others."

Following the great curve which they were traveling it was a full five miles to the point on the river they wished to reach. The forest, they knew, was full of warriors, some hunting, perhaps, but many thrown out on the great encircling movement intended to enclose the five. Now, the trailers, with deadly peril all about them, gave a superb exhibition of skill. There was no danger of any one losing his rifle, because no blade of grass rustled, nor did any leaf give back the sound of a brushing body. They were endowed peculiarly by birth and long habit to the life they lived and the dangers they faced. Their hearts beat high, but not with fear. Their muscles were steady, and eye and ear were attuned to the utmost for any strange presence in the forest.

Henry led, Paul followed, Long Jim came next, then Silent Tom, and Shif'less Sol defended the rear. This was usually their order, the greatest trailer at the head of the line, and the next greatest at the end of it. They invariably fell into place with the quickness and precision of trained soldiers.

A panther, not as large and fierce as the one that Henry had driven in fright down the ravine, saw them, looking upon human beings for the first time. It was his first impulse to make off through the woods, but they were soundless and in flight, and curiosity began to get the better of fear. He followed swiftly, somewhat to one side, but where he could see, and the silent line went so fast that the panther himself was compelled to extend his muscles. He saw them come to a brook. The foremost leaped it, the others in turn did the same, landing exactly in his footsteps, and they went on without losing speed. Then the panther turned back, satisfied that he could not solve the problem his curiosity had raised.

Henry caught a yellow gleam through the leaves, and he knew that it was the Ohio. In two or three minutes, they were at the low shore, although the opposite bank was high. Both were wooded densely. The stream itself was here a full mile in width, a vast mass of water flowing slowly in silent majesty. They thought they saw far up the channel a faint reflection of the Indian fires, but they were not sure. Where they stood the river was as lone and desolate as it had been before man had come. The moonlight was not good, and their view of the farther shore was dim, leaving them only the certainty that it was lofty and thick with forest.

"Paul, you and Jim and Tom lie here, where this little spit of land runs out into the water," said Henry. "There's good cover for you to wait in, and Sol and I will come down the river in our new canoe, or we won't."

"At any rate come," said Paul.

"You can trust us," replied Henry, and he and the shiftless one started at once along the edge of the river toward the northeast, where the Indian camp lay. Henry reckoned that it was about three miles away, but it would have to be approached with great care. As they advanced they kept a watch on the farther shore also, and rounding a curve in the river they caught their first sight of its reflection.

"It's fur up the stream," said Shif'less Sol, "an' I cal'late it's 'bout opposite the big camp. Thar must be some warriors passin' back an' forth from band to band, an' that, I reckon, will give us our chance fur a canoe."

"Yes, if we can make off with it without being seen," said Henry. "A pursuit would spoil everything. We'd have to abandon the canoe and retreat back from the southern shore."

"'Spose we go a leetle further up," said Shif'less Sol. "The bank's low here, but it's high enough to hide us, an' the bushes are mighty thick. The nearer we come to the Indian camp the greater the danger is, but the greater is our chance, too, to git a canoe."

"That's right, Sol. We'll try it."

They edged along yard by yard and soon could see through the intervening trees and bushes the light of the great camp, from which came a monotonous hum.

"A lot of 'em are dancin' the scalp dance," said the shiftless one. "Will you 'scuse me, Henry, while I laugh a leetle to myself?"

"Of course, Sol, but why do you want to laugh?"

"'Cause they're dancin' the scalp dance when they ain't goin' to take no scalps. It's ourn they're thinkin' of, but I kin tell you right now, Henry, that a year from today they'll be growin' squa'rly on top o' our heads, right whar they are this minute."

"I hope and believe you're right, Sol. Isn't that a canoe putting out from the far shore?"

"Yes, a big one, with four warriors in it, an' they're comin' straight across to the main camp, paddlin' like the strong men they are."

"Yes, I can see them clearly now, as they come nearer the middle of the stream. That would be a good canoe for us, Sol. It looks big enough."

"But I'm afraid we ain't goin' to hev it, Henry. It's comin' straight on to the main camp, an' it'll be tied to the bank right in the glow o' thar fires. Hevin' wanted that canoe, ez we both do, we'd better quit wantin' it an' want suthin' else."

Henry laughed softly.

"You're a true philosopher, Sol," he said.

"You hev to be in the woods, Henry. Here we learn to take what we can, an' let alone what we can't. I guess the wilderness jerks all the foolishness out o' a man, an' brings him plum' down to his level. Ain't I right 'bout thar comin' straight to the main camp?"

46

"Yes, Sol, and they'll land in a few more minutes. Those are big warriors, Miamis as their paint and dress show. Well, they're out of our reckoning, so we'd better move a little farther up."

"We'll be shore to find canoes tied to the bank, an' thar will be our chance. Ef our luck's good we'll git it, an' I find that luck is gen'ally with the bold."

The situation into which they had entered was one of extreme danger, but their surprising skill as trailers helped them greatly. The bank at this point was about eight feet high, with rather a sharp slope, covered with a dense growth of bushes, in which their figures were well hidden, but they were so near now to the main camp that its luminous glow passed over their heads, and lay in a broad band of light on the yellow surface of the river. A canoe put out from the southern shore, and was paddled by two warriors to the northern bank. Evidently there was constant communication between the two forces.

From the bank above them came the steady drone of the scalp song, and they heard the measured beat of the dance. Voices, too, came to them as they advanced a little farther, and once Henry distinguished that of Blackstaffe, although he was not able to understand the words. The light from the great fire was steadily growing stronger on the river and it would be a peril, disclosing their movements, if they took a canoe. From the southern forest came the cries of wolves and owls which were the signals of the Indians to one another, and Henry felt sure they were talking of the five. He was thoroughly convinced now that their trail had been discovered, and that the warriors, sure they were in the ring, were seeking to draw in the steel girdle enclosing them. And unless the canoe was secured quickly it was likely they would succeed. The two paused, their minds in a state of painful indecision.

"What do you think, Henry?" whispered the shiftless one.

"Nothing that amounts to anything."

"When you don't know what to do the best thing to do is to do nothin'. 'Spose we jest wait a while. We're well kivered here, an' they'd never think o' lookin' so close by fur us, anyway. Besides, hev you noticed, Henry, that it's growin' a lot darker? 'Tain't goin' to rain, but the moon an' all the stars are goin' away, fur a rest, I s'pose, so they kin shine all the brighter tomorrow night."

"It's so, Sol, and a good heavy blanket of darkness will help us a lot."

They lay perfectly still and waited with all the patience of those who know they must be patient to live. A full hour passed, and the welcome darkness increased, the heavens turning into a solid canopy, black and vast. The light from the great campfire sank, and its luminous glow no longer appeared on the river. The stream itself showed but faintly yellow under the darkness. Henry's heart began to beat high. Nature, as it so often did, was coming to their help. The droning song of the scalp dance had ceased and with it the voices of the warriors talking. No sound came from the river, save the soft swish of the flowing waters, and now and then a gurgle and a splash, when some huge catfish raised part of his body above the surface, and then let it fall back again.

Another canoe came presently from the northern shore. Henry and Shif'less Sol, although they could not see it at first, knew it had started, because their keen ears caught the plash of the paddles.

"It's a big one, Henry," whispered Shif'less Sol. "How many paddles do you make out by the sound?"

"Six. Is that your count, too?"

"Yes. Now I kin see it. One, two, three, four, five, six. We wuz right in the number an' it's a big fine canoe, jest the canoe we want, Henry, an' it'll land 'bout twenty yards 'bove us. Somethin' tells me our chance is comin'!"

"I hope the something telling you is telling you right. In any case you're correct about their landing. It will be almost exactly twenty yards away."

The great canoe emerged from the darkness, six powerful Miamis swinging the paddles, and it came in a straight line for the bank, leaving a trailing yellow wake. Henry admired their strength and dexterity. They were splendid canoemen, and he never felt any hatred of the Indians. He knew that they acted according to such guidance as they had, and it was merely circumstances that placed him and his kind in opposition to them and their kind.

The light but strong craft touched the bank gently, and the six canoemen stepped out, a figure that appeared among the bushes confronting them. Henry, with a thrill, recognized Blackstaffe, and the canoe must have arrived on an errand of importance or the renegade would not have been there to meet the six warriors.

"You will come into the camp and hear the reports of the scouts," said Blackstaffe, speaking in Miami, which both Henry and the shiftless one understood perfectly. "It will take some time to do this, because not all of them have returned yet. Then two of you had better go back with the canoe, while the others stay here to help us. I think we have these five rovers trapped at last, and we'll make an end of 'em. They've certainly caused us enough trouble, and I'm bound to say they're masters of forest war."

48

One of the warriors tied the canoe to a bush with a willow withe, and then all six following Blackstaffe disappeared among the trees, going toward the campfire.

"At least Blackstaffe compliments us before sending us to the next world," whispered Henry.

"Ez fur me," Shif'less Sol whispered back, "I ain't goin' to no next world, jest to oblige a villyun renegade. Besides, I like this wilderness o' ours too much to leave it fur anybody. They think they're mighty smart an' that they're plannin' somethin' big right now, but all the same they're givin' us our chance."

"What do you mean, Sol?"

"Didn't you hear the villyun say that two o' the warriors wuz to go back with the boat?"

"Well, what of it?"

"Then two warriors is goin' to be me an' you, Henry."

"Of course. I ought to have thought of it, too."

"Thar must be sent'nels on the bank, but waitin' 'bout ten minutes we'll git into the canoe an' paddle off. The sent'nels will know that two warriors are to go back in it, an' they'll think we're them. This darkness which has come up, heavy an' black, on purpose to help us, will keep 'em from seein' that we ain't warriors. When we git into the middle o' the river, whar thar eyes can't even make out the canoe, we'll go down stream like a flash o' lightnin', pick up the boys and then be off ag'in like another flash o' lightnin'."

"A good plan, Sol, and we'll try it. As you say, luck is always on the side of the bold, and I don't see why we can't succeed."

But to wait the necessary fifteen minutes was one of the hardest tasks they ever undertook. It would not do to take the canoe at once, as suspicion would certainly be aroused. They must conform to Blackstaffe's own plan. It seemed to them that they must actually hold themselves with their own hands to keep from creeping forward to the canoe, yet they did it, though the minutes doubled and redoubled in length, and then tripled; but, after a time that both judged sufficient, they slid forward, and Henry's knife cut the willow withe. Then they lifted themselves gently into the canoe, took up two of the paddles and were away.

Henry's back was to the southern bank, and despite all his experience and courage shivers ran through his body at the thought that a bullet from the forest might strike him any moment. Yet he did not wish to seem in a hurry, and restrained his eagerness to paddle with all his might.

"Softly, Sol, softly," he said. "We must not be in too much haste."

"Don't I know it, Henry? Don't I know that we must 'pear to be the two warriors whose business it is to take back the canoe? Ain't I jest strainin' an' achin' to make the biggest sweep with my paddle I ever swep', an' ain't my mind pullin' ag'inst my hands all the time, tryin' to keep 'em at the proper gait? Are you shore you ain't felt no bullet in your back yet, Henry?"

"No, Sol. What makes you ask such a question?"

"'Cause I reckon I wuz so much afeared o' one that I imagined the place whar it's track would be in me, ef it had been really fired. My fancy is pow'ful lively at sech a time."

"There has been no alarm, at least not yet, and we're near the middle of the river. The canoe must be invisible, although I can see the fires on either shore. Now, Sol, we'll turn down stream and paddle with all our might, showing what canoemen we really are!"

It was with actual physical as well as mental joy that they turned the prow of the canoe toward the southeast, that is, with the current, and began to do their best with the paddles. They no longer had that horrible fear of a bullet in the back, and muscles seemed to leap together with the spirit into greater strength and elasticity.

"Come on you, Henry," said Shif'less Sol exultantly. "Keep up your side! Prove that you're jest ez good a man with the paddle ez me! We ain't makin' more'n a mile a minute, an' fur sech ez we are that's nothin' but standin' still!"

The two bent their powerful backs a little and their great arms swept the paddles through the water at an amazing rate. The soul of Shif'less Sol surged up to the heights. He became dithyrambic and he spoke in a tone not loud, but full of concentrated fire and feeling.

"Fine, you Henry, you!" he said. "But we kin do better! The canoe is goin' fast, but one or two canoes in the hist'ry o' the world hez gone ez fast! We must go faster by ten or fifteen miles an hour an' set the record that will stan'! It's so dark in here I can't see either bank, but I wish sometimes I could, warriors or no warriors! Then I could see 'em whizzin' by, jest streaks, with all the trees and bushes meltin' into one another like a green ribbon! Now, that's the way to do it, Henry! Our speed is jumpin'! I ain't shore whether the canoe is touchin' the water or not! I think mebbe it's jest our paddles that dip in, an' that the canoe is flyin' through the air! An' not a soun' from 'em yet! They haven't discovered that the wrong warriors hev took thar boat, but they will soon! Now we'll turn her in toward the southern bank, Henry, 'cause in the battin' o' an eye or two we'll be whar the rest o' the boys are a-lyin' hid in the bushes! Now, slow an' slower! I kin see the trees an' bushes separatin' tharselves, an' thar's the bank, an' now I see the face o' Long Jim, 'bout seven feet above

50

the groun'! He's an onery, ugly cuss, never givin' me all the respeck that's due me, but somehow I like him, an' he never looked better nor more welcome than he does now, God bless the long-armed, long-legged, fightin', gen'rous, kind-hearted cuss! An' thar's Paul, too, lookin' fur all the world like a scholar, crammed full o' book l'arnin', 'stead o' the ring-tailed forest runner, half hoss, half alligator, that he is, though he's got the book l'arnin' an' is one o' the greatest scholars the world ever seed! An' that's Tom Ross, with his mouth openin' ez ef he wuz 'bout to speak a word, though he'll conclude, likely, that he oughtn't, an' all three o' 'em are pow'ful glad to see us comin' in our triumphal Roman gallus that we hev captured from the enemy."

"Galley, Sol, galley! Not gallus!"

"It's all the same, galley or gallus. We hev got it, an' we are in it, an' it's a fine big canoe with six paddles, one for ev'ry one o' us an' one to spare! Now here we are ag'in the bank, an' thar they are ready to jump in!"

There was no time for hesitation, as a long and tremendous war whoop from a point up the stream seemed to surcharge the whole night with rage and ferocity. It was evident that the warriors had discovered that the wrong men had taken the canoe, as they were bound to do soon, and the chase would be on at once, conducted with all the power and tenacity of those who devoted their lives to such deeds.

"They'll know, of course, that we've come down the stream, not daring to go against the current," said Henry, "and they'll follow with every canoe they have."

"An' more will run along either bank hopin' fur a shot," said the shiftless one, "an' so while we turn our canoe into a shootin' star ag'in we'll hev to remember to keep in the middle o' the stream. A lot o' the dark that helped us to git the canoe is fadin' away, leavin' us to make our race fur our lives mostly in the open."

The great war whoop came again, filling the forest with its fierce echoes, and then followed silence, a silence which every one of the five knew would be broken later by the plash of paddles. The valley Indians had great canoes, sometimes carrying as many as twenty paddles, and when twenty strong backs were bent into one of them it could come at greater speed than any five in the world could command.

But this five, calm and ready to face any danger, put their rifles where they could reach them in an instant, and then their canoe shot down the stream.

CHAPTER V
THE PROTECTING RIVER

The Ohio was the great stream of the borderers. It was the artery that led into the vast, rich new lands of the west, upon its waters many of them came, and upon its current and along its banks were fought thrilling battles between white men and red. Many a race for life was made upon its bosom, but none was ever carried on with more courage and energy than the one now occurring.

They kept well to the middle of the stream, which was still of great width, a full mile across, where they would be safe from shots from either shore, until the river narrowed, and although they sent the canoe along very fast, they did not use their full strength, keeping a reserve for the greater emergency which was sure to come.

Meanwhile they worked like a machine. The arms of five rose together and five paddles made a single plash. In the returning moonlight the water took on a silver color, and it fell away in masses of shimmering bubbles from the paddle blades. Before them the river spread its vast width, at once a channel of escape and of danger. The forest yet rose on either bank, a solid mass of green, in which nothing stirred, and from which no sound came.

The silence, save for the swish of the paddles, was brooding and full of menace. Paul, so sensitive to circumstance, felt as if it were a sullen sky, out of which would suddenly come a blazing flash of lightning. But to Henry the greatest anxiety was the narrowing of the river which must come before long. The Ohio was not a mile wide everywhere, and when that straightening of the stream occurred they would be within rifle shot of the warriors on one bank or the other. And while the Indians were not good marksmen, it was true that where there were many bullets not all missed.

A quarter of an hour passed, and they heard the war-whoop behind them, and then a few moments later the faint, rhythmic swish of paddles. The moonlight had been deepening fast, and Henry saw two of the great canoes appear, although they were yet a full half mile away. But they came on at a mighty pace, and it was evident that unless bullets stopped them they would overtake the fugitives. Henry put aside his paddle, leaving the work for the present to the others, and studied the long canoes. He and his comrades might strain as they would, but in an hour the big boats filled with muscular warriors would be alongside. They must devise some other method to elude the pursuit. A shout from Paul caused him to turn.

A peninsula from the south projected into the river, making its width at this point much less than half a mile, and upon the spit, which was bare, stood several Indian warriors, rifle in hand and waiting.

"Turn the canoe in toward the northern shore," said Henry. "We must chance a shot from that quarter, dealing with the seen danger, and letting the unseen go. Sol, you and Tom take your rifles, and I'll take mine too. Paul, you and Jim do the paddling and we'll see whether those warriors on the sand stop us, or are just taking a heavy risk themselves."

The canoe sheered off violently toward the northern bank, but did not cease to move swiftly, as Paul and Jim alone were able to send it along at a great rate. Henry, with his rifle lying in the hollow of his arm, watched a large warrior standing on the edge of the water.

"I'll take the big fellow with the waving scalp lock," he said.

"The short, broad one by the side o' him is mine," said Shif'less Sol. "Which is yours, Tom?"

"One with red blanket looped over his shoulder," replied the taciturn rover.

"Be sure of your aim," said Henry. "We're running a gauntlet, but it's likely to be as much of a gauntlet for those warriors as it is for us."

Perhaps the Indians on the spit did not know that the canoe contained the best marksmen in the West, as they crowded closer to the water's edge, uttered a yell or two of triumph and raised their own weapons. The three rifles in the canoe flashed together and the big warrior, the short, broad one, and the one with the red blanket looped over his shoulder, fell on the sand. One of them got up again and fled with his unhurt comrades into the forest, but the others lay quite still, with their feet in the water. As the marksmen reloaded rapidly, Henry cried to the paddlers:

"Now, boys, back toward the middle of the river and put all your might in it!"

Paul and Long Jim swung the canoe into the main current, which had increased greatly in strength here, owing to the narrowing of the stream, and their paddles flashed fast. Two of the Indians who had fled into the woods reappeared and fired at them, but their bullets fell wide, and Henry, who had now rammed in the second charge, wounded one of them, whereupon they fled to cover as quickly as they did the first time.

Shif'less Sol and Tom Ross had also reloaded, but put their rifles in the bottom of the boat and resumed their paddles. The danger on the land spit had been passed, but the great canoes behind them were hanging on tenaciously and were gaining, not rapidly, but with certainty. Henry swept them again with a measuring eye, and he saw no reason to change his calculations.

"They'll come within rifle shot in just about an hour," he repeated. "We'd pick off some of them with our bullets, but they'd keep on coming anyhow, and that would be the end of us."

Such a solemn statement would have daunted any but those who had escaped many great dangers. Imminent and deadly as was the peril, it did not occur to any of the five that they would not evade it, the problem now being one of method rather than result.

"What are we going to do, Henry?" asked Paul.

"I don't know yet," replied the leader, "but we'll keep going until something develops."

"Thar's your development!" exclaimed the shiftless one, as a rifle was fired from the northern shore, and a bullet plashed in the water just ahead of them. Then came a second shot from the same source which struck the inoffensive river behind them. They were now being attacked from both banks while the great canoes followed tenaciously.

"We don't have to bother about one thing," said Paul grimly. "We know which way to go, and it's the only way that's open to us."

But the threat offered by the northern shore did not seem to be so menacing. The river began to widen again and rapidly, and the scattered shots fired later on came from a great distance, falling short. Those discharged from the southern bank also missed the mark as widely. Henry no longer paid any attention to them, but was examining the forest and the curves of the river with a minute scrutiny. His look, which had been very grave, brightened suddenly, and a reassuring flash appeared in his eye.

"What is it, Henry?" asked Shif'less Sol, who had noticed the change.

"We've been along here before," replied the great youth. "I know the shores now, and it's mighty lucky for us that we are just where we are."

The shiftless one looked at the northern, then at the southern forest, and shook his head.

"I don't 'pear to recall it," he said. "The woods, at this distance away, look like any other woods at night, black an' mighty nigh solid."

"It's not so much the forest, because, like you, I couldn't tell it from any other, as it is the curve of the river. I thought I saw something familiar in it a little while ago, and now I know by the sound that I'm right."

"Sound! What sound?"

"Turn your ears down the river and listen as hard as you can. After a while you'll hear a faint humming."

"So I do, Henry, but I wouldn't hev noticed it ef you hadn't told me about it, an' even ef I do hear it I don't know what it means."

"It's made by the rush of a great volume of water, Sol. It's the Falls of the Ohio, that not many white men have yet seen, a gradual sort of fall, one that boats can go over without trouble most of the time, but which, owing to the state of the river, are just now at their highest."

"An' you mean fur them falls to come in between us an' the big canoes? You're reckonin' on water to save us?"

"That's what I have in mind, Sol. The falls are dangerous at this stage of the river, no doubt about it, but we're not canoemen for nothing, and with our lives at stake we'll not think twice before shooting 'em. What say you, boys?"

"The falls fur me!" replied the shiftless one, quickly.

"Nothin' could keep me from takin' the tumble. I jest love them falls," said Long Jim.

"It's that or nothing," said Paul.

"On!" said Silent Tom.

"Then ease a little with your paddles," said Henry. "The Indians know, of course, that the falls are just ahead, and I notice they are not now pushing us so hard. It follows, then, that the falls are at a dangerous height they don't often reach, and they expect to trap us."

"In which they will be mighty well fooled."

"I think so. I'll sit in the prow of the boat and do my best with my paddle to guide. I believe we can shoot the falls all right, but maybe we'll be swamped in the rapids below. But we're all good swimmers, and, if we do go over, every fellow must swim for the northern bank, where the Indians are fewest. Some one of us must manage to save his rifle and ammunition or we'd be lost, even if we happened to reach the land. Still, it's possible that we can keep afloat. It's a good canoe."

55

"A good canoe!" exclaimed the shiftless one, in whom the spirit of achievement and of triumph was rising again. "It's the finest canoe on all this great river, and didn't I tell you boys that them that's bold always win! Jest when our last chance 'peared to be gone, these falls wuz put squar'ly in our track to save us! Will they wreck us? No, they won't! We'll shoot 'em like a bird on the wing!"

He looked back at their pursuers, and gave utterance suddenly to a long, piercing shout of defiance. The Indians in the canoes replied with war whoops that Henry could read easily. They expressed faith in speedy triumph, and joy over the destruction of the five. He saw, moreover, that they were using only half strength now, preferring to take their ease while the game struggled vainly in the net. But as well as many of these warriors knew the five they did not know them to the full.

The shiftless one waited until their last war whoop died, and then, sending forth once more his long, thrilling note of defiance, he burst again into his triumphal chant.

"Steady now with the paddles, boys," he cried, "an' we'll ride the water ez ef we'd done nothin' else all our lives! Oh, I love rivers, big rivers, speshully when they hev a strong current like this that takes your boat 'long an' you don't hev to do no work! Now it reaches up a thousand hands that grab our canoe an' sail 'long with it! Don't paddle any more, boys, but jest hold yourselves ready to do it, when needed! The river's doin' all the work, an' it never gits tired! Look, now, how the current's a-rushin', an' a-dancin', an' a-hummin'! Look at the white water 'roun' us! Look at the water behind us, an' hear the roarin' before us! Thar, she rocks, but never min' that! Wait till the water comes spillin' in! Then it will be time to use the paddles!"

He burst once more into that irrepressible yell of defiance, and then he cried exultantly:

"They slow up! They're gittin' afeard! We've made the race too fast fur 'em! Come on, you warriors! Ain't you ready to go whar we will? These falls are fine an' we jest love to play with 'em! We are goin' to sail down 'em, an' then we're goin' to sail back up 'em ag'in! Don't you hear all that roarin'? It's the tumblin' o' the water, an' it's singin' a song to you, tellin' you to come!"

The shiftless one's own tremendous song had a thrilling effect upon his comrades. Their spirits leaped with it. The rushing canoe was now dancing upon the surface of the river, but somehow they were not afraid. They were at that reach of the river where a great city was destined to grow upon the southern shore, and which was to be the scene, a year or two later, of other activities of theirs, but now both banks were in solid, black forest, and no human habitation had yet appeared.

The canoe was rocking dangerously and all five began to use the paddles now and then, as the white water foamed around them. It required the utmost quickness of eye and hand to keep afloat, and the flying spray soon wet them through and through. Yet the soul of Shif'less Sol was still undaunted. He sang his song of victory, and although most of the words were lost amid the crash and roar of the waters, their triumphant note rose above every other sound, and found an echo in the hearts of the others.

Henry, looking back, saw that the long canoes had turned and were making for the southern shore. Great as was the prize they sought, they would not dare the falls, and half the battle was won.

"They don't follow!" he shouted at the top of his voice. "And now for the miracle that will keep us afloat!"

The canoe raced down the watery slope and the spray continued to drench them, though they had taken the precaution to cover up their rifles and ammunition. But their surpassing skill had its reward. The descent soon became more gradual, the torrents of white water sank, and then they slid forward in the rapids, still going at a great rate, but no longer in danger.

"An' we've left the enemy behind!" sang the shiftless one, looking back at the white masses. "He thought he had us, but he hadn't! He turned back at the steep slope, but we came on! Thar's nothin' like havin' a fall between you an' a lot o' pursuin' Injun canoes, is thar, Paul?"

Paul laughed, half in amusement and half in nervous relief.

"No, Sol, there isn't, at least not now," he replied. "It looks as if these falls had been put here especially to save us."

"I like to think so, too," said the shiftless one.

The river was still very wide and they kept the canoe in its center, although they no longer dreaded Indian shots, feeling quite sure that no warriors were on either shore below the falls. So they went on three or four miles, until Paul asked what was the next plan.

"We must talk it over, all of us," said Henry. "The canoe is of no particular use to us except as a way of escape from immediate danger."

"But it and the falls together saved us," said Shif'less Sol. "Oh, it's a good boat, a fine boat, a friendly boat!"

"I hate to desert a friend."

"It must be done. We can't stay forever on the river in a canoe. That would merely invite destruction. The Indians can take their canoes out of the water, carry them around the falls and resume the pursuit."

"O' course I know you're right, Henry. I wuz jest droppin' a tear or two over the partin' with our faithful canoe. We make fur the north bank, I s'pose."

"That seems to me to be the right course, because the warriors will be thicker on the south side. We'll keep our policy of defense against them by resuming the offense. What say you, Paul?"

"I choose the north bank."

"And you, Jim?"

"North, uv course."

"And you, Tom?"

"North."

"And Sol and I have already spoken. We'll make for the low point across there, sink the canoe and go into the forest. The Indians will be sure in time to pick up our trail and follow us, but we'll escape 'em as we've escaped twice already."

"Red Eagle and Yellow Panther will come for us now," said Paul. "It's their turn next."

"Let 'em," said Long Jim in sanguine tones. "They can't beat us."

They were now out of the rapids and were paddling swiftly toward the northern shore, with their eyes on a small cove, where the bushes grew thick to the water's edge. When they reached it they pushed the canoe into the dense thicket and sank it.

"After all," said Shif'less Sol, "we're not partin' wholly with our friend. We know whar he is, an' he'll wait here until some time or other when we want him ag'in."

Gathering up their arms, ammunition and supplies, they traveled northward through the dense forest until they came to a small and well sheltered valley, where they concluded to rest, it being full time, as collapse was coming fast after their great exertions and intense strain. Nevertheless, Silent Tom was able to keep the first watch, while the others threw themselves on the ground and went to sleep almost instantly.

Tom had promised to awaken Shif'less Sol in two hours, but he did not do so. He knew how much his comrades needed rest, and being willing to sacrifice himself, he watched until dawn, which came bright, cold at first, and then full of grateful warmth, a great sun hanging in a vast disc of reddish gold over the eastern forest.

Silent Tom Ross, in his most talkative moments, was a man of few words, at other times of none, but he felt deeply. A life spent wholly in the woods into which he fitted so supremely had given him much of the Indian feeling. He, too, peopled earth, air and water with spirits, and to him the wild became incarnate. The great burning sun, at which he took occasional glances, was almost the same as the God of the white man and the Manitou of the red man. He had keenly appreciated their danger, both when Henry was at the hollow, and when they were in the canoe on the river, hemmed in on three sides. And yet they had come safely from both nets. The skill of the five had been great, but more than human skill had helped them to escape from such watchful and powerful enemies.

Tom Ross, as he looked at the faces of his comrades, knitted to him by so many hardships and perils shared, was deeply grateful. He took one or two more glances at the great burning sun, and the sky that looked like illimitable depths of velvet blue, and then he surveyed the whole circle of the forest curving around them. It was silent there, no sign of a foe appeared, all seemed to be as peaceful as a great park in the Old World. Tom said no words, not even to himself, but his prayer of thanks ran:

"O Lord, I offer my gratitude to Thee for the friends whom Thou hast given me. As they have been faithful to me in every danger, so shall I try to be faithful to them. Perhaps my mind moves more slowly than theirs, but I strive always to make it move in the right way. They are younger than I am, and I feel it my duty and my pleasure, too, to watch over them, despite their strength of body, mind and spirit. I have not the gift of words, nor do I pray for it, but help me in other things that I may do my part and more."

Then Tom Ross felt uplifted. The dangers passed were passed, and those to come could not press upon him yet. He was singularly light of heart, and the wind sang among the leaves for him, though not in words, as it sang often for Henry.

He took another look at his comrades, and they still slept as if they would never awake. The strain of the preceding nights and days had been tremendous, and their spirits, having gone away with old King Sleep to his untroubled realms, showed no signs of a wish to come back again to a land of unlimited peril. He had promised faithfully to awaken one of them long ago for the second turn at the watch, and he knew that all of them expected to be up at sunrise, but he had broken his promise and he was happy in the breaking of it.

Nor did he awaken them now. Instead he made a wide circle

through the forest, using his good eyes and good ears to their utmost. The stillness had gone, because birds were singing from pure joy at the dawn, and the thickets rustled with the movements of small animals setting about the day's work and play. But Silent Tom knew all these sounds, and he paid no attention to them. Instead he listened for man, man the vengeful, the dangerous and the deadly, and hearing nothing from him and being sure that he was not near, he went back to the place where the four sleepers lay. Examining them critically he saw that they had not stirred a particle. They had been so absolutely still that they had grown into the landscape itself.

Tom Ross smiled a deep smile that brought his mouth well across his face and made his eyes crinkle up, and then, disregarding their wishes with the utmost lightness of heart, he sat himself down, calmly letting them sleep on. He produced from an inside pocket a long stretch of fine, thin, but very strong cord, and ran it through his fingers until he came to the sharp hook on the end. It was all in good trim, and his questing eye soon saw where a long, slender pole could be cut. Then he put thread and hook back in his pocket, and sat as silent as the sleepers, but bright-eyed and watchful. No one could come near without his knowledge.

Shif'less Sol awoke first, yawning mightily, but he did not yet open his eyes.

"Who's watchin'?" he called.

"Me," replied Ross.

"Is it day yet?"

"Look up an' see."

The shiftless one did look up, and when he beheld the great sun shining almost directly over his head he exclaimed in surprise:

"Why, Tom, is it today or tomorrer?"

"It's today, though I guess it's well on to noon."

"Seein' the sun whar it is, an' feelin' now ez ef I had slep' so long, I thought mebbe it might be tomorrer. An' it bein' so late an' me sleepin', too, it looks ez ef the warriors ought to hev us."

"But they hevn't, Sol. All safe."

"No, Tom, they hevn't got us, an' now, hevin' learned from your long an' volyble conversation that it ain't tomorrer an' that we are free, 'stead o' bein' taken captive an' bein' burned at the stake by the Injuns, I'm feelin' mighty fine."

"Sol, you talk real foolish at times. How could we be took by the Injuns an' be burned alive at the stake, an' not know nothin' 'bout it?"

"Don't ask me, Tom. Thar are lots o' strange things that I

60

don't pretend to understan', an' me a smart man, too. Here, you, Jim Hart! Wake up! Shake them long legs an' arms o' yours an' cook our breakfast!"

Silent Tom began to laugh, not audibly, but his lips moved in such a manner that they betrayed risibility. The shiftless one looked at him suspiciously.

"Tom Ross," he said, "what you laughin' at?"

"You told Long Jim to cook breakfast, didn't you?"

"I shorely did, an' I meant it, too."

"He ain't."

"Why ain't he?"

"Because he ain't."

"Ef he ain't, then why ain't he?"

"Because thar ain't any."

"Thar ain't any breakfast, you mean?"

"Jest what I say. He ain't goin' to cook breakfast, 'cause thar ain't any to cook, an' thar ain't no more to say."

Henry and Paul, awakening at the sound of the voices, sat up and caught the last words.

"Do you mean to tell us, Tom," exclaimed Paul, "that we have nothing to eat?"

"Shorely," said Silent Tom triumphantly. "Look! See!"

All of them examined their packs quickly, but they had eaten the last scrap of food the day before. Silent Tom's mouth again stretched across his face with triumph and his eyes crinkled up.

"Right, ain't it?" he asked exultantly.

"Look here you, Tom Ross," exclaimed Shif'less Sol, indignantly, "you'd rather be right an' starve to death than be wrong an' live!"

"Right, ain't I?"

"Yes, right, ain't you, 'bout the food, an' wrong in everythin' else. Ef you say 'ain't' to me ag'in, Tom Ross, inside o' a week, I'll club you so hard over the head with your own gun that you won't be able to speak another word fur a year! The idee o' you laughin' an' me plum' dead with hunger! Why, I could eat a hull big buffler by myself, an' ef he wuzn't cooked I could eat him alive, an' on the hoof too, so I could!"

Tom Ross continued to laugh silently with his eyes and lips.

"What are we to do?" asked Paul in dismay. "If we were to find game we wouldn't dare fire at it with the Indians perhaps so near."

"True," said Tom Ross.

"And if we can't fire at it we certainly can't catch it with our hands."

61

"True," said Tom Ross.

"And then are we to starve to death?"

"No," said Tom Ross.

Paul did not ask anything more, but his questioning look was on the silent man.

"Fish," said Tom Ross, showing his line and hook.

"Where?" asked Shif'less Sol.

"Fine, clear creek, only hundred yards away."

"Do you know that it hez any fish in it?"

"Saw 'em little while ago. Fine big fellers, bass."

"Then be quick an' ketch a lot, 'cause the pangs o' starvation are already on me."

Tom Ross cut the slim pole that he had already picked out and measured with his eye, took squirming bait from the soft earth under a stone, just as millions of boys in the Mississippi valley have done, and started for the creek, Paul being delegated to accompany him, while Henry, Long Jim and the shiftless one proceeded to build a fire in the most secluded spot they could find. There was danger in a fire, but they could shield the smoke, or at least most of it, and the risk must be taken anyhow. They could not eat raw the fish which they did not doubt for a moment Tom Ross would soon bring.

Meanwhile Paul and Tom reached the banks of the creek, which was all the silent one had claimed for it, fifteen feet wide, two feet deep, clear water, flowing over a pebbly bottom. Tom tied his string to the pole, and threw in the hook and bait.

"You watch, I fish," he said.

Paul, his rifle in the crook of his arm, strolled a little bit down the stream, examining the forest and listening attentively for any hostile sound. Since it was his business to protect the fisherman while he fished, he meant to protect him well, and no enemy could have come near without being observed by him. And yet he had enough detachment from the dangers of their situation to drink deep in the beauty of the wilderness, which was here a tangle of green forest, shot with wild flowers and cut by clear running waters.

But he did not go so far that he failed to hear a thump where Tom Ross was sitting, and he knew that a fine fish had been landed. Presently a second thump came to his ear, and, glancing through the bushes, he saw Tom taking the fish off the hook, a look of intense satisfaction on his face. Then the silent fisherman threw in the line again and leaned back luxuriously against the trunk of a tree, while he waited for his third bite. Paul smiled. He knew that Silent Tom was happy, happy because he had prepared for and was achieving a necessary task.

Paul went on in a circuit about the fisherman, crossing the creek lower down, where it was narrower, on a fallen log, and discovered no sign of a foe, though he did come to a bed of wild flowers, the delicate pale blue of which pleased him so much that he broke off two blossoms and thrust them into his deerskin tunic. Then he came back to Silent Tom, to find that he had caught four fine large fish, and, having thrown away his pole, was winding up his line.

"'Nuff," said the silent one.

"I think so, too," said Paul, "and now we'll hurry back with 'em."

"Look like a flower garden, you!"

"If I do I'm glad of it."

"Like it myself."

"I know you do, Tom. I know that however you may appear, and that however fierce and warlike you may be at times, your character rests upon a solid bedrock of poetry."

Tom stared and then smiled, and by this time the two had returned with their spoils to a little valley in which a little fire was burning, with the blaze smothered already, but a fine bed of coals left. The fish were cleaned with amazing quickness, and then Long Jim broiled them in a manner fit for kings. The five ate hungrily, but with due regard for manners.

"You're a good fisherman, Tom Ross," said Shif'less Sol, "but it ought to be my job."

"Why?"

"'Cause it's the job o' a lazy man. I reckon that all fishermen, leastways them that fish in creeks an' rivers, are lazy, nothin' to do but set still an' doze till a fish comes along an' hooks hisself on to your bait. Then you jest hev to heave him in an' put the hook back in the water ag'in."

"There's enough of the fish left for another meal," said Henry, "and I think we'd better put it in our packs and be off."

"You still favor a retreat into the north?" said Paul.

"Yes, and toward the northeast, too. We'll go in the direction of Piqua and Chillicothe, their big towns. As we've concluded over and over again, the offensive is the best defensive, and we'll push it to the utmost. What's your opinion, Sol? Who do you think will be the next leader to come against us?"

"Red Eagle an' the Shawnees. I'm thinkin' they're curvin' out now to trap us, an' that Red Eagle is a mighty crafty fellow."

They trod out the coals, threw some dead leaves over them,

and took a course toward the northeast. It seemed pretty safe to assume that the ring of warriors was thickest in the south, and that they might slip through in the north. Time and distance were of little importance to them, and they felt able to find their rations as they went in the forest.

They had been traveling about an hour at the easy walk of the border, when they heard a long cry behind them.

"They've found the dead coals o' our fire," said Shif'less Sol.

"Which means that they're not so far away," said Paul.

"But we've been comin' over rocky ground, an' the trail ain't picked up so easy. An' we might make it a lot harder by wadin' a while up this branch."

The brook fortunately led in the direction in which they wished to go. They walked in it a full half mile, and as it had a sandy bottom their footprints vanished almost at once. When they emerged at last they heard the long cry again, now from a point toward the east, and then a distant answer from a point in the west. Shif'less Sol laughed with intense enjoyment.

"Guessin'! Jest guessin'!" he said. "They've found the dead coals an' they know that we wuz thar once, but that now we ain't, an' it's not whar we wuz but whar we ain't that's botherin' 'em."

"Still," said Paul, "the more distance we put between them and us the better I, for one, will like it."

"You're right, Paul," said Shif'less Sol. "I guess we'd better shake our feet to a lively tune."

They increased their walk to a trot, and fled through the great forest.

CHAPTER VI
THE OASIS

The five continued their flight all that day, seeing no enemies and hearing no further signal from them. But Henry knew intuitively that the warriors were still in pursuit. They would spread out in every direction, and some one among them would, in time, pick up the trail. After a while, they permitted their own gait to sink to an easy walk, but they did not veer from their northeastern course. Henry, all the time, was a keen observer of the country, and he noticed with pleasure the change that was occurring.

They were coming to a low sunken land, cut by many streams, nearly all sluggish and muddy. The season had been rainy, and there was an odor of dampness over all things. Great thickets of reeds and cane began to appear, and now and then they trod into deep banks of moss.

"Perhaps we'd better turn to the north and avoid it," said Paul. "This marsh region seems to be extensive."

Henry shook his head.

"We won't avoid it," he said. "On the contrary it's just what we want. I'm thinking that we're being watched over. You know the forest fire came in time to save us, then the falls appeared just when we needed 'em, and now this huge marsh, extending miles and miles in every direction, cuts across our path, not as an enemy, but as a friend."

"That is, we are to hide in it?"

"Where could we find a better refuge?"

"Then you lead the way, Henry," said Shif'less Sol. "Ef you sink in it we'll pull you out, purvidin' you don't go in it over your neck."

Henry went ahead, his wary eye examining the ground which had already grown alarmingly soft save for those trained for such marchings. But he was able to pick out the firm places, though the earth would quickly close over their footsteps, as they passed, and, now and then, they walked on the upthrust roots of trees, their moccasins giving them a securer hold.

It was precarious and dangerous work, but they went deeper and deeper into the heart of the great swamp, through thickets of bushes, cane and reeds, the soil continually growing softer and the vegetation ranker and more gloomy. Often the canes and reeds were so dense that they had difficulty in seeing their leader, as he slipped on ahead. Sometimes snakes trailed a slimy length from their path, and, hardened foresters though they were, they shuddered. Occasionally an incautious foot sank to the knee and it was pulled out again with a choking sigh as the mud closed where it had been. Mosquitoes and many other buzzing and stinging insects assailed them, but they pressed on without hesitation.

They came to a great black pond on which marsh fowl were swimming, but Henry led around its miry edges, and they pressed on into the deeper depths of the vast swamp. He judged that they had now penetrated it a full two miles, but he had no intention of stopping. The four behind him knew without his telling for what he was looking. The swamp, partly a product of an extremely rainy season, must have bits of solid ground somewhere within its area, and, when they came to such a place, they would stop. Yet it would be all the better if they did not reach it for a long time, as the farther they were from the edge of the swamp the safer they could rest.

No island of firm earth appeared, and the traveling grew more difficult. Often they helped themselves along with vines that drooped from scrubby trees, swinging their bodies over places that would not bear their weight, but always, whether slow or fast, they made progress, penetrating farther and farther into the huge blind maze.

The sun was low when they stopped for a long rest, hoping they would reach refuge very soon.

"I don't think the warriors kin ever find us in here," said Long Jim, "but what's troublin' me is whether we'll ever be able to git out ag'in."

"Mebbe you wouldn't be so anxious to show yourse'f, Jim Hart, on solid ground ef you could only see yourse'f ez I see you," said Shif'less Sol. "You're a sight, plastered over with black mud, an' scratched with briers an' bushes. Lookin' at you, an' sizin' you up, I reckon that jest now you're 'bout the ugliest man in this hull round world."

"Ef I ain't, you are," said Long Jim, grinning. "Fact is, thar ain't a beauty among us. I don't mind mud so much, but I don't like it when it's black an' slimy. How fur do you reckon this flooded country goes, Henry?"

"Twenty miles, maybe, Jim, but the farther the better for us. Here's an old fallen log which I think will hold our weight. Suppose we stop here and rest a little."

They were glad enough to do so. When they sat down they heard the mournful sigh of a light wind through the black and marshy jungle, and the splash now and then of a muskrat in the water. Their refuge seemed dim and inexpressibly remote, as if it belonged to the wet and ferny world of dim antiquity. But every one of the five felt that they were safe, at least for the present, from pursuit.

"We might plough a trail a yard deep," said Shif'less Sol, "but the mud would close over it ag'in in five minutes, an' Red Eagle with five hundred o' the best trailers in the hull Shawnee nation couldn't foller us."

"It's strange and grim," said Paul, "but, when you look at it a long time there's a certain kind of forbidding beauty about it, and you're bound to admit that it's a friendly swamp, since it's hiding us from ruthless pursuers."

"Perhaps that's why you find the beauty in it," said Henry. "Come on, though. The Shawnees are not likely to reach us here, but we must find some snug place in which we can camp."

"After all," said Paul, "we're like travelers in a great desert looking for an oasis."

"We ain't as hungry ez all that," said Long Jim.

"You won't get angry if I laugh, Jim, will you?" asked Paul.

"Don't mind me. Go ahead an' laugh all you want."

"An oasis is not something to eat, Jim. It's a green and watered place in an ocean of sand."

"Seems to me that we waste time lookin' fur a place that's more watered than all these we're crossin'. What I want is a dry place, a piece out uv that ocean uv sand you're talkin' 'bout."

"The conditions are merely reversed. My illustration holds good."

"What did you say, Paul? Them wuz mighty big words."

"Never mind. You'll find out in due time. Just you pray for an oasis in this swamp, because that is what we want, and we want it bad."

"All right, Paul, I'm prayin'. I ain't shore what I'm prayin' fur, but I take your word fur it."

Henry rose and led on again, anxious of heart. They were well hidden, it was true, in the great swamp, but they must find some place to lay their heads. It was impossible to rest in the black ooze that surrounded them, and if they did not reach firmer ground soon he did not know what they would do. The sun was already low, and, in the east, the shadows were gathering. Around them all things were clothed in gloom. Even that touch of forbidding beauty, of which Paul had spoken was gone and the whole swamp became dark and sinister.

67

Henry was compelled to walk with the utmost care, lest he become engulfed, and finally all of them cut lengths of cane with which they felt about in the mire before they advanced.

"Pray hard, Long Jim," said Paul. "Pray hard for that oasis, because the night will soon be here, and if we don't find our oasis we'll have to stand in our tracks until day, and that's a mighty hard thing to do."

"I wuz never wishin' an prayin' harder in my life."

"I think your prayer is answered," interrupted Henry, who was thrusting here and there with his cane. "To the right the ground seems to be growing more solid. The mire is not more than a foot deep. I think I'll venture in that direction. What do you say, boys?"

"Might ez well try it," said Shif'less Sol. "It may be a last chance, but sometimes a last chance wins."

Henry, feeling carefully with the long, stout cane, plunged into the slough. He was more anxious than he was willing to say, but at the same time he was hopeful. As the swamp was due, at least in large part, to the great rains, it must have firm ground somewhere, and he had noticed also in the thickening twilight that the bushes ahead seemed much larger than usual. A dozen steps and the mire was not more than six inches deep. Then with a subdued cry of triumph he seized the bushes, pulled himself among them, and stood not more than moccasin deep in the mud.

"It's the best place we've come to yet," he said. "I can't see over the thicket, but I'm hoping that we'll find beyond it some kind of a hill and dry ground."

"I know we will," said Long Jim, confidently. "It's 'cause I wished an' prayed so hard. It's a lucky thing, Paul, that you had me to do the wishin' an' prayin', 'stead o' Shif'less Sol, 'cause then we'd hev walked into black mire a thousan' feet deep. Ef the prayers uv the sinners are answered a-tall, a-tall, they're answered wrong."

Shif'less Sol shook his head scornfully.

"Let's go on, Henry," he said, "afore Long Jim talks us plum' to death, a thing I'd hate to hev happen to me, jest when we're 'bout to reach the promised land."

Henry pushed his way through dense bushes and trailing vines, and he noticed with intense joy that all the time the earth was growing firmer. The others followed silently in his tracks. In five minutes he emerged from the thicket, and then he could not repress an exclamation of pleasure. They had come upon a low hill, an acre perhaps in extent, as firm as any soil and well grown with thick low oaks. Where the shade was not too deep the grass was rich, and the five, the others repeating Henry's cry of joy, threw themselves upon it and luxuriated.

68

"It's fine," said Shif'less Sol, "to lay here an' to feel that the earth under you ain't quiverin' like a heap o' jelly. I turn from one side to the other an' then back ag'in, an' I don't sink into no mud, a-tall, a-tall."

"An' this, Paul, is the o-sis that you wuz talkin' 'bout, an' that I wished an' prayed into the right place fur us?" said Long Jim.

"Oasis, Jim, not o-sis," said Paul.

"Oasis or o-sis, it's jest ez good to me by either name, an' I think I'll stick to o-sis, 'cause it's easier to say. But, Paul, did you ever see a finer piece uv land? Did you ever see finer, richer soil? Did you ever see more splendiferous grass or grander oaks?"

"I feel about it just as you do," laughed Paul.

Henry lay still a full ten minutes, resting after their tremendous efforts in the swamp, then he rose, walked through their oasis and discovered that at the far edge a fine large brook was running, apparently and in some mysterious way, escaping at that point the contamination of the mud, although he could see that farther on it lost itself in the swamp. But its cool, sparkling waters were a heavenly sight, and, walking back, he announced his discovery to the others.

"All of you know what you can do," he said.

"We do," said Paul.

"First thought in my mind," said Shif'less Sol.

"An' we'll do it," said Long Jim.

"Now!" said Silent Tom.

They took off their clothing, scraped from it as much mud as they could, and took a long and luxurious bath in the brook. Then they came out on the bank and let themselves dry, the night which had now fully come, fortunately being warm. As they lay in the grass they felt a great content, and Long Jim gave it utterance.

"An o-sis is a fine thing," he said. "I'm glad you invented 'em, Paul, 'cause I don't know what we'd a-done without this un."

Henry rose and began to dress. The others did likewise.

"I think we'd better eat the rest of Tom's fish and then go to sleep," he said. "Tomorrow morning we'll have to hold a grand council, and consider the question of food, as I think we're very likely to stay in here quite a while."

"Are you really looking for a long stay?" asked Paul.

"Yes, because the Indians will be beating up the woods for us so thoroughly that it will be best for us not to move from our hiding place. It's a fine swamp! A glorious swamp! And because it's so big and black and miry it's all the better for us. The only problem before us is to get food."

69

"And we always get it somehow or other."

They wrapped themselves in their blankets to keep off any chill that might come later in the night, lay down under the boughs of the dwarf oaks, and slept soundly until the next day, keeping no watch, because they were sure they needed none. Tom Ross himself never opened his eyes once until the sun rose. Then the problem of food, imminent and pressing, as the last of the fish was gone, presented itself.

"I think that branch is big enough to hold fish," said Tom Ross, bringing forth his hook and line again, "an' ef any are thar they'll be purty tame, seein' that the water wuz never fished afore. Anyway I'll soon see."

The others watched him anxiously, as he threw in his bait, and their delight was immense, when a half hour's effort was rewarded with a half dozen perch, of fair size and obviously succulent.

"At any rate, we won't starve," said Henry, "though it would be hard to live on fish alone, and besides it's not healthy."

"But we'll get something else," said Paul.

"What else?"

"I don't know, but I notice when we keep on looking we're always sure to find."

"You're right, Paul. It's a good thing to have faith, and I'll have it, too. But we can eat fish for several meals yet, and then see what will happen."

They devoted the morning to a thorough washing and cleaning of their clothing, which they dried in the sun, and they also made a further examination of the oasis. The swamp came up to its very edge on all three sides except that of the brook, and a little distance beyond the brook it was swamp again. It would have been hard to imagine a more secluded and secure retreat, and Henry dismissed from his mind the thought of immediate pursuit there by the Indians. Their present problems were those of food and shelter.

"I think," he said, "that we ought to build a bark hut. There's a natural site between the four big trees which will be the corners of our house, and the ground is just covered with the kind of bark we want."

In the warm sunshine and with a clear sky above them they seemed to have no need of a house, but all of them knew how quickly the weather could change in the great valley. It would be hard to stand a fierce storm on the oasis, and one of the secrets of the great and continued success of the five was to prepare for every emergency of which they could think.

Long practice had given them high skill, and four of them set

70

to work with their tomahawks to build a hut of bark and poles, working swiftly, dextrously and mostly in silence, while Silent Tom went back to the fishing. They toiled that day and at least half the night with poles and bark, and by noon the next day they had finished a little cabin, which they were sure would hold, with the aid of the great trees, against anything. It had a floor of poles smoothed with dead leaves, one small window and a low door, over which they purposed to hang blankets if a blowing rain came.

Throughout their hard labors they had an abundance of fish, but nothing else, and they not only began to long for other food, but health demanded it as well.

"Ef Long Jim Hart offers fish to me, ag'in," said the shiftless one, "I'll take it an' cram it down his own throat."

"And then how'll you live?" asked Paul.

"I think I'll take Long Jim hisself an' eat him, beginnin' at his head, which is the softest part o' him."

"Now that the cabin is done," said Henry, "maybe we can devote some attention to hunting."

"Huntin' in black mud that'll suck you down to your waist in a second?" said Shif'less Sol.

"I think I might find a pathway on the other side of the stream, and this swamp ought to hold a lot of game. Bears love swamps, and I might run across a deer."

"Would the Indians hear you if you fired?" asked Paul.

"No, we're too far in for the sound of a rifle to reach 'em. Still, I won't start today. I suppose we can stand the fish until tomorrow."

"We have to stand 'em," said Shif'less Sol, "an' that bein' the case I think I'll look ag'in at our beautiful house which hasn't a nail or a spike in it, but is jest held together by withes an' vines, but held together well jest the same."

"Ain't it fine?" said Long Jim with genuine admiration. "It's jest 'bout the finest house that ever stood on this o-sis."

"That, at least, is true," said Paul.

They did not sleep in the cabin that night, as they intended to use it only in bad weather, but made good beds on the leaves outside. Shif'less Sol was the first to awake, and it was scarcely dawn when he arose. Happening to look toward the brook delight overspread his face like a sunrise, and laughing softly to himself he took his own rifle and Long Jim's. Then he crept forward without noise, and making sure of his aim, fired both rifles so closely together that one would have thought it was a double barreled weapon.

The four leaped to their feet, and, clearing the sleep from their eyes, ran in the direction of the shots. But the shiftless one was already walking proudly back toward them.

"What is it, Sol?" cried Paul.

"Only these," replied Shif'less Sol, and he held up a fat wild duck in either hand. "They wuz swimmin' in the branch, waitin' to be cooked an' et by five good fellers like us, an' seein' they wuz in earnest 'bout it I hev obliged 'em. So here they are, an' you, Long Jim, you, you set to work at once an' cook 'em, 'cause I'm mighty hungry fur nice fat duck, not hevin' et anythin' but fish fur the last year or two."

"Jest watch me do it," said Long Jim. "Ain't I been waitin' fur a chance uv this kind? While I'm cookin' 'em you fellers will stan' 'roun', an' them sav'ry smells will make you so hungry you can't bear to wait, but you'll hev to, 'cause I won't let you touch a duck till it's br'iled jest right. Are thar any more whar these come from, Sol?"

"Not jest at this minute, Jim, but thar wuz, an' thar will be. A dozen jest ez good ez these fat fellers flew away when I fired, an' whar some hez been more will come."

"Curious we didn't think of the wild fowl," said Henry. "We noticed that the swamp had big permanent ponds besides running water, and it was a certainty that wild ducks and wild geese would come in search of their kind of food, which is so plentiful in here."

"Maybe we can set up traps and snares and catch game," said Paul. "It will save our ammunition, and besides there would be no danger that a wandering Indian in the swamp might hear our shots and carry the news of our location."

"Wise words, Paul," said Henry. "We must put our minds on the question of traps."

"But not this minute," said Long Jim. "Bigger things are to the front. Here, you lazy Sol, he'p me clean these ducks, an' Paul, you an' Tom build me a fire quicker'n lightnin'. The sooner you do what I tell you the sooner you'll git juicy duck to eat."

They worked rapidly, with such an incentive to effort, and soon the savory odors of which Long Jim had boasted incited their hunger to an extreme pitch. He did not keep them waiting long, and when they were through nothing was left of the ducks but bones.

"It would be better to have bread, too," said Paul, as he sighed with satisfaction, "but since we can't have it we must manage to get along without it."

"Mustn't ask fur too much," said Silent Tom.

"Sol," said Henry, "after we rest an hour or so suppose you and I set the snares for the ducks and geese. Likely no human being has ever been in here before, and they won't be on guard against us.

The rest of you might do more work on the house. We ought to provide food and shelter as well as we can before stormy weather comes."

While Henry and the shiftless one were busy down the stream, the other three put more strength into the hut, lashing the poles and bark fast with additional tenacious withes and feeling all the interest that people have when they erect a fine new house.

"It's surely a tight little cabin," said Paul, standing off and examining it with a critical eye. "I don't think a drop of rain could get in even in the heaviest storm. There, did you hear that?"

"Yes, a rifle shot," said Long Jim. "It wuz Henry or Sol, but it don't mean no enemy. They hev got some kind uv game that they didn't expect."

The shot was followed in a few moments by a shout of triumph, and Henry and Sol emerged from the swamp carrying between them a small but very fat black bear.

"Thar's rations fur some time to come," said Long Jim. "I guess he wuz huntin' berries in the swamp when Sol or Henry picked him off, an' I'm shore thar'll be more uv the same kind. It begins to look like a mighty fine swamp to me."

It was the shiftless one who had shot the bear, and he was proud of his triumph, as he had a right to be, having secured such a supply of good food, because there was nothing better that the forest furnished than fat young bear. It did not take experts, such as they, long to clean the bear, and cut its flesh into strips for drying.

"I think our snares will hold something in the morning," said Henry, "and that will be a big help, too. What was it you said about the swamp, Jim?"

"I said it wuz gittin' to be a mighty fine swamp. First time I saw it I thought it wuz an ugly place, ugliest I ever seed, but now it's growin' plum' beautiful. Reckon it's the safest place now in all the wilderness. Knowin' that, helps it a lot, an' its yieldin' up good food helps it more. The sun is gildin' the trees, an' the bushes an' the mud an' the water a heap, an' all them things don't hurt my eyes when they linger on 'em."

"Jim is turnin' into a poet," said the shiftless one, "but I reckon he hez cause. I'm gittin' to feel 'bout the swamp jest ez he does. It's a splendid place, jest full o' beauty!"

They slept under the trees again, putting the strips of bear meat in the house to secure them from marauders of the air, and awoke the next morning to find the swamp still improving. Powerful factors in the improvement were two ducks and a fat wild goose caught in the snares, and, with more fish from Silent Tom, they had a variety for breakfast.

73

"I jest love wild goose," said Shif'less Sol, "speshully when it's fat an' tender, an' I'm thinkin' this swamp is a good place for wild geese. When we come in here we didn't think what a fine home we wuz findin'. Since the tribes an' the renegades have sworn to wipe us out, an' we're hid here so snug an' so tight, I don't keer how long I stay."

"Nor me either," said Long Jim. "This o-sis makes me think sure uv that island in the lake on which we stayed once, but it's safer here. Nothin' but the longest kind uv chance would make the warriors find us."

"That's true," said Henry thoughtfully. "We might have searched the whole continent, and we couldn't have discovered a better refuge, for our purpose. I know we can lie hid here a long time and let them hunt us."

Shif'less Sol began to laugh, not loud, but with great intensity, and his laugh was continued long.

"What you laffin' at, you Sol Hyde?" asked Long Jim suspiciously.

"Not at you, Jim," replied the shiftless one. "I wuz thinkin' 'bout them renegades, Wyatt and Blackstaffe. I would shorely like to see 'em now, an' look into thar faces, an' behold 'em wonderin' an' wonderin' what hez become o' us that they expected to ketch between thar fingers, an' squash to death. They look on the earth, an' they don't see no trail o' ourn. They look in the sky an' they don't see us flyin' 'roun' anywhar thar. The warriors circle an' circle an' circle an' they don't put their hands on us. That ring is tight an' fast, an' we can't break out o' it. We ain't on the outside o' it, an' they can't find us on the inside o' it. So, whar are we? They don't know but we do. We hev melted away like witches. Them renegades is shorely hoppin', t'arin' mad, but the madder they are the better we like it. 'Scuse me, Jim, while I laff ag'in, an' it wouldn't hurt you, Jim, if you wuz to laff with me."

"I think I will," said Long Jim, and action followed word. Later in the day Henry and Paul penetrated a short distance deeper into the swamp, but did not find another oasis like theirs. The entire area seemed to be occupied by mire and ponds and thickets of reeds and cane, mingled with briars. They stirred up another black bear, but they did not get a chance for a shot at him, and they also saw the footprints of a panther. They returned to the oasis satisfied with their exploration. The swampier the swamp and the greater its extent the safer they were.

That night as they slept under the trees they were awakened by the rushing of many wings. When they sat up they found the sky

74

dark above them, although the moon was shining and all the stars were out. It was a flight of wild pigeons and they had settled in countless thousands on the trees of the oasis. The five with sticks knocked off as many as they thought they could use, and stored them for the night in the hut. They devoted the next day to picking and dressing their spoils, the living birds having gone on, and on the following day, Henry, who had entered the swamp on another trip of exploration, returned with the most welcome news of all. He had discovered a salt spring only a short distance away, and with labor they were able to boil out the salt which was invaluable to them in curing their food supply.

"Now, if we had bread, we'd be entirely happy," said Paul.

"Shucks, Paul," said Shif'less Sol with asperity, "you're entirely happy ez it is. Never ask too much an' then you won't git too little. This splendid, magnificent swamp o' ourn furnishes everythin' any reasonin' human bein' could want."

Henry shot another black bear, very small but quite fat and tender, and he was quickly added to their store. More wild ducks and wild geese were caught in the snares, and they had now been on the oasis more than a week without the slightest sign from their foes. Danger seemed so far away that it could never come near, and they enjoyed the interval of peace and quiet, devoted to the homely business of mere living.

Then came a day when great mists and vapors rose from the swamp, and the air grew heavy. Everything turned to a sullen, leaden color. Henry glanced at their hut.

"We have built in time," he said. "All this heaviness and cloudiness foretells a storm and I think we'll sleep under a roof tonight. What say you, Sol?"

"I shorely will, Henry. Them that wants to lay on the ground, an' take a wettin' kin take it, but, ez fur me, a floor, a roof an' four walls is jest what I want."

"Everybody will agree with you on that," said Paul.

No one spoke again for a long time. Meanwhile the vapors and mists thickened and the skies became almost as black as night. The whole swamp, save the little island on which they sat, was lost in the dusk, and a wind, heavy with damp, came moaning out of the vast wilderness. Thunder rumbled on the horizon, then cracked directly overhead, and flashes of lightning cut the blackness.

The five retreated to their hut, and, with a mighty rushing of wind and a great sweep of rain, the storm burst over the oasis.

CHAPTER VII
INTO THE NORTH

When the wilderness was under the beat of wind or rain or hail or snow Henry and Paul, if sheltered well, never failed to feel an increase of comfort, even of luxury. The contrast between the storm without and the dryness within gave an elemental feeling of relaxation and content that nothing else could supply. It had been so at the rocky hollow, and it was so here.

Their first anxiety had been for the little house. Being built of poles and bark it quivered and trembled, as the wind smote it hard, but it held fast and did not lose a timber. That apprehension passed, they looked to see whether it would turn the rain, and noted with joy in their workmanship and pleasure in their security that not a drop made its way between the poles and bark.

These early fugitive fears gone, they settled down to ease and observation of the storm, being able to leave the door open about a foot, as the wind was driving against the back of the house. It was almost as dark as night, with gusts that whistled and screamed, and the rain seemed to come in great waves of water. Despite the dusk, they saw leaves torn from the trees and whirled away in showers. Every phase and change of the storm was watched by them with the keenest attention and interest. Weather was a tremendous factor in the life of the borderer, and he was compelled to guide most of his actions by it.

"How long do you think it will last, Sol?" asked Henry.

"I don't see no break in the clouds," replied the shiftless one. "This wind will die after a while, but the rain will keep right on. I look for it to last all today, an' all the night that's comin'."

"I think you're right, Sol, an' it's a mighty big rain, too. The whole swamp except our island will be swimming in water."

"But it won't be no flood, that is, like the big flood," said Long Jim. "But ef one did come I wouldn't mind it much ef we had an ark same ez Noah. Ef you could only furgit all them poor people that got theirselves drowned it would be mighty fine, sailin' 'roun' in an ark a mile or so long, guessin' at the places whar the towns hev stood, an' lettin' down a line now an' then to sound fur the tops uv the highest mountains in the world."

"You wouldn't hev no time fur lettin' down lines fur mountain tops, Jim Hart," said Shif'less Sol.

76

"An' why wouldn't I hev time fur lettin' down lines fur anythin' I wanted, you lazy Solomon Hyde?"

"'Cause it would be your job to feed the animals, an' to do it right you'd hev to git up early in the mornin' an' work purty nigh to midnight all the forty days the flood lasted. Me an' Henry an' Paul an' Tom would spen' most o' our time settin' on the edge o' the ark with our umbrellers h'isted, lookin' at the scenery, while you wuz down in the bowels o' the ark, heavin' in more meat to the lions an' tigers, which wuz allus roarin' fur more."

"I wouldn't feed no animals, not ef every one uv 'em starved to death. Besides, what would be the use uv it? 'Cause when the flood dried up the woods would soon be full uv 'em ag'in."

"Jim Hart, hevn't you no sense a-tall, a-tall? Ef all the animals wuz drowned, ev'ry last one o' 'em, how could the woods be full o' 'em ag'in?"

"Don't ask me, Sol Hyde. Thar are lots uv things that are too deep fur you an' me both. Now, how did the animals git into the woods in the fust place?"

"I can't answer, o' course."

"Nor can I, but I reckon they'd git into the woods in the second place, which is after the flood, we're s'posin', jest the same way they did in the fust place, which wuz afore the flood, an' that, I reckon, settles it. I don't feed no wild animals, nohow."

"What will the big storm and the deluge of rain mean to us, anyway?" asked Paul.

"It will help us," replied Henry promptly. "I've been worried about all those mists and vapors rising from the decayed or sodden vegetation. There was malaria in them. Our systems have resisted it, because the life we lead has made us so tough and hard, but maybe the poison would have soaked in some time or other. Now the flood of clean rain will freshen up the whole swamp. It will lay the mists and vapors and wash everything till it's pure."

"An' it will flood the swamp so tremenjeously," said the shiftless one, "that fur days thar will be no gittin' in or gittin' out. Anybody that tries it will sink over his head afore he goes a hundred yards."

"Which makes us all the more secure," said Paul. "It certainly appears as if the elements fight for us. For a week at least we're as safe here as if we were surrounded by a stone wall, a thousand feet thick and a mile high. And in that time I intend to enjoy myself. It will be the first rest in two or three years for us to have, absolutely free from care. Here we are with good shelter, plenty of food, nothing to do, and, such being the happy case, I intend to take a big sleep."

He rolled himself in a blanket, stretched his body on a bed of leaves, and soon was in slumber. The others also luxuriated in a mighty sleep, after their great labors and anxiety, and the little hut that they had builded with their own hands not only held fast against the wind, but kept out the least drop of water. The rain, true to Shif'less Sol's prediction, lasted all night, but the morning came, beautiful and clear, with a pleasant, cool touch.

The swamp was turned into a vast lake, and they shot two deer that had taken refuge from the flood on their oasis. Henry, despite the rising waters, was able to reach the salt spring, and they cured the flesh of the deer, adding to it a day or two later several wild turkeys that alighted in their trees. They continued to prepare themselves for a long stay, and they were not at all averse to it. Rest and freedom from danger were a rare luxury that every one of the five enjoyed.

Henry's assumption that the great rain would freshen the swamp proved true. All the mists and vapors were gone. There was no odor of decaying wood or of slime. It seemed as if the place had been cleaned and scrubbed until it was like a fine lake. Silent Tom caught bigger fish than ever, and they agreed that they were better to the taste, although they agreed also that it might be an effect of fancy. The island itself was dry and sunny, but from their home they looked upon a wilderness of bushes, cane and reeds, growing in what was now clear water. The effect of the whole was beautiful. The swamp had become transformed.

"It will all settle back after a while," said Henry quietly.

But a second rain, though not so hard and long as the first, filled up the basin again, and they foresaw a delay of at least two weeks before it returned to its old condition. They accepted the increased time with thankfulness, and remained in their camp, doing nothing but little tasks, and gathering strength for the future.

"I should fancy that the warriors would hunt us here some time or other," said Paul. "Shrewd and cunning as they are, and missing us as they have, they'd think to penetrate it!"

"It seems so to me," said Henry. "Red Eagle is a great chief, and, after he searches everywhere else for us and fails to find us, he'll try for a way into this swamp, unlikely though it looks as a home."

"But lookin' at the water an' the canes, an' the reeds an' the bushes I've figgered it out that he can't come fur two weeks," said

Shif'less Sol, "an' so I've made up my mind to enjoy myse'f. Think o' it! A hull two weeks fur a lazy man to do nothin' in! An' I reckon I kin do nothin' harder an' better than any other man that ever lived. Ef it wuzn't fur gittin' stiff I wouldn't move hand or foot fur the next two weeks. I'd jest lay on my back on the softest bed I could make, an' Long Jim Hart would come an' feed me three times ev'ry day."

"I think," said Henry, "we'd better build a raft. It'll help us with both the fishing and the hunting, and with plenty of willow withes we ought to hold enough timbers together."

The raft was made in about a day. It was a crude structure, but as it was intended to have a cruising radius of only a few hundred yards, pushing its way through strong vegetation, to which the bold navigators could cling, it sufficed, proving to be very useful in visiting the snares and decoys they set for the wild ducks and wild geese. The swamp, in truth, now fairly swarmed with feathered game, and, had they cared to expend their ammunition, they could have killed enough for twenty men, but they preferred to save powder and lead, and rely upon the traps, and fish which were abundant.

The skies were very clear now and they watched them for threads of Indian smoke which could be seen far, many miles in such a thin atmosphere, but the bright heavens were never defiled by any such sign. It was the opinion of Henry that the main Indian band, under Red Eagle, had gone northward in the search, but it would be folly to leave the swamp now, since other detachments had certainly been left to the southward. The ring might be looser and much larger, but it was sure to be still there, and it was not hard for such as they, trained in patience and enjoying a rare peace, to wait. Thus the days passed without event, and the five felt their muscles growing bigger and stronger for the great tasks bound to come. But a curious feeling that war and danger were half a world away grew upon them. They were in love for a time with peace and all its ways. They were reluctant even to shoot any of the larger wild animals that wandered through the swamp, and they felt actual pain when they slew the wild ducks and wild geese caught in their snares.

"I'm bein' gentled fast," said Shif'less Sol. "Ef this keeps on fur a month or so I won't hev the heart to shoot at any Injun who may come ag'inst me. I'll jest say: 'Here, Mr. Warrior, hop up an' take my skelp. It's a good skelp, a fine head o' hair an' I wuz proud o' it. I would like to hev kep' it, but seein' that you want it bad, snatch it off, hang it in your wigwam, tell the neighbors that thar is the skelp o' Solomon Hyde, an' I'll git along the best I kin without it.'"

"You may feel that way now, Sol," said Long Jim, "but you jest wait till the Injun comes at you fur your skelp. Then you'll change your mind quicker'n lightnin', an' you'll reach fur your gun, an' blow his head off."

"Reckon you're right, Jim," said the shiftless one.

Silent Tom stared at them in amazement.

"What's the matter, Tom?" asked Paul. "Why do you look at them in that manner?"

"Agreed!" replied Silent Tom.

"What?"

"Agreed!"

"Agreed? Oh, I understand what you mean! Sol and Jim hold the same opinion about something."

"Yes. Fust time!"

"Don't you be worried, Tom Ross," said Shif'less Sol, "I'll see that it never happens ag'in."

"Me, too," said Long Jim Hart. "You see, Tom, that wuz the only time in his life that Sol wuz ever right when he wuz disputin' with me, an' me bein' a truthful man had to agree with him."

Another week passed and the atmosphere of peace and content that clothed the great marsh grew deeper. The waters subsided somewhat, but it was still impossible to pass from the oasis to the firm land without, except in a canoe, and that they did not have. Nor was it likely that the Indians would produce a canoe merely to navigate a flooded marsh. While sure that none would come, all nevertheless kept a good watch for a possible invader.

The weather began to turn cooler and the first fading tints appeared on the foliage. It was the time when one season passed into another, usually accompanied by rains and winds, but they were more numerous than usual this year. The strong little hut again and again proved its usefulness, not only as a storehouse, but as a shelter, although it was so crowded now with stores that scarcely room was left for the five to sleep there. The skins of the two bears had been dressed and Henry and Paul slept upon them, while much of their cured food hung from pegs which they contrived to fix into the walls.

As the waters sank still farther, they noticed that the swamp was full of life. What had seemed to be a waste was inhabited in reality by many of the people of the wilderness. The five had approached it from the west, and now Henry, who was able to go farther east than they had been before, found a small beaver colony at a point on the brook, where there was enough firm ground to support a little grove of fine trees.

The beavers had dammed the stream and were already building their houses for the distant winter. Henry, hidden among the bushes, watched them quite a while, interested in their work, and observing their methods of construction. He could easily have shot two or three, and beaver tail was good to eat, but he had no thought of molesting them, and, after he had seen enough, drew off cautiously, lest he disturb them in their pursuits.

He saw many muskrats and rabbits and also the footprints of wildcats. A magnificent stag, standing knee deep in the water, looked at him with startled eyes. He would have been a grand trophy, but Henry did not fire, and, a moment or two later, the stag floundered away, leaving the young leader very thoughtful. What had the big deer been doing in such difficult territory? It would scarcely come of its own accord into so deep a marsh, and Henry concluded that it must have fled there for refuge from hunters, and the only hunters in that region were Indians. Then they must still be not far away from the marsh!

It was such a serious matter and he was so preoccupied with it that a huge black bear, springing up almost at his feet, passed unnoticed. The bear lumbered away, splashing mud and water, stopping once to look back fearfully at the strange creature that had disturbed it, but Henry went on, caring nothing for bears or any other wild animals just then.

When he returned, however, he was bound to take notice of the vast quantity of wild fowl in the swamp. Every pond or lagoon swarmed with wild ducks and wild geese, and hawks and eagles swooped from the air, splashed the water, and then rose again with fish in their talons. Two big owls, blinking in the light, sat on the bough of an oak. Another flight of wild pigeons streamed southward. The life of the swamp was so multitudinous that Henry and his comrades could have lived in it indefinitely, even without bread.

When he was back on the oasis he said nothing of his meeting with the deer and the significance that he had read in it, thinking it not worth while to cause alarm until he had something more tangible. Another week, and there was a perceptible increase in the autumnal tints. All the green was gone from the leaves. Red and yellow dyes, not yet glowing, but giving promise of what they would be, appeared. The early flights southward of more wild fowl, taking time by the forelock, increased, and in the minds of some of the five came thoughts of leaving the swamp.

"They must have given up the pursuit by this time," said Paul. "They wouldn't hunt us forever."

"Looks that way to me, too," said Long Jim.

Henry shook his head.

"Some of the warriors have gone away," he said, "but not all of them. Red Eagle, the Shawnee chief, is a man who thinks, and a man who holds on. He knows that we couldn't sink through the earth or fly above the clouds, and the time will come when he will look into this matter of the swamp. It appears to be impenetrable, but he will conclude at last that there is a way."

"I'm o' your mind," said Shif'less Sol. "When you're carryin' on a war it ain't jest a matter o' guns an' ammunition, an' the lay o' the land. You've got to think what kind o' a gen'ral is leadin' the warriors ag'inst you. You must take his mind into account. Ain't that so, Paul? Wuzn't it true o' that old Roman, Hannybul?"

"Hannibal was not a Roman, not by a great deal, Sol, as I told you before."

"Well, he wuz a Rooshian, or mebbe an Eyetalian. What diff'unce does it make? He wuz some kind o' a furriner, an' ef what you tell us 'bout him is true, Paul, as I reckon it is, it wuz his mind that led his men on to victory over the Rooshians an' the Prooshians an' the French an' the Dutch."

"Over the Romans, Sol."

"Ez I told you once, Paul, it makes no diff'unce. They're all furriners, an' all furriners are jest the same. Hannybul wuz the kind that wouldn't give up. You've talked so much 'bout him, Paul, that I kin see him in my fancy an' I know jest how he done. Often a big battle seemed to be goin' ag'inst him. His men hev shot away all thar powder an' bullets. The Shawnees an' the Miamis an' the Wyandots are comin' on hard, shoutin' the war whoop, swingin' thar glitterin' tomahawks 'bout thar fierce heads. The Romans already feel the hands o' the warriors on thar skelps, an' they are tremblin', ready to run. But Hannybul swings his rifle, clubs the leadin' Injun over the head with it, an' yells to his men: 'Come on, fellers! Draw your hatchets an' knives! Drive 'em into the brush! We kin whip 'em yet!' An' the Romans, gittin' courage from thar leader, go in an' thrash the hull band. Now, that's the kind o' a leader Red Eagle is. I give him credit fur doin' a power o' thinking an' holdin' on. Braxton Wyatt and Blackstaffe will say to him: 'Come, chief, let's go away. They slipped through our lines in the night, an' they're somewhar up on the shore o' one o' the big lakes, a-laffin' an' a-laffin' at us. We'll go up thar, trail 'em down an' make 'em laff if they kin, a-settin' among the live coals.' But that Red Eagle, wise old chief that he is, will up an' say: 'They haven't got through. They couldn't without bein' seen by our scouts an' watchers. An' since they haven't passed, it follers that they're somewhar inside the ring. So, we'll jest thresh out ev'ry inch o' ground in thar, ef it takes ten years to do it.'"

Silent Tom looked at him with admiration.

"Mighty long speech," he said. "How do you find so many words?"

"Oh, they're all in the dictionary," replied the shiftless one, "an' a heap more, too. I'm an eddicated man, ez all o' you kin see, though bein' jealous some o' you won't admit it. Thar are nigh onto a million good words in the dictionary, an' ev'ry one o' 'em is known to me. Ev'ry one o' 'em would reckernize me ez a friend, an' would ask me to use it ef I looked at it, but I'm mighty pertickler an' I take only the best ones. Returnin' to the subject from which we hev traveled far, I think we'd better be on the lookout fur old Red Eagle an' his Shawnees."

"Think so, too," said Silent Tom.

Henry announced the next morning that he would start at once on a scout, and that he probably would go outside the swamp.

"I go with you, o' course," said Shif'less Sol.

"I think it best to travel alone."

"Why, you couldn't git along without me, Henry!"

"I'll have to try, Sol."

"I wouldn't talk you to death," said Silent Tom.

Long Jim and Paul also wanted to go, but the young leader rejected them all, and they knew that it was a waste of time to argue with him. He started in the early morning and they waved farewell to him from the oasis.

Henry was not averse to action. The long period of idleness on the island, much as he had enjoyed it, was coming to its natural end, and his active mind and body looked forward to new events. The swamp had returned to the state in which they had found it, and remembering the path by which they had come he had no great difficulty in making his journey.

Three hundred yards away and the oasis was hidden completely by the marshy thickets. He could not even see the tops of the trees, and he reflected that it was the merest chance that had led them there. It was not likely that the chance would be repeated in the case of any of Red Eagle's warriors, and perhaps it would be better for all of the five to stay snug and tight on the oasis, even if they did not move until full winter came. But second thought told him that Red Eagle would surely thresh up the swamp. The reasoning of Shif'less Sol was correct, and it was better to go on and see what was being prepared for them by their enemies.

His progress was necessarily slow, as he was compelled to pick his way, but he had plenty of strength and patience, and noon found him near the outer rim, where he paused to watch the sky. Henry had an idea that he might see smoke, betraying the presence of Indian bands, but not even his keen eyes were able to make out any dark traces against the heavens, which had all the thinness and clearness of early autumn. Reflection convinced him, however, that if Red Eagle were meditating a movement against the swamp he would avoid anything that might warn its occupants. He abided by his second thought, and began anew his cautious progress toward the edge of the bushes and reeds.

The ending of the swamp was abrupt, the marshy ground becoming firm in the space of a few yards, and Henry, emerging upon what was in a sense the mainland, crept into a dense clump of alders, where he lay hidden for some time, examining from his covert the country about him. He did not see or hear anything to betoken a hostile presence, but, as wary as any wild animal that inhabited the forest, he ventured forth, still using every kind of cover that he could find.

His course took him toward the east, and a quarter of a mile passed, his eye was caught by the red gleam of a feather in the grass. He retrieved it, and saw at once that it was painted. Hence, it had fallen from the scalplock of an Indian. It was not bedraggled, so it had fallen recently, as the winds had not beaten it about. It was sure, too, that a warrior or warriors had gone that way within a few hours. He searched for the trail, stooping among the bushes, lest he fall into an ambush, and presently he came upon the faint imprint of moccasins, judging that they had been made by about a half dozen warriors.

The trail led to the east, and Henry followed it promptly, finding as he advanced that it was growing plainer. Other and smaller trails met it and merged with it, and he became confident that he would soon locate a large band. He was no longer dealing with supposition, he had actualities, the tangible, before him, and his pulses began to leap in expectation. The shiftless one and he had been right. Red Eagle had never left the neighborhood of the swamp, and Henry believed that he would soon know what the wily old Indian chief was intending. There was a certain exhilaration in matching his wits against those of the great Shawnee, and he knew that he would need to exercise every power of his mind to the utmost. He followed the trail steadily about a half hour as it led on among trees and bushes, and he reckoned that it was made now by at least twenty warriors who had no wish to conceal their traces. Presently he came to one of the little prairies, numerous in that region, and as the trail led directly into it he paused, lest he be seen and be trapped when he was in the open.

But as he examined the prairie from the shelter of the bushes, he became convinced that the warriors must have increased their speed when they crossed it, and were now some distance ahead. At the far edge, two buffaloes, a bull and a cow, and two half-grown calves, were grazing in peace. Two deer strolled from the forest, nosed the grass and then strolled back again. The wild animals would not have been so peaceful and unconcerned, if Indians were near, and, trusting to his logic, Henry boldly crossed the open. The four buffaloes sniffed him and lurched away to the shelter of the trees, thus proving to him that they were vigilant, and that he was the only human being in their neighborhood.

He entered the forest again and followed on the broad trail, increasing his own speed, but neglecting nothing of watchfulness. The country was a striking contrast to the great swamp, firm soil, hilly and often rocky, cut with many small, clear streams. He judged that the swamp was the bowl into which all these rivulets emptied.

Reaching the crest of one of the low hills he caught a red gleam among the bushes ahead of him and he sank down instantly. He knew that the flash of scarlet was made by a fire, and he suspected that the warriors whom he was following had gone into camp there. Then he began his cautious approach after the border fashion, creeping forward inch by inch among the bushes and fallen leaves. It was necessary to use his utmost skill, too, as the dry leaves easily gave back a rustle. Yet he persisted, despite the danger, because he needed to know what band it was that sat there in the thicket.

A hundred yards further and he looked into a tiny valley, where was burning a fire of small sticks, over which Indian warriors were broiling strips of venison. But the majority of the band sat on the ground in a half circle about the fire, and Henry drew a long breath when he saw that Red Eagle, the Shawnee chief, was among them. Then he no longer had the slightest doubt that the hunt was at its full height, that the Shawnees were still using every device they knew to destroy the five who had troubled them so much.

Red Eagle was a man of massive features and grave demeanor, one of the great Indian chiefs who, their circumstances considered, were inferior in intellectual power to nobody. Henry watched him as he sat now with his legs crossed and arms folded, staring into the flames. He was a picturesque figure, and he looked the warlike sage, as he sat there brooding. The little feathers in his scalplock were dyed red, his leggings and moccasins were of the same color, and a blanket of the finest red cloth was draped about his shoulders like a Roman toga. He was a man to arouse interest, respect and even admiration.

Red Eagle did not speak until the strips of meat were cooked and eaten and all were sitting about the fire, when he arose and addressed them in a slow, solemn and weighty manner. Henry would have given much to understand the words, as he believed they referred to the five and might tell the chief's plans, but he was too far away to hear anything except a murmur that meant nothing.

He saw, however, that Red Eagle was intensely earnest, and that the warriors listened with fixed attention, hanging on every word and watching his face. Their only interruptions were exclamations of approval now and then, and, when he finished and sat down, all together uttered the same deep notes. Then eight of the warriors arose, and to Henry's great surprise, came back on the trail.

He recognized at once that a sudden danger had presented itself. The Shawnees would presently find his trail mingled with theirs, and they were sure to give immediate pursuit. He thrust himself back into the bushes, crawled a hundred yards or so, then rose and ran, curving about the fire and passing to the eastward of it. Three hundred yards, and he sank down again, listening. A single fierce shout came from the portion of the band that had turned back. He understood. They had come upon his trail, and in another minute Red Eagle would organize a pursuit by all the warriors, a pursuit that would hang on through everything.

Henry, knowing well the formidable nature of the danger, felt, nevertheless, no dismay. He had matched himself against the warriors many times, and he was ready to do so once more. He swung into the long frontier run that not even the Indians themselves could match in speed and ease.

It was characteristic of him that he did not turn toward the swamp, in which he could speedily have found refuge. Instead, wishing to draw the enemy away from his comrades, he offered himself as bait, and fled on the firm ground toward the east.

CHAPTER VIII
THE BUFFALO RING

Henry, feeling some alarm at first over the discovery of his trail, soon felt elation instead. He was at the very height of his powers. The long rest on the oasis had restored all his physical vigor. Every nerve and muscle was flexible and strong, as if made of steel wire. His eye had never before been so clear, nor his ear so acute, and above all, that sixth sense, the power of divination almost, which came from a perfect correlation of the five senses, developed to the utmost degree, was alive in him. Nothing could stir in the brush without his knowing it, and, welcoming the pursuit, the spirit of challenge was so strong in him that he threw back his head and uttered a long, thrilling cry, the note of defiance, just as the trumpet of the mediæval knight sang to his enemy to come to the field of battle.

Then he continued his flight toward the northwest, not too fast, because he wished his trail to remain warm for the warriors who followed, but stooping low, lest some wanderers from the main band should see him as he ran. No answer came to his cry, but he knew well enough that the Indians had heard it, and he knew, too, that it filled them with rage because any of the five had been bold enough to defy their full power.

Reaching the crest of one of the low hills in which the region abounded, he looked toward the southwest and saw the vast maze of the swamp in which his comrades lay hidden. He had not been able to think of any plan to turn aside the forces of Red Eagle, but now it came to him suddenly. He intended when the pursuit ended to be far away from the swamp, and then he could rejoin the four at some other point.

He reached a brook, leaped it and passed on. He could have followed the bed of the stream, hiding his trail for a space, but he knew the pursuers would soon find it again, and after all he did not wish his trail to be hidden. He laughed a little as he planted his moccasin purposely in a soft spot in the earth, and noticed the deep imprint he left. There was no warrior so blind who would not see the trace, and he sped on, leaving other such marks here and there, and finally sending forth another thrilling note of defiance that swelled far over the forest, a cry that was at once an invitation, a challenge and a taunt. It bade the warriors to use the utmost speed, because they would need it. It asked them to pursue, because the one who fled wished to be followed, and so wishing, he did not hide his trail from them. He would be bitterly disappointed if they did not come. It told them, too, that if they did come, no matter how great their speed, the hunters could never catch the hunted.

He stopped two minutes perhaps, long enough for the fleetest of the warriors to come within sight. Just as their brown bodies appeared among the trees he uttered his piercing cry a third time and took to flight again at a speed greater than any of theirs. Two shots were fired, but the bullets cut only the uncomplaining leaves, falling far short. He gained a full hundred yards, and then he turned abruptly toward the north. His sixth sense, in which this time the supreme development of hearing was predominant, warned him that other warriors were coming up from the south. In truth they were approaching so fast that they uttered a cry of triumph in reply to his own cry, but, increasing his speed, he merely laughed to himself once more, knowing that he had evaded the trap. His elation grew. His plan was succeeding better than he had hoped. One after another he was drawing the Indian bands upon his trail, and he hoped to have them all. He hoped that Red Eagle would lead the pursuit and he hoped that Blackstaffe and Wyatt would be there.

His ear had given warning before, and now it was his eye that told him of the menace. He caught a glimpse of a flitting figure in the north, and then of two more. And so a third band was bearing down upon him, but from a point of the compass opposite the second. Any one of ordinary powers might well have been trapped now, but he yet had strength in reserve, and now he put forth an amazing burst of speed that carried him well ahead of all three bands.

Then he entered another low region covered with bushes and reeds, and, lest they lose his trail, he took occasion, as he fled, to trample down a clump of reeds here and a bush there. On the far side of this sunken land he came to a creek, in which the water rose to his knees, but he forded it without hesitation, and even took the time to make a plain trail after he had crossed.

He knew that the warriors would pursue, in spite of every obstacle, and he knew, too, that they would divine who it was whom they followed. Using a new burst of speed, he widened the gap as he surmised to a full quarter of a mile. And then he let his gait sink to not much more than a long walk, wishing to recover his full physical powers. His spirit of elation remained. In very truth, he was enjoying himself, and he felt that he could lead them on forever. He was even able to note the character of the country as he passed, the numerous brooks, the splendor of the forest, the brown leaves as they fell before the light wind, and then a great patch of early blackberries hanging ripe and rich. He paused a moment or two, long enough to gather many of the berries and eat them, noting that they were the juiciest and best he could recall to have tasted.

Then he came into a country that the animal kingdom seemed to have made its own. He could not remember having seen anywhere else such an abundance of game. Buffaloes, puffing and snorting, ran to one side as he crossed the little prairies. Deer, some big and some little, sped away through the thickets. Bears, hidden in their coverts, gazed at him with curious eyes. Rabbits leaped away in the grass, squirrels ran in alarm out on the farthest boughs, and flocks of wild fowl rose with a whirr and a rush.

Henry was so sure of himself, so sure he could not be overtaken, that he noted the character of this country which seemed to be so much favored by the creatures of earth and air. Some time, when all their present dangers were over, he and his comrades would come back there and have a pleasant and peaceful hunt. Doubtless it had been neglected a long time by the Indians, who were in the habit of using a region for a season or two and then of letting it lie fallow until the wild animals should forget and come back again.

He ascended a hill larger and higher than the others, and bare, being mostly a stony outcrop. Here he sat down in the shadow of a ledge and took long breaths. He felt that the pursuit was then fully a mile behind, and he could afford to stop for a little while. From the lofty summit he saw a great distance. Toward the southwest was where the swamp lay, but, despite the height, it was invisible now. Behind him was the deep forest through which his pursuers were coming, to the north lay the same forest, but to the east he caught a shimmer of blue through the browning leaves. It was so faint that at first he was not certain of its nature, but a second look told him it was one of the little lakes often to be found in the country north of the Ohio.

His flight, as he was making it, would take him straight against that body of blue water, impassable to him then, and as he drew a deep breath of gratitude he felt that he was in truth being watched over by a supreme power. If not, why were all the turns of chance in his favor? Why had he stopped to rest a moment or two by the stony ledge, and why in doing so had he caught a glimpse of the lake which soon would have been an insuperable bar across his path, enabling the Indians to hem him in on either flank?

He breathed his thanks, and then he lay back against the ledge for another minute or two of rest. Near grew a dwarf oak, still thick in green foliage, and as if by command the wind suddenly began to sing among its leaves, and the leaves, as if touched by the hand of a master artist, gave back a song. Henry had heard that song before. It came to him in his greatest moments of spiritual exaltation. Always it was a song of strength and encouragement, telling him that he would succeed, and now its note was not changed.

He opened his eyes, sure that his pursuers were not yet within rifle shot, and rising, refreshed, passed over the hill and into the forest again, curving now toward the north. When he was sure he was well hidden by the bushes, he ran at great speed, intending to pass between the northern wing of his pursuers and the lake. They, of course, had known of the water there and were expecting to catch him in the trap, and as he ran he heard the two wings calling distantly to each other. His silent laugh came once more. He had invisible guides who always led him out of traps, and he had heard the voice that sang to him so often saying this pursuit, like so many others, might be long, but in vain.

Fifteen minutes more, and he caught another view of the lake, which appeared to be about two miles long and a quarter of a mile across, a fine sheet of water, on which great numbers of wild fowl swam, or over which they hovered. It was heavily wooded on all sides, and had he not seen it earlier it would surely have proved an obstacle leading to his capture or destruction. The pursuing bands, evidently believing that the trap had been closed with the fugitive in it, began to exchange signals again, and Henry discerned in their cries the note of triumph. It gave the great youth satisfaction to feel that they would soon be undeceived.

Now he called up all the reserves of strength that he had been saving for some such emergency as this, and sped toward the northeast at a pace few could equal, cleaving the thickets, leaping gullies, and racing across the open. The lake on his right came nearer and nearer, but he was rapidly approaching the northern end, and he knew that he would pass it before the band pursuing in that quarter could close in upon him.

Now the critical time came and he increased his speed to the utmost, running through a thicket, passing the extreme northern curve of the lake, and entering a wood where only firm ground lay before him. The great obstacle was passed and he felt a mighty surge of triumph. He was for the time being primitive and wild, like the warriors who pursued him, thinking as they thought, and acting as they acted. Feeling now that he was victorious anew, he raised his voice and sent forth once more that tremendous thrilling cry, a compound of triumph, defiance and mockery. Yells of disappointment came from the deep woods behind him, and to hear them gave him all the satisfaction he had anticipated.

He kept a steady course toward the east, not running so fast as before, but maintaining a steady pace, nevertheless. As he ran he began to think now of hiding his trail, not in such a manner that it could be lost permanently, that being impossible, but long enough for him to take rest. However great one's natural powers might be and however severely and often one might have been hardened in the fire, one could not run on forever. He must lie down in the forest by and by, and the time would come, too, when he must sleep.

He glanced up at the sun and saw that the day would not last more than two hours longer. There were no clouds and the night was likely to be bright, furnishing enough light for the warriors to find an ordinary trail, and willing to delude them now he began to take pains to make his own trail one that was not ordinary. He resorted to all the usual forest devices, walking on hard ground, stones and fallen trees, and wading in water whenever he came to it, methods that he knew would merely delay the warriors, but that could not baffle them long.

He did not hear the bands signaling again and he surmised that the one on the south would pass around the southern end of the lake, reuniting with the other as soon afterward as possible. Nevertheless he curved off in that direction, and, sinking now to a long walk, he went steadily ahead, until the great sun went down in a sea of gold behind the forest and night threw a dusky veil over the wilderness. Then he stopped entirely, and standing against a huge tree trunk, with which his figure blended in the night, he took deep breaths.

At first he felt weakness. No one, no matter how powerful and well trained, could run so long without putting an immense strain upon the nerves, and for a little space bushes and trees danced before him. Then the world steadied itself, his heart ceased to beat so hard and the suffusion of blood retreated from his head. He saw nothing nor heard anything of his foes, but he knew that the pursuit would not cease. He felt that this was his great flight, one that might go on for days and nights, in which every faculty he had would be tested to the utmost, but he was willing for it to be so. The longer the flight continued the further he would draw away from the Indian power, and that was what he wished most of all. He would make such a fugitive as the chiefs had never known before.

Henry stood a full fifteen minutes beside the brown trunk of the tree, of which in the dark he seemed to be a part, and so great was his physical power and elasticity that the time was sufficient to restore all his strength. When he thought he caught a glimpse of a bush moving behind him, he resumed the long running walk that covered ground so rapidly. An hour later he came to a brook, in the bed of which he walked fully a mile. But he did not expect this to bother his pursuers very long. They would send warriors up and down either bank until in the moonlight they struck the trail anew, and then they would follow as before. But it would give him time, and not doubting that he would find some new circumstance to aid him, it came sooner than he had expected or hoped.

Less than half a mile farther he encountered the wreckage left by a hurricane of some former season, a path not more than three hundred yards wide, a perfect tangle of fallen trees, amid which bushes were already growing. The windrow led two or three miles to the northeast, and he walked all the way on the trunks, slipping lightly from tree to tree. It was now late, and as the night fortunately began to turn considerably darker, he bethought himself of a place in which to sleep, because in time sleep one must have, whether or not a fugitive.

As he considered, he heard ahead of him a faint puffing and blowing which he knew to come from buffaloes, and their presence indicated one of the little prairies in which the country north of the Ohio abounded. He made his way through the bushes, came to the prairie and saw that it was black with the herd.

The buffalo, although numerous east of the Mississippi, invariably grazed in small bands, owing to the wooded nature of the country, and the present herd, four or five hundred at least, was the largest that Henry had ever seen away from the Great Plains. As the wind was blowing from him toward them, and they showed, nevertheless, no sign of flight, he surmised that the weaker members had been harassed much by wolves, and that the herd was unwilling to move from its present place of rest. They shuffled and puffed and panted, but there was no alarm.

He stood a few moments and gazed at them, his look full of friendliness. The Indians hunted the buffalo and they also hunted him. For the time being these, the most gigantic of North American animals, were his brethren, and then came his idea.

A little ridge ran into the prairie, terminating in a hillock, and it was clear of the buffaloes, as they naturally lay in the lower places. Henry walked down among the buffaloes along the ridge until he came to the hillock, where he took the blanket from his back, wrapped it about him, and reclined with his head on his arm. The buffaloes puffed and snorted and some of them moved uneasily, but they did not get up. Perhaps Henry was wholly a wild creature himself then and they discerned in him something akin to themselves, or perhaps they had been harassed by wolves so much that they would not stir for anything now. But as the human intruder lay soundless and motionless, they, too, settled into quiet.

Henry's friendly feeling for the buffaloes increased, and it had full warrant. He was surrounded by an army of sentinels. He knew that if the Indians attempted to cross the prairie, coming in a band, they would rise up at once in alarm, and if he fell asleep he would be awakened immediately by such a multitudinous sound. Hence he would go to sleep, and quickly.

If the buffaloes felt their kinship with Henry, he felt his kinship with them as strongly. Since they had sunk into silence they were like so many friends around him, ready to fend off danger or to warn him. From the crest of the low mound upon which he lay he saw the big black forms dotting the prairie, a ring about him. Then he calmly composed himself for the slumber which he needed so much.

But sleep did not come as speedily as he had expected. Wolves howled in the forest, and he knew they were real wolves, hanging on the flank of the buffalo herd, cutting out the calves or the weak. The big bull buffaloes moved and snorted again at the sound, but, when it was not repeated, returned to their rest, all except one that lumbered forward a step or two and then sank down directly on the little ridge by which Henry had come to his hillock, as if he were a rear guard, closing the way to the fugitive. He saw in it at once an omen. The superior power that was watching over him had put the buffalo there to protect him, and, free from any further apprehension, he closed his eyes, falling asleep without delay.

Henry always felt afterward that he must have been wholly a creature of the wild that night, else the buffaloes would have taken alarm at his presence and probably would have stampeded. But the kinship they recognized in him must have endured, or they had been harried so much by the wolves that they did not feel like moving because of an intruder who was so quiet and harmless that he was really no intruder at all. The huge bull, crouched across the path by which he had come, puffed and groaned at intervals, but he did not stir from his place. He was in very truth, if not in intent, a guardian of the way.

And yet, while Henry slept amid the herd, the pursuit of him was conducted with the energy, thoroughness and tenacity of which the Indians were capable. The spirit of the great Shawnee chief, Red Eagle, had been stung by his failure to overtake the fugitive, whom he knew to be the youth Ware, their greatest foe, and he was resolved that Henry should not escape. With him now were the renegades Blackstaffe and Wyatt, and they, too, urged on the chase. They felt that if Henry could be taken or destroyed, the four would fall easier victims, and then the eyes of the woods that watched so well for the settlers would have gone out forever.

All through the night the warriors ranged the forest, hunting for the trail. The moon and the stars returned, bringing with them a light that helped, and an hour or two after midnight a Shawnee found traces that led toward the prairie. He called to his comrades and they followed it to the prairie, where they lost it. The Indian warriors, looking cautiously from the brush, saw in the open the clustered black forms, looming gigantic in the moonlight, and they heard the heavings and puffings and groanings of the big bulls. Directly in front of them, across a low narrow ridge, lay the biggest bull of them all, a buffalo that stirred now and then as if he were glad to rub his body against the soil, which was rougher there than elsewhere. On the far side of the prairie, wolves yapped and barked, longing to get at the calves inside the ring of their elders.

The warriors crept away and began the entire circuit of the open, looking for the lost trail. It had entered it on the western side, and it would pass out somewhere, probably on the eastern. Red Eagle, Blackstaffe and Wyatt themselves came up and directed the chase, but they were mystified when their runners, completing the entire circling movement, reported that there was no sign of the trail's reappearance. Red Eagle, after taking thought, refused to believe it. The fugitive had surpassing skill, as all of them knew, but a human being could not take a flight through the air, like an eagle or a wild duck, and leave no trail behind him. They must have overlooked the traces in the moonlight, and he sent out the warriors anew, to right and to left.

Henry meanwhile slept the sleep of one who was weary and unafraid. He had not only the feeling, but the conviction, as he lay down, that he was within an inviolable ring of sentinels, and having dismissed all care and apprehension from his mind, he fell into a slumber so deep that for a long time nothing could disturb it. The yapping and barking of the wolves fell upon an unhearing ear. The puffings and groanings of the buffaloes were merely whispers to dull him into more powerful sleep. When the Indian scouts, not fifty yards away, looked at the body of the big bull that blocked the path, nothing whispered to him that danger was near. Nor was the whisper needed, as the danger passed as quickly as it had come.

He awoke at the first streak of dawn, stirred a little in his blanket, but did not rise yet. He saw the buffaloes all around him and realized that his faith in them had not been misplaced. The great bull, like a black mountain, still barred the path to him.

It was warm and snug in his blanket and he yawned prodigiously. It would have been pleasant to have remained there a few hours longer, but when one was pursued by a whole Indian nation he could not remain long in one place. He took the last strips of venison from his pack and ate them as he lay. Meanwhile the buffaloes themselves began to move somewhat, as if they were making ready for their day's work, and Henry wondered at their disregard of him. Perhaps his presence for a night, and the fact that he had been harmless, removed their fear of him.

He rose to his knees, and then suddenly sank back again. He had caught the gleam of red feathers in the forest to the west, and he knew they were in the scalplock of a Shawnee. Raising his head cautiously he saw several more. It was a small band passing toward the north. But he had too much experience to imagine that they were chance travelers. Beyond a doubt they were a part of Red Eagle's army, and that army had come up in the night and had surrounded him.

He lay back and listened. An Indian call arose in the west and another in the east, and then they came from north and south and points between. They were on all sides of him and he had been trapped as he slept. He saw that the danger was the most formidable he had yet encountered, but he did not despair. It was characteristic of him that when there seemed to be no hope, he yet had hope, and plenty of it. His heart beat a little faster, but he lay quiet in his blanket, taking thought with himself.

He had been aided before by storms, but there was not the remotest chance now of one. The sun was rising in the full splendor of an early autumn morning, and the thin, clear air had the brightness of silver. The blue skies held not a single cloud. Far over his head a flock of wild fowl in arrow formation flew southward, and for the moment they expressed to him, as he lay in the snare, the very quintessence of freedom. But he spent no time in vain longings. His eyes came back to the earth and that which surrounded him. Once more he caught the gleam of feathers in the forest and he was sure that the line about the prairie was now continuous.

He must find a way through that line, and he poured all his mind upon one point. When one thinks for life, one thinks fast and hard. Stratagem after stratagem flitted before him, to be cast aside one after another. Meanwhile the buffaloes were stirring more and more, and some of them began to nip at the dry grass of the prairie, but the big black bull on the little ridge remained crouched and motionless. He was not fifteen feet away and between him and Henry lay fragments of dead wood which had been blown from the forest by some old wind. His eyes alighted upon them idly, but remained there in interest, and then, in a sudden burst of intuition, came his plan. Hesitating not a single instant, he prepared for it.

Henry slid forward, recovered a long dead stick, and rapidly whittled from it a lot of shavings. He never knew why the buffaloes did not take alarm at his presence and actions, but he always supposed that the mystic tie of kinship still endured. Then using his flint and steel with all the energy and power that imminent danger could inspire, he lighted first the shavings and then the end of the long stick.

The buffaloes at last began to puff and snort and show alarm, and Henry, springing to his feet, whirled the torch in a circle of living fire around his head. The whole herd broke in an instant into a frightful panic, and with much snorting and bellowing rushed away in a black mass toward the east. He threw down his torch, and grasping his rifle and throwing his pack over his shoulder, followed close upon them, so close that not even the keenest eye in the forest could have distinguished him from the herd in the great cloud of dust that quickly rose.

It was for this cloud of dust that he had bargained. The soil of the prairie became dry in the autumn, and the tramplings of four or five hundred huge beasts churned it into a powder which the wind picked up and blew into a blinding stream. Henry felt it in his eyes, his nose, his ears and his mouth, but he was glad and he laughed aloud in his joy. The rush and bellowings of the buffaloes made it a mighty roar, and the soul within him was wild and triumphant, as became one who was the very spirit and essence of the wilderness. He shouted aloud like Long Jim Hart, knowing that his voice would be lost in the thunder of the herd and could not reach the Indians.

"On, my gallant beasts!" he cried. "Charge 'em! Break their line! They can't stand before you! Faster! Faster!"

He struck one of them across the body with the butt of his rifle, but the herd was already running as fast as it could, while the cloud of dust was continually rising in greater and thicker volume. In the midst of this cloud, and hanging almost bodily to the herd itself, Henry was invisible as he rushed on, shouting his battle song of triumph and defiance, although no word of it reached the warriors who had lain in the brushwood and who were now fleeing in fright before the rush of the mad herd.

Mad it certainly was, said Red Eagle, for the chief himself, with Wyatt and Blackstaffe, had been directly in its path, and they had been compelled to run in undignified haste, while the great pillar of dust, filled with the dim figures of buffaloes, crashed and thundered past, trampling down bushes, crushing saplings, and driving off to the east, the pillar of dust still visible long after the buffaloes were deep in the forest. Red Eagle stared after it. He was a wise old chief, and he had seen buffaloes before in a panic, but he did not understand the cause of this sudden and terrific flight.

"It is strange," he said, "but we must let them run. We will go back now and look for Ware."

CHAPTER IX
THE COVERT

It was one of the most thrilling moments in the life of Henry Ware. He was in a kind of exaltation that made him equal to any task or danger, and rather to court, instead of avoiding them. His feeling of kinship with the herd that was saving him had grown stronger with the dawn. The dust entering his eyes and mouth, nose and ears, had a singular quality like burned gun powder that excited him and stimulated him to efforts far beyond the normal. He was for the time being a physical superman out of that old dim past, and he was scarcely conscious of anything he was doing, save that he ran with the great beasts, and was their friend.

His exalted state increased. He continued to shout to the buffaloes to run faster, and to hurl challenge and defiance at the warriors who could not hear him. Once more he swung his clubbed rifle and hit a buffalo on the side, not in anger, but as a salute from one hardy friend to another, and the buffalo, uttering a bellow, rushed on with mighty leaps.

Although he could not see them for the dust, Henry knew now by the crashing and crackling of boughs that they were among the bushes, but they did not trouble him, as the herd, like a huge wedge, first clearing the way trampled everything under foot. How long the race lasted and how long they ran he never knew, but after a lapse of time that was surcharged with an enormous elation and an unexampled display of physical power the herd began to recover in some degree from its panic. Its speed decreased. The great cloud of dust that had wrapped Henry around and that had saved him sank fast. Then he came suddenly to himself, out of the exalted regions of the spirit in which he had been dwelling. His throat was sore from excessive shouting and the sting of the dust, and it was a few minutes before he was able to clear his eyes and see with his usual keenness. Then he found that his body, too, ached from his flight with the buffaloes and his excessive exertions.

But he had escaped. Nothing could alter the fact. When he had been surrounded so completely by powerful foes that his destruction seemed inevitable a miraculous way had been opened through their lines. Kindly chance had drooped about him an impenetrable veil and he had passed his enemies unseen. His first

97

emotion was of deep thankfulness and gratitude to the power that had saved him.

The pace of the herd sank to a walk. The light wind caught the last streamers of dust and carried them away over the trees. Then some of the buffaloes, puffing with exhaustion, stopped, and Henry, coming back wholly to himself, turned aside into the deep forest. But he gave a parting wave of his hand to the great animals that had enabled him to make his invisible flight. Never again would he kill a buffalo without reluctance.

An immense weariness came suddenly upon him. One could not run so far with a herd without draining to their depths the reservoirs of human endurance, but he would not let his body collapse. He knew he must put the danger far behind him before it was a danger passed or even a danger deferred. Calling upon his will anew, he turned toward the southeast and walked many miles through a stony region. Here again he felt that he was watched over by the greater powers, as leaping from stone to stone it was easy to hide his trail, for the time at least. When the last ounce of strength was exhausted he came to a blue pool, ten or fifteen yards across, clear and deep.

He looked at the pool and was about to make another effort to go on, but the blue waters crinkled up and laughed under a light wind, and looked so inviting that he concluded to take the risk. He still felt the dust in eye and ear, mouth and nose. He knew that it was caked upon his face by perspiration, until it had become a mask, and now his whole body tingled like fire with the tiny particles that had stopped up the pores. And there was the pool, clear, blue and beautiful, inviting him to come.

Delaying not an instant longer he threw off his clothing and sprang into the water. It was cold, but it was full of life. New strength shot into every vein. He dived again and again, but without noise, and then, swimming about a minute or two, emerged clean, shining and refreshed. While he stretched himself, flexing and tensing his muscles and drying his body in the sun, a stag, seeking water, came through the forest on the other side of the pool. Perhaps that sense of kinship was felt by the stag, too. It may be that Henry was in spirit an absolute creature of the wild that morning, and by some unknown transmission of knowledge the stag knew it.

However it was, the great deer took no fright, but, sniffing the air once or twice, looked at the great youth, and the great youth looked back at him. Henry would not have harmed any inhabitant of the forest then, and the deer may have read it in his eye, as after his first hesitation he came boldly to the pool and drank his fill. Henry on the other side was dressing rapidly. When the stag had drunk enough he raised his head and gazed out of great mild eyes at the human being who was perhaps the first he had ever seen. Then he turned and stalked majestically into the forest, his mighty antlers visible after his body was hidden.

Henry, lying down in the brown grass, remained a half hour by the pool, and he became a part of the wilderness, recognized as such by the others that dwelled in it. Wild fowl descended upon the water, swam there a while and then flew away, but not because of him. A black bear made havoc in a patch of berries, and paid no attention to the youth.

When he started anew he still kept to the northeast, but he was uncertain about his immediate action. He did not doubt that Red Eagle and his host would pick up his trail some time or other, and would follow with a patience that nothing could discourage. It would not be wise to turn back to the oasis and his comrades, as that would merely bring upon them the attack that he had drawn aside. Not knowing what to do he kept on in his present course until certainty should come to him.

Hunger assailed him and, imitating the bear, he ate great quantities of berries which were numerous everywhere in the forest. They were not substantial food, but they must suffice for a time. After a while, when he felt that he was far beyond the hearing of Red Eagle's men, he would shoot game, though in his present mood he did not like to kill anything that lived in the forest. But he knew that he must, in time, overcome his reluctance, as such a frame as his, in the absence of bread, could not live without meat.

He saw ahead of him a line of blue hills, much such a region as that in which lay their warm, stony hollow, and he believed that he might find kindred shelter there. At least it would be safer from pursuit, and, keeping a straight course, he reached the ridges in about two hours. He found an abundance of rocky outcrop, so much of it that he was able to walk on it a full mile without putting a foot on earth, but there was no deep hollow, although he did come to a tiny valley or cup among the stones, well sheltered from the winds, and here he lay for a long time on a bed that he made for himself on dead leaves. Toward night he went out and was fortunate enough to find a wild turkey, which, overcoming his reluctance, he shot. Then he cleaned it, and, daring all dangers, lighted a fire in the cup and cooked it.

But before taking a bite of the turkey he made a wide and careful circuit about the dip to discover whether any wandering warrior had seen the glow of his little fire, and, satisfied that none had been within sight, he returned and ate, putting what was left in his pack for future use. Then he lay down again and felt very grateful. The stars were out, and, in their courses, they had undoubtedly fought for him. He did not ascribe his great successes in the face of obstacles that seemed insurmountable to any especial virtue in himself, but the idea that, for some unknown cause, he was favored by the greater powers was still strong within him. He could but thank them and looking up at the sky he did so without words.

Then, feeling sure that his trail could not be found for hours, he wrapped his blanket about his body and pillowing his head on a heap of leaves fell asleep. The sense of watching remained so strong that it was alive while he slept, and about midnight it awakened him to see what a noise meant. It was, however, only the hungry whining of two wolves, drawn by the odor of the turkey, and, throwing a stick at them, he went back to sleep.

He did not awaken again until morning, and then he felt so warm and snug in his blanket and on the bed of leaves that he was loath to move. The dawn was clear and cold, the first frost of the season touching his blanket with white, and he yawned mightily. While his body was refreshed, his spirit was not as high as it had been the night before, and he would have been glad for the pursuit to stop, a day at least, while he dawdled there among the hills. He reflected that his four comrades were probably lying at their ease in the oasis, and the thought brought a certain envy, though the envy contained no trace of malice. He wished that he was back with them, but the wish vanished in an instant, and he was his old self, ingenious, resourceful, resolute.

He rose from his bed, folded the blanket into the usual tight square, which he fastened on his back, and took a look at his surroundings. There was no human presence save his own, but innumerable tracks showed him that the hills were full of game. Then sharp hunger assailed him, and he ate another portion of the wild turkey, calculating that enough would be left for several more meals. He considered himself extremely lucky in securing the turkey, as it undoubtedly would be dangerous now to fire his rifle, since the warriors must have come much nearer in the course of the night.

Going to the crest of the highest hill, whence he could get a long view, he saw smoke in the west, not more than three miles away, and he was quite certain it was made by some portion of Red Eagle's band. They would not allow so much smoke to rise, unless it was intended as a signal, and his eyes followed the circle of the horizon in search of the answer.

From his lofty perch he saw far over the tumbled mass of hills to the eastern sky, and there he caught a faint trace across the sunlit blue. It was miles away and only eyes of the keenest, like his, would

100

have noticed the vague smudge, but he did not doubt that it was a response to the first signal. They could not see from the first to the third smoke, but there must be a second in between, probably to the north, where the hills shut out his view, and the messages were transmitted from the extremes through it.

He gazed a long time at the eastern smoke, trying to read what it was saying. The warriors of Red Eagle's band were not likely to have gone so far in the night, and, at last, he came to the conclusion that Yellow Panther and the Miamis had come up. The more he thought about it the more thoroughly he was convinced that it was so, and that his situation had become extremely dangerous again. The Shawnees were bound to pick up his trail in time, they would find that it led into the hills, and then, by means of signals of one kind or another, they would tell their allies, the Miamis, to close in on him. They would also send warriors to both north and south, and he would be surrounded completely.

Henry did not despair. It was characteristic of him that his spirits should rise to the highest when the danger was greatest. The lassitude of the soul that he had felt for a few moments disappeared and once more he was alert, powerful, with all his marvelous senses attuned, and with that sixth sense which came from the perfect coordination of the others ready to help him.

He examined as well as he could from his summit the maze of hills in which he stood, and it seemed to him to be a region three or four miles square, a network of crests, ridges, cups, and narrow valleys like ravines. He resolved that for the present, at least, he would make no attempt to break from it and pass the Indian lines. He would be for a day or two the needle in the haystack. One might move from cover to cover and evade pursuit for a long time in a tumbled and tangled mass of country fifteen or sixteen miles square, covered moreover with heavy vegetation of all kinds.

He had been the panther before, now he would be the fox, and leaping from stone to stone, and from fallen trunk to fallen trunk he plunged into the very heart of the maze, finding it wilder and even more broken than he had hoped. Small streams were flowing in several of the gullies or ravines, and there were pools, around which reeds and bushes grew thickly. At least he would not suffer for water while he lay in hiding.

Near the center of the little wilderness was a valley larger than the others, but before he descended into it he climbed a hill, and took another long look around the whole horizon. The smoke signals had increased to nearly a dozen, making a complete circuit of the hills, and it would have been obvious, even to an intelligence much less acute than his, that they were sure he was in the hills, and had drawn their lines about him.

Well, it would be a chase, he said to himself grimly. He did not particularly like the rôle of fox, but once he had undertaken it he would play it to the last detail. He went down into the valley which was like a bowl filled with a vast mass of bushes and briars, many of the briars covered with ripe berries, a fact of which he made a mental note, as he might need those berries later on, and picked a way through them until he came to the other slope, which was as rough and broken as if it had been taken up by an earthquake, shaken for several days, and then allowed to lie as the pieces fell. There were many blind openings, like the box cañons of the west, running back into the hills, and they were crossed by other gullies and ravines, and he decided that he would find a temporary covert somewhere among them.

As he wandered about in the maze of bushes and stones, he did not neglect the least possible precaution to hide all traces of footsteps, and he knew that he had left a trail invisible like that of a bird through the air. There were many able warriors among the Shawnees and Miamis, but if they found him at all it must be by currying the maze as if with a comb, and not by following directly in his path.

A ravine that he was following led a little distance up the slope, and then another crossed it at right angles. A small stream, rising above, flowed down the first ravine, and he resolved that he would not go far from it, as he could not lie long in hiding without water. The smaller cross ravine, which was pretty well choked with briars and bushes, ended under an overhanging stony ledge, and here he stopped.

As the place had a floor of dead leaves and was sheltered well he thought it likely that in some former time it had been a den of a large wild beast, but it could not have been put to such a use recently, as there was no odor. He was thankful that he had found the ledge. It would protect him from any rain except one driven fiercely into the face of it by the wind, and, if it came to the last resort and he had to make a fight, it would prove a formidable little fortress.

Having located his refuge he went back to the stream and took a long, deep drink of the water, which was cold and good. Then he returned to the ledge and lay down in its shadow, his eyes on the briars and bushes, through which alone one could approach.

He saw a few coarse hairs in the crevices of the rocks and he was confirmed in his opinion that it had once been a lair. Perhaps the original owner would return to it and claim it while he was

102

there, and Henry smiled at the thought of the meeting. It would not be easy to displace him. The feeling that he too was wild, a creature of the forest, was growing upon him. He was hunted like one and he began to display their characteristics, lying perfectly still, facing the opening and ready to strike, the moment a foe appeared. However dangerous may have been the wild beast that once lived under the ledge it was far less formidable than its successor.

Henry was at his ease, watching the briars and bushes and with his rifle thrust forward a little, but a sort of cold rage grew upon him. It was the rage that a fierce animal must feel, when hunted beyond endurance, it turns at last. He rather hoped that one or two of their scouts would appear and try to force the ravine. They would pay for it richly, and he would take some revenge for being forced into such a hard and long flight.

But no scalplock appeared in the bushes, nor did he hear any sound of advancing men. But he was not deceived by the false appearance of peace. The Shawnees and Miamis had drawn their lines about the hills and they would search until they found. Now they had two great chiefs instead of one, both Red Eagle and Yellow Panther, to drive them on. Meanwhile he would wait patiently and take his ease until they did find him.

He was conscious of the passage of time, but he took little measure of it until he noticed that the sun was low. Then he ate another portion of the turkey, rolled himself into a new position on the leaves, and resumed the patient waiting which was not so hard for one trained as he had been in a school, the most important rule of which was patience.

The entire day passed. At times he dozed, but so lightly that the slightest movement in the thickets would have awakened him. He was neither lonely nor afraid, and his sense of comfort grew. He had been carried back farther than he knew into the old primitive world, in which shelter and ease were the first of all things. He was content now to wait any length of time while the warriors searched for him, and he was so still, he blended so thoroughly into his surroundings, that the other people of the maze accepted him as one of themselves.

He saw a splash of flame over his head, and a scarlet tanager, alighting on a bush not a yard from him, prinked and preened itself, until it felt that its toilet was perfect, when it deliberately flew away again. It had not shown the slightest fear of the motionless youth, and Henry was pleased. He intended no harm to the creatures of the forest then, and he was glad they understood it.

A small gray bird, far less brilliant in plumage than the tanager, alighted even nearer, and poured forth a flood of song to which Henry listened without moving. Then the gray bird also flew away, not in fear, but because its variable mind moved it to do so. It too had come as a friend and it departed without changing. A rabbit hopped through the brush, stared at him a moment or two, and then hopped calmly out of sight. Its visit had all the appearance of a friendly nature, and Henry was pleased once more.

When the twilight came, he crept through the bushes to the little stream in the ravine and drank deep again. His glance caught a pair of red eyes gleaming through the dusk and he saw a wildcat treading lightly. But the cat did not snarl or arch its back. Instead it moved away without any sign of hostility and climbed a big oak, in the brown foliage of which it was lost to Henry's sight. In his mind the thought grew stronger that he was being accepted as a brother to the wild, and it gave him a thrill, a compound of pleasure and of wonder. Had he really reverted so far? It seemed to be so, for the time, at least.

He crawled back through the bushes to his lair, ate another portion of the wild turkey and disposed his lodgings for the night, which he foresaw was going to be cold, drawing the dead leaves into a heap with a depression in the center, in which he could lie with the blanket over him.

The full dark had now come, and, as he finished his bed, he heard a light step which caused him to seize his rifle and sit silent, awaiting a possible enemy. The light step was repeated once, twice, thrice, and then stopped. But he knew it was not that of a human being. He had heard the pad, pad of an animal too often to be mistaken, and his tension relaxed, though he still waited.

He gradually made out an ungainly figure in the dusk, and then two small red eyes. The figure moved about a little and the eyes seemed to question. Henry smiled once more to himself. It was a large black bear, and he knew instinctively that it had not come as an enemy. Its visit was one of inquiry, perhaps of search for an old and comfortable home, which it remembered dimly. As it stared at him, showing no sign of fright and making no movement to run away, he knew then that he was in truth in a former home of the bear.

He was sorry that he had dispossessed any one. He would not willingly keep from his home a friendly and worthy black bear, but since it was the only home of the kind he needed that he could find, he must keep his place. The bear was not hunted as he was, and required less to give him comfort and shelter. He could improvise elsewhere a home that would suffice for him.

He waved his hand, but the bear did not withdraw, uttering instead a low growl which had some of the quality of a purr, and which was not at all hostile. Henry felt real grief at ousting such an amiable animal, and he realized anew that he had become, in fact, a creature of the wild. It was obvious that the bear looked upon him as a brother, else it would have taken to hasty flight long since. Instead it continued to stare at him, as if asking to come in that it might have a share of the leaves. But Henry shook his head. There was room for only one, and while not selfish he needed it worse than the bear, which, after a minute more of gazing, uttered another growling purr and then shambled away among the bushes. Henry felt real sorrow at its departure. Obviously it had been a good and kind bear, and he was regretful at having crowded it out of house and home.

But as bears were adaptable creatures and the dispossessed tenant would find quarters elsewhere, he settled himself back to further rest and contemplation. The lair under the ledge was really a better place than he had at first thought it. The leaves were so abundant that he had a soft bed, and they contributed not only to warmth in themselves, but he was able to throw them up in little ridges beside him, where they would cut off the cold air. He felt himself splendidly hidden, and both body and mind were invaded by a dreamy sense of peace and ease.

Believing that the invasion of the valley would yet be delayed some time, he dared to go to sleep, though he awoke at frequent intervals. All these awakenings told him that the warriors had not yet come nor was their vanguard even at hand. The bear was not the only wild animal to inhabit the valley and now and then he saw their dim figures moving in the leisurely manner that betokened no alarm brought by sight, scent or sound. He silently made them his sentinels, his watchers, the bear, the rabbit, the squirrel, the wildcat and even the tawny yellow panther.

Morning broke, the air heavy and clouds betokening rain. He strengthened his banks of leaves with some dead wood, and, after eating half the remaining portion of wild turkey, crouched again in the lair. In an hour it began to rain, not to the accompaniment of wind, but came down steadily, as if it meant to fall all day long.

Having a good shelter Henry was glad of the rain, as he knew that it would cause the warriors further delay in the search. The wilderness, cold and dripping with water, is a funereal sight, full of discomforts, and savage man himself avoids it if he can. The warriors, feeling that they had the fugitive within the inescapable circle, would wait. Henry would willingly wait with them. He had but one problem that troubled him greatly, and it was food. But perhaps the ravens would provide, as they had provided for the holy man in the olden time.

As he had foreseen, the chilling rain fell all day long, and no sign came from his pursuers. The valley grew sodden. He saw pools standing in low places, and cold vapors arose. At night he ate the last of the turkey, and, resolutely dismissing the question of more food from his mind for the time, fell asleep again and slept well.

The second dawn came, clear and cool, and the foliage and the earth dried rapidly under the bright sun. Henry's powerful frame craved breakfast but there was none, and, from necessity, he made up his mind to do without, as long as he could. But the cravings became so strong by noon that he stole out to the blackberry briars and ate his fill of the berries. He also found some ripening wild plums and ate those, too. Fruit alone was not very staying and he also saw the risk of disclosing his trail, but he felt that he must have it. One might talk lightly of enduring hunger, but to endure it was much harder. If he only had two or three more wild turkeys he felt that he might defy the siege.

That afternoon he heard the signals of Indians, showing that they were in the maze, looking for him. They imitated the cries of birds and animals, but they did not deceive him a single time. None was nearer than a quarter of a mile, and he was sure that they had a long hunt before them. Then he resolved upon a daring venture. If the coming night was dark he would make the Indians themselves provide him with food. It was tremendously risky, but the kind of life he lived was full of such risks.

His plan in mind, he watched the setting of the sun. It had mists and vapors around it, and he knew that he was about to have what he wished. Then the night settled down, heavy and dark, and he slipped cautiously from his lair. The last signal that he had heard came from the south and he advanced in that direction.

He calculated that boldness, as usual, might win. The warriors, daring themselves, nevertheless would not dream of an inroad upon them by the fugitive himself, and were likely to be careless in their night camp. It was possible that they would leave their own food where he could reach it unseen.

His progress was slow, owing to the extremely rough and broken nature of the ground, and his own great caution, a caution that made no sound, and that left no trail, as he always walked on rock. In an hour he saw the glimmer of a fire, and then he redoubled his caution, as he approached.

CHAPTER X
THE BEAR GUIDE

The fire was just beyond the thicket of reeds, and Henry addressed himself to the task of penetrating them without noise, a difficult thing to do, but which he accomplished in about five minutes, stopping just short of the outer edge, where he was still hidden well.

He was then able to see a small opening in which about a dozen warriors lay around a low fire, with two who were sentinels sitting up but nodding. He saw by their paint that they were Miamis, and thus he was confirmed in his belief that Yellow Panther had come with a large force from his tribe.

He knew that the sentinels had been set largely as a matter of form, since the Indians in the bowl itself would not anticipate any attack from a lone fugitive. The true watch would be kept on the outermost rim. So reasoning he waited, hoping that the two sentinels who were nodding so suggestively would fall asleep. Even as he looked their nods began to increase in violence. Their heads would fall over on their shoulders, hang there for a few moments and then their owners would bring them back with a jerk.

Indians, like white people, have to sleep, and Henry knew that the two warriors must have been up long, else they would not have to fight so hard to keep awake. That they would yield before long he did not now doubt, and he began to watch with an amused interest to see which would give in first. One was an old warrior, the other a youth of about twenty. Henry believed the lad would lead the way, and he was justified in his opinion, as the younger warrior, after bringing his head back into position two or three times with violent jerks, finally let it hang, while his chest rose with the long and deep breathing of one who slumbers. The older man looked at him with heavy-laden eyes and then followed him to the pleasant land of oblivion.

Henry now examined the camp with questioning eyes. In such a land of plentiful game they would be sure to have abundant supplies, and he saw there a haunch of deer well cooked, buffalo meat, two or three wild turkeys and wild ducks. His eyes rested longest on the haunch of the deer, and, making up his mind that it should be his, he began to creep again through the undergrowth to the sheltered point that lay nearest it, a task in which he exercised to the utmost his supreme gifts as a stalker, since these were the most critical moments of all.

The haunch lay not more than eight feet from the reeds, and he believed he could reach it without awakening any of the warriors. Once the older sentinel opened his eyes and looked around sleepily, and Henry instantly stopped dead, but it was merely a momentary return from slumberland, to which the man went back in a second or two, and then the stalker resumed his slow creeping.

At the point he sought, he slipped noiselessly into the open, seized the haunch and slid back in the same way, stopping in the shelter of the reeds to see if he had been noticed. But all the warriors still slept, and, thankful once more to the greater powers who had favored him, he made his way back to his shelter, provisioned now for several days. Then he ate a hearty supper, gathering more of the berries as a sauce, and drinking from the little stream.

He was well aware that the Indians, when they missed the haunch, would know that he lay somewhere in the bowl; but, with starvation as the alternative, he was compelled to take the risk. Before dawn, it rained again, removing all apprehensions that he may have felt about his trail, and he took a nap of two or three hours, relying upon his heightened senses to give him an alarm, if they drew near, even while he slept.

The next dawn came, cold and raw, with the rain ceasing after a while, but followed by a heavy fog that filled the whole bowl. Henry, sharp as his eyes were, could not see twenty feet in front of him, and, just like the bear that had once occupied it, he lay very close in his lair. The confinement was growing irksome to one of his youth and strength, as he felt his muscles stiffening, but it was necessary, because he heard the signals of the Indians to one another through the fog, sometimes not more than two or three hundred yards away. Their proximity, he knew, was due to chance, as there was nothing to disclose to them where he lay. They were merely following the plan of threshing out all the hay in the haystack in order to find the needle, and he knew that they would complete it even to the last wisp.

Another day and night passed in the lair, and the inactivity, confinement and suspense became frightful. He began to feel that he must move, even if he plunged directly into the Indian ranks, and the warriors permitted no doubt that they were near, since the calls of birds and animals were frequent. Two or three times he heard shots, and he knew it was the warriors killing game. He resented it, as all the animals in this little valley had proved themselves his friends, and he felt an actual grief for those that had been slain.

It was the truth that in these days of hiding and waiting Henry was reverting to some ancient type, not one necessarily ruder or more ferocious, but a primitive golden age in its way, in which man and beast were more nearly friends. There was proof in the fact that birds hopped about within a foot or two of him and showed no alarm, and that a rabbit boldly rested among the leaves not a yard away.

It would be, in truth, his happy valley were it not for the presence of the Indians. But they were drawing nearer. Call now answered to call, and they were only a few hundred yards away. He divined that they had threshed up most of the maze, and that a close circle was being drawn about him in the bowl. The next night, when he went out for water, he caught a glimpse of warriors stalking in the brush, and he did not believe that his lair would hide him more than a day or two longer. He must find some way to creep through the ring, but, for the present, he could think of none.

Another day passed, and he did not sleep at all in the night that followed, as the warriors were so near now that his keen ear often heard them moving, and once the sound of the men talking to one another came to him distinctly. It was obvious that he must soon make his attempt to break through the ring. Fortunately the night was foggy again, and while he was deliberating anew, concentrating all the power of his mind upon the attempt to find a plan, he heard a faint rustle in the thicket directly in front of him, and he instantly threw his rifle forward, sure that the warriors were upon him. Instead, a shambling figure poked its head through the thicket and looked curiously at him out of little red eyes.

It was the black bear that he had ousted, and Henry thought he saw sympathy as well as curiosity in the red eyes. The bear, far from upbraiding him for driving it from its home, had pity, and no fear at all. He could not see any sign of either alarm or hostility in the red eyes. The gaze expressed kinship, and his own was reciprocal.

"I hope the warriors won't get you, but you're running a mighty big risk," was his thought. Then came a second thought quick upon the heels of the first. How had the bear come through the ring of the warriors? Had the Indians seen it they would certainly have shot at it, because they loved bear meat. Not only had no shot been fired, but the bear was deliberate and free from apprehension. Then like lightning came a third thought. The bear had come in some providential way to save him. It had been sent by the greater powers.

109

There was something almost human in the gaze of the bear and Henry could never persuade himself afterward that its look did not have understanding. It began to withdraw slowly through the thicket, and, rising up, taking his rifle, blanket and supplies, he followed. A strange feeling seized him. He was transported out of himself. He believed that the miraculous was going to happen. And it happened.

The bear led ten or fifteen feet ahead, and then turned sharply to the right, where apparently it would come up dead against the blank stone wall of the hill. But it turned to look once at Henry and disappeared in the wall. He stood in amazement, but followed nevertheless. Then he saw. There was a narrow cleft in the stone, the entrance to which was completely hidden by three or four bushes growing closely together. The wariest eye would have passed over it a hundred times without seeing it, but the bear had gone in without hesitation, and now Henry, parting the bushes, went in, too.

He found a ravine not more than three feet wide that seemed to lead completely through the hill. The foliage met above it, and it was dark there, but he saw well enough to make his way. He could also trace the dim figure of the bear shambling on ahead, and his heart made a violent leap as he realized that in very truth and fact he was being led out of the Indian ring. Chance or intent? What did it matter? Who was he to question when favors were showered upon him? It was merely for him to take the gifts the greater powers gave, and, with voiceless thanks, he followed the lead of the animal which shambled steadily ahead.

The narrow ravine, or rather crack in the stone, might have ended against a wall, or it might have led up to the crest of the hill where Indian warriors lay watching, but he knew that it would do neither. He felt with all the certainty of actual knowledge that it would go on until it came out on the far side of the circling hills, and beyond the Indian ring.

He walked a full mile, his dumb guide leading faithfully. Sometimes the ravine widened a little, but always the foliage met overhead, and he was never able to catch more than glimpses of the sky. At last the width increased steadily, and then he came out into the forest with the hills behind him. The form of the bear was disappearing among the trees, but Henry sent after him his voiceless thanks. Again he felt that he could not question whether it was chance or intent, but must accept with gratitude the great favor that had been granted to him. Behind him, as reminders, came from far across the hills the faint calls of wolf and owl, the cries of the Indians to one another, as the chiefs directed the closing in of the ring upon the fugitive who was no longer there, the fugitive who had been guided in a miraculous manner to the only way of escape.

He sat down upon a fallen tree trunk, laughing silently at the chagrin his pursuers would feel when they came upon the lair, the empty lair. Braxton Wyatt would rage, Blackstaffe would rage, and while Red Eagle and Yellow Panther might not rage openly, they would burn with internal fire. Then his laughter gave way to far more solemn feelings. Who was he to laugh at two great Indian chiefs who certainly would have taken or slain him had it not been for the intervening miracle?

Henry's heart was filled with admiration and gratitude. He had been a friend for a day or two to the beasts of the forest and one of them had come to his rescue. The feeling of reversion to a primitive golden age was still strong within him, and doubtless the bear, too, had really felt the sense of kinship. He looked in the direction in which the shambling animal had gone, but there was no sign of him. Perhaps he had disappeared forever, because his mission was done.

Again came the calls of animals to one another, the cries of the owl and wolf, and then their own natural voices, in which Henry now, in fancy or in fact, detected the note of chagrin. They had found the lair at last, and they had found it empty! A long yell, fiercer than any of the others, confirmed him in the belief, and despite the solemnity of his own feelings at such a time, when he had been saved in such a manner, he was compelled to laugh silently, but with intense enjoyment.

Then he addressed himself to his new problems. Because he had escaped with his life, it did not mean that his troubles were ended. The warriors would come quickly out of the maze and Red Eagle and Yellow Panther, with the host at their command, would send innumerable scouts and trailers in every direction to find his new traces. It would be with them not only a question of removing their enemy, but a matter of pride as well, and they were sure to make a supreme effort.

It was his knowledge of the minds of the chiefs that had kept him from turning back to the oasis and his comrades. To return would be merely to draw a fresh attack upon them, and he resolved to continue his flight to the northeast. It was characteristic of him that he should not be headlong, exhausting himself, but he sat down calmly, ate a slice of the deer meat, and waited until he should hear the Indian signals again. They came presently from the segment of the circling hills nearest to him, and he knew that the pursuit had been organized anew and thoroughly. Then he rose and fled in the direction he had chosen.

He did not stop until the next night, covering a distance of about thirty miles, and although he heard nothing further then from the warriors, he knew the pursuit was still on. But he was so far ahead that he believed he could take rest with safety, and, creeping into a thicket, he made his bed once more among the leaves of last year. He slept soundly, but awakening at midnight, he scouted a bit about his retreat. Finding no evidence that the enemy was near, he slept again until dawn. Then he renewed the flight, turning a little more toward the north.

He yet had enough of the deer meat to last, with economy, three or four days, and he did not trouble himself for the present about the question of a further food supply. Instead he began to rejoice in his own flight. He was now fifty or sixty miles further north than the oasis, and as the country was higher and some time had elapsed since his departure, autumn was much more advanced. It was a season in which he was always uplifted. It struck for him no note of decay and dissolution. The crispness and freshness that came into the air always expanded his lungs and made his muscles more elastic and powerful. He had the full delight of the eye in the glorious colors that came over the mighty wilderness. He saw the leaves a glossy brown, or glowing in reds or yellows. The sumac bushes burned like fire. Everything was sharp, clear, intense and vital.

There was never another forest like that of the Mississippi Valley, a million square miles of unbroken woods, cut by a myriad of streams, varying in size from the tiniest of brooks to the great Father of Waters himself. Henry loved it and gloried in it, and he knew it well, too. It now contained various kinds of ripening berries that served as a sauce for his deer meat, and occasionally he would crack some of the early nuts that had ripened and fallen. The need for food would not be strong enough for some days yet to make him fire upon any of his new comrades, the wild animals.

But it is true that Henry still remained a creature of that primitive golden age. Never were his senses more acute. The lost faculties of man when he lived wholly in the woodland came back to him. He detected the presence of the hidden deer in the thickets, and he knew that the buffaloes were on the little prairies long before he came to them. He might have shot any number of the big beasts with ease, but he passed them by as he continued his steady flight into the north.

He had not seen any sign of his pursuers in two days, and now he stopped for them to come up, meanwhile eating plentifully in a berry patch. The berries were rich and large, and he took his time and ease, enjoying his stay there all the more because of his new comrades. Two black bears preyed upon the farther edge of the patch, and he laughed at them when their noses were covered with crimson stains. They seemed to be friendly, but he did not put the tie of friendship to too severe a test by approaching closely. Instead, he watched them from a little distance, when, after having eaten enormously, they played with each other like two boys, pushing and pulling, their reddened noses giving them the look of the comedians they were.

A stag watched the sportive bears from a little distance, standing body deep among the bushes, and regarding them with gravity. It pleased Henry to see a twinkle of amusement in the great eyes of the deer, which kept his ground unafraid, despite the presence of his usual enemy, man.

The bears, which were young, and hence festive, continued their sport, encouraged, perhaps, by a gathering and appreciative audience. A wildcat ran out on a long bough, looked at them and yowled twice. As they paid no attention to him, he concluded that it was best to be in a good humor after all, as obviously nobody meant him any harm. So he lay on the bough and watched the game. His eyes showed green and yellow in the sunlight, but it pleased Henry to think that they also held a look of laughter.

Three gray squirrels rattled the bark of an oak that overhung the berry patch. Then came a fox squirrel, with his more glowing color and big bushy tail, and all four looked at the bears. Sometimes they seemed glued to the bark. Then they would scuttle a short distance, to become glued again. Their beady eyes were twinkling. Henry could not see them, but he knew it must be so.

A slender nose and a pointed head pushed through the bushes, and then a long, strong figure followed. A great gray wolf! A beast of prey, but no thought of the hunt seemed to be in his mind now. He was about twenty feet from the rolling bears, and he regarded Henry with a look that said very plainly: "I enjoy the sport, but I would not do it myself." Henry gave back the look in kind, and the two, who would have been natural enemies at any other time, stood at opposite sides of the berry patch, looking with grave amusement at the sportive animals which still tumbled about, crushing the ripe berries under them, until not only their noses but almost their entire bodies were streaked with red stains.

A tiny spot appeared in the blue sky far overhead, grew with astonishing swiftness, as a great bald eagle, descending with the utmost velocity, and then abruptly checking its flight, alighted on the bough of a tree over Henry's head, where it sat, its eyes upon the comedy passing in the berry patch. At any other time the eagle would have regarded the youth as his natural enemy, but now there was no hostility between them. They were merely innocent spectators.

A rabbit, disturbed in its cosy nest under the briars, hopped out, sat on a little mound and looked on with interest, unafraid of the bears, the wolf, the eagle or the human being. A red bird flew in a circle over the berry patch and then alighted among the leaves of a tree, where it burned in a splash of flame against the glossy brown. Another bird, in a more sober garb, poured forth a joyous song.

The wilderness was at peace. Moreover, it was witnessing a comedy, presented by the true comedians of the forest, the young bears, and Henry's sense of kinship grew stronger. It gave him a feeling of great warmth, too, to see that they were not afraid of him. In a measure and for the time at least he was received into the forest family.

A quarter of an hour passed, and the comedy was not yet finished, but Henry heard a lone far cry in the south, and he knew it was the signal of warrior to warrior. In a minute the answering signal was given, but much nearer, and the two bears stopped in their play, standing up, their stained noses in the air and their streaked bodies quivering with apprehension. A third time came the call, and the figures of the bears stiffened. Then they slid through the berry patch and disappeared in the forest, going like shadows. The eagle unfolded his wings, shot upward like a bolt and was lost in the vast blue vault. The wolf vanished so silently that Henry found himself merely looking at the place where he had been. The rabbit disappeared from the mound. The spot of flame on the glossy brown that marked the presence of the tanager was gone, and the sober brown bird ceased to sing. The forest idyll was over and Henry was alone in the berry patch.

He felt bitter anger against the approaching warriors. Before he had regarded them merely as enemies whose interests put them in opposition to him. In their place, doubtless, he would do as they were doing, but now, seeking his death, they had broken the wilderness peace. A desire for revenge, a wish to show them that pursuers as well as pursued could be in danger, grew upon him, and, as he fled again, he used little speed, allowing them to gain until he saw one of the brown figures among the tree trunks. Then he fired, and, when the figure fell, he uttered a shout of triumph in the Indian fashion. A yell of rage answered him, and now, reloading as he ran, he fled at a great rate. Twice he heard the distant cries, and then no more, but he knew that Shawnees and Miamis still followed on. The death of the warrior would be an additional incentive to the pursuit. He would seem to them to be taunting them, and, in truth, he was.

But he had been refreshed so much by his stay in the berry patch that his speed now was amazing, wishing to leave them far behind as usual when the time came for sleep. A river, narrow but deep, suddenly threw itself across his path. It was an unwelcome obstruction, but, managing to keep his arms and ammunition dry, he swam it. The water was cold, and when he was on the other side he ran faster than ever in order to keep the blood warm in his veins and dry his clothing.

There was but little sunshine now, and a raw, damp wind came out of the northwest. He looked at the skies anxiously, and they gave back no assurance. He knew the region had been steadily rising, and he had his apprehensions. In an hour they were justified. The raw, damp wind brought with it something that touched his face like the brush of a feather. It was the year's first flake of snow, premature and tentative, but it was followed soon by others, until they became a thin white veil, driven by the wind. The brown leaves rustled and fell before them, and the appearance of the forest, that had been glowing in color an hour or two before, suddenly became wintry and chill. The advance of twilight made the wilderness all the more somber, and Henry's anxiety increased. He must find shelter for the night somewhere, and he did not yet know where.

He came out upon the crest of a low ridge, and searched the forest with his eyes, hopeful that he might find again a rocky hollow equipped with dead leaves, or even a windrow matted with bushes and vines, but he saw neither. He beheld instead, and to his great surprise, a smoke in the north, a smoke that must be large or it would not be so plain in the dusk. He studied it, and finally came to the conclusion that it marked the presence of an Indian village. This region was not known to him, but as obviously it was a splendid hunting ground it was not at all strange that he should come upon such a town.

It was Indian smoke, but it beckoned to him, because there was warmth beneath it. It was not likely to be a large village, but the skin lodges and the log cabins perhaps would give ample protection against snow and cold. In every age, whether stone, cave or golden, man had to have something over his head on winter nights, and Henry, acting upon his usual belief that boldness was the best policy, went straight toward the village. He had some sort of an idea that he might pilfer the hospitality of his enemies. That would be a great joke upon them, and the more he thought of it the better he liked it.

115

He used the last precaution as he approached. He was quite sure that the village stood in the woods, and he did not really fear anything except the stray curs usually found around Indian homes. But none barked as he drew near and he began to believe that his luck would find the place without them. Presently he saw the lights of two or three fires glimmering through the bushes, and then he came to a heap of bones, those of buffalo, wild turkey, deer, bear and every other kind of game, like one of the kitchen middens of ancient man in Europe. He drew at once the conclusion that the village, though small, was as nearly permanent as an Indian village could be.

He went closer. Nobody sat by the fire. Apparently there was no watch, which was not strange, as here in the heart of their own country no enemy was likely to come. He counted fourteen lodges, four small log cabins and a larger one standing among the trees apart from the others. Thin threads of smoke rose from the four cabins and several of the tepees, but not from the larger cabin. It was certain now that there were no dogs, as, scenting him, they would have given tongue earlier. The fortune in which he trusted had not betrayed him.

His eyes passed again over the lodges and the smaller cabins and rested on the larger one, which was built of poles and had a wooden figure, carved rudely, standing at every one of the four corners. He noted these figures with intense satisfaction, and, having followed bold tactics, he became yet bolder, creeping through the forest toward the long cabin.

The snow was still falling in fine, feathery flakes, not enough to make a real snow, but enough to cause great discomfort, and he exercised all his skill and caution.

While the Indians slept, yet someone among them always slept lightly, and he knew better than to bring such a swarm of hornets upon him. He reached the long cabin and saw in it a door opening toward the eastern forest and away from the village.

The door was closed with a heavy curtain of buffalo robe, but lifting it without hesitation he entered. Then he stood a little while near the entrance until his eyes grew accustomed to the dusk. The room, which had a floor of bark, was empty save for skins of buffalo or other animals hanging from poles, and two curtained recesses, in which stood totem figures like those at the corners of the house.

Henry knew that it was a council house or house of worship. He had known that as soon as he saw the figures outside. No one would enter it until the chiefs came from a greater village to hold council or make worship. Any possible trail that he might have left

116

would soon be covered by the falling snow, and, going within one of the curtained alcoves, he lifted the wooden figure there a little to one side. Then he spread one of the buffalo robes within the space and, folding his blanket about himself, lay down upon it. Soon he was asleep, while nearly a hundred of his enemies, men, women and children, also slept but fifty yards away.

Henry did not awaken while the night lasted. He had reached the limit of endurance, and every nerve and muscle in him cried aloud for rest. Moreover, his freedom from apprehension conduced to quick and sound slumber, and it was long after daylight when his eyes opened and he stretched himself. He remembered at once where he was, and he felt a great sense of comfort. It was very warm and pleasant on the buffalo robe, with his blanket wrapped about his body, and sitting up he looked out through a narrow crevice between the poles.

He saw a cold morning, with a skim of snow on the ground, already melting fast before the sun, and destined to be gone in a half hour, fires that had been built anew until they burned brightly, and squaws cooking before them, while warriors, with blankets drawn about their shoulders, sat near and ate. Children ran about, also eating or doing errands. It was a homely wilderness scene, and Henry knew at once that these people had nothing to do with the great hunt for him that was being conducted by Red Eagle and Yellow Panther, though they would seize him quickly enough if they knew of his presence.

They were neither Miamis nor Shawnees, nor any other tribe he knew. They might be a detached fragment of some northwestern tribe with which he had never come in contact, or they might be a tiny tribe in themselves. In the vast American wilderness old tribes were continually perishing, and new tribes were continually being formed from the pieces of the old. The people of this village seemed to Henry a fine Indian race, much like the great warrior nation, the Wyandots. The men were well built and powerful, and the women were taller than usual.

He saw that it was a village of plenty. It was usually a feast or a famine with the Indians, but now it was unquestionably a period of feast. The squaws were broiling buffalo, deer, wild turkey, smaller game and fish over the coals. They were also cooking corn cakes, and Henry looked at these hungrily. It had been many days since he had eaten bread, and, craving it with a fierce craving, he resolved to pilfer some of the cakes if a chance offered.

The odors, so pleasant in his nostrils and yet so tantalizing, reminded him that he had with him the haunch of venison, of which

117

a large portion was yet left. He ate, but it was cold. There was no water to drink with it, and he was not satisfied. His resolve to become an uninvited guest at their table, as well as under their roof, grew stronger.

Yet he liked these Indians and he became convinced that they were in truth a little tribe of their own or a fragment split off from a larger tribe, buried here in the woods, to be the germ of bigger things. He was seeing them at their best, leading, amid abundance, the life to which they had been born and which they loved. All, men, women and children, ate until they could eat no more. Then they idled about, the sun driving away the last of the snow and warming earth and air again. In a cleared space the half-grown boys began to play ball with the earnestness and vigor the Indians always showed in the game. The men, full and content, sat on their blankets and looked on. Thus the morning passed.

In the hours before noon Henry did not chafe. He rather enjoyed the rest; but in the latter half of the day he grew impatient. He longed to be up and away again, but there would be no chance to leave until night, and he forced himself to lie still. He yet had no fear that any one would come into the council room. Such chambers were little used, unless the occasion was one of state.

The afternoon was warm. The cold and light snow of the night before had been premature, and the vanguard of autumn returned to its normal state. While many leaves had fallen, more remained, and the colors were deeper and more vivid than ever. The whole forest burned with red fire. Through a narrow opening among the trees Henry saw a small field, full of ripened maize, with yellow pumpkins between the stalks. The sight made him hungrier than ever for bread.

About the middle of the afternoon, the warriors who were lying on their blankets rose suddenly and stood in an attitude of attention. They seemed to be listening, rather than looking, and Henry strained his ears also. He heard what appeared to be an echo, and then one of the warriors in the village replied with a long, thrilling whoop that penetrated far through the forest.

He divined at once that the pursuit was at hand, not because the warriors had been led there by his trail, which in truth was invisible now, but because some portion of the net they had spread out must in time reach the village.

The whole population gathered in the cleared space where the fires had burned and looked toward the southern forest. Henry, from his crack between the poles, saw ripples of interest running among them, the warriors exchanging sober comment with one another, the women and children not hesitating to talk and chatter as in a white village when visitors of interest were approaching. It was on the whole a bright and animated picture, and he did not feel any hostility to a soul in that lost little town in the wilderness.

Another cry came in five minutes from the forest, and now it was clear and piercing. A warrior in the village replied, and then they all waited, a vivid, eager crowd, to see who came. The whole space was within visible range of Henry's crevice, and he watched with equal interest.

A tall figure emerged from the forest, the figure of an elderly man, powerful despite his years, and with a face of authority. It was Red Eagle, head chief of the Shawnees, and behind him came the renegades, Wyatt and Blackstaffe, and twenty warriors. Despite their haughty bearing they showed signs of weariness.

The chief of the village stepped forward and gravely saluted Red Eagle, who replied with equal gravity. They exchanged a few words, and with a wave of the arms the chief made them welcome. The fires were built anew, and, the guests sitting about them, smoked with their hosts a pipe of peace which was passed from one to another. Then food was brought and Red Eagle, his warriors and the renegades ate.

Henry would have given much to hear what they said, but he knew they would not speak of their errand for a while. Some time must be allowed for courtesy and for talk that had nothing to do with their purpose. Nevertheless he saw that Red Eagle and all his band were worn to the bone, and he was glad. He had led them on such a chase as they had never pursued before, and he would lead them yet farther. He could afford to laugh.

The guests ate hungrily and the women continued to serve food to them until they were satisfied. Then all except the adult male population of the village withdrew, and Red Eagle rose to address his hosts.

CHAPTER XI
THE GREATER POWERS

When the Shawnee chief rose to talk he stood at one side of the open space, scarcely twenty feet from the corner of the council house in which Henry lay hidden, and as he said what he had to say in the usual oratorical manner of the Indians upon such occasions, the youth easily heard every word.

Red Eagle spoke in Shawnee, which Henry surmised was a kindred language to that of the village, and which it was obvious they easily understood. He told them a startling tale. He said that far in the south five white scouts and foresters, two of whom were only boys in years, although one of the boys was the largest and strongest of the five, had kept the Indians from destroying the white settlements in Kain-tuck-ee. By trick and device, by wile and stratagem, they had turned back many an attack. It was not their numbers, but the cunning they used and the evil spirits they summoned to their aid that made them so powerful and dangerous. Until the five were removed the Indians could not roam their ancient hunting grounds in content.

So the Shawnees, the Miamis, the Wyandots, the Delawares and the kindred tribes had organized to pursue the five to the death. They had struck the trail of one, the youth who was the largest, the strongest and the most formidable of them all, and they had never ceased to follow it. Twice they had drawn around him a ring through which it seemed possible for nothing human to break, but on each occasion he had called to the evil spirits, his friends, and they had answered him with such effect that he had vanished like a bird at night.

Murmurs of wonder came from the listening crowd. Truly, the young white warrior was of marvelous prowess, and it would not be well for one of them alone to meet him, when he not only had his formidable weapons, but could summon to his help spirits yet more dreadful. They cast apprehensive glances at the deep woods into which he had fled.

Red Eagle was an impressive orator, and the forest setting was admirable. The great Shawnee chief stood full six feet in height, his brow was broad and his eyes clear and sparkling. He made but few gestures, and he spoke in a full voice that carried far. Before him were the people of the village, and behind him was the great forest, blazing in autumn red. The renegades, Blackstaffe and Wyatt, stood near, each leaning against a tree trunk, following closely all that Red Eagle said. They, too, wished the destruction of the great youth, but their enmity to him was baser than that of the Indians, since it was an innate jealousy and hatred, and not a hostility based upon difference of race and interest.

When Henry looked at the renegades the desire to laugh was strong again. What rage they would feel if they ever came to know that when Red Eagle was making his address with his veteran warriors around him, the fugitive, for whose capture or death a red army had striven in vain for days, lay at his ease within fifty or sixty feet of them, a buffalo robe of the Indians' themselves, his bed, and one of their own houses his shelter!

Red Eagle continued, in his round, full voice, telling them he had tracked the fugitive northward, his warriors picking up the trail again, and that he must have passed near their village. He wished to know if they had seen any trace of him, and he asked their help in the hunt. A middle-aged man, evidently the head of the village, replied with equal dignity, but in a dialect that Henry could not understand. Still, he assumed that it was a full assent, as, a few minutes after he had finished, ten warriors of the village, taking their weapons, went into the forest, and Henry knew that they were looking for him or his trail. But Red Eagle, his warriors and the renegades remained by the fire, still resting, because they were weary, very weary, no fugitive before ever having led them such a troublesome chase.

Red Eagle, the Shawnee chief, was a statesman as well as a warrior. While it was true that young Ware was helped by evil spirits, he felt that the pursuit must be maintained nevertheless. Ware was the great champion of the white people, who far to the south were cutting down the forest and building houses. He had acquired a wonderful name. His own deeds were marvelous, but superstition had added to the terror that he carried among the Indians. He must be removed. The necessity for it grew greater and more pressing every day. All the Indian power must be turned upon him, and when the task was achieved they could deal with his four comrades. He had talked over the problem with Yellow Panther, first chief of the Miamis, a man full of years, wise in council and great on the war path, and he had agreed with him fully that the pursuit must be maintained, even if it went to the Great Lakes, or those other great lakes in the far misty Canadian region beyond.

Now, Red Eagle, as he rested by the fire and received the

121

hospitality of the tiny tribe in the wilderness, was very thoughtful. Intellect as well as prowess had made him a great chief; like the one whom he pursued, he loved the forest, and when he looked upon it now, in all its glowing colors of autumn, the glossy browns, the blazing reds and the soft yellows, he was not willing for a single one of its trees to be cut down. And while he meant to carry the pursuit to the very rim of the world he knew, if need be, he did not withhold admiration and a certain liking for the fugitive.

Red Eagle glanced at the renegades, who had sat down now before the fire and who were in a half doze. Although they were useful to the Indians, who valued them for many reasons, he felt a strong aversion toward them at that moment. He knew that if Ware were taken they would clamor at once for his life. None would be more eager for the torture than they, but Red Eagle had another plan in his mind. The principle of adoption was strong among the Indians. Captives were often received into the tribes, and Ware, with death as the alternative, might become a splendid young adopted son for him and, in time, the greatest chief of the Shawnees. He would not come as a renegade, like Blackstaffe and Wyatt, but as a valiant prisoner taken fairly in battle, to whom was left no other choice.

It was to the credit of Red Eagle's heart and brain, as he sat deeply pondering, that he evolved such a plan, but he made one mistake. High as he estimated the mental and physical powers of the fugitive to be, he did not estimate them high enough. Few would have had the strength of will that Henry displayed then to lie quiet in the council house while his enemies were all about him and the warriors were searching the forest around for his trail. It was fortunate, in truth, that the snow had come and passed, hiding any possible traces he might have left.

His conviction that he was safe, for the present at least, remained. He knew there was no occasion for the chiefs to enter the sacred building in which he lay, and the others would not dare to do so. Nothing troubled him at present but thirst. His throat and mouth were dry and craved water, as one in the desert, but he knew that he must endure.

Late in the day, the warriors of the village who had gone out to look for his trail began to return, and when they had made their reports, Henry knew by the disappointment evident on the faces of Red Eagle and the renegades, that they had found nothing. He saw the Shawnee chief give orders to his own men, half of whom plunged into the forest to the northward and disappeared. They reckoned that he had gone on, and, spreading out in the usual fan fashion, would continue the pursuit. But it seemed that Red Eagle, with the remainder of his immediate force and the renegades, intended to pass the night in the village.

A supper of great abundance and variety was served to the Shawnee chief and his men, and, when he saw the pure fresh drinking water brought to them, Henry raged inwardly. They had not taken him yet, but already he was being put to the torture. It was bitter irony that he should suffer so much for water when the forest contained countless streams and pools. He shut his teeth tight together and waited for the coming of the night, now not far away. The lack of water would drive him out of the council house, and in the dark he must seize anything that looked like an opportunity.

He hoped for the clouds again and another veil of snow, however thin, but his hopes were not fulfilled. When the slow dusk came, he lifted the buffalo curtain and emerged from his corner, feeling an intense relief, despite the shooting pain, because he could stand up again. Then he stretched and rubbed himself until all the soreness was gone from his muscles, and, standing there, tried to think of a way to escape.

His eyes, used to the dark of the room, fell upon a great headdress of twisted buffalo horns, profusely decorated with feathers. A long coat of buffalo skin adorned with feathers and porcupine quills in strange designs lay beside it upon the poles. He had seen many such equipments. It was a sort of regalia worn by Indian dancers, and now and then by great chiefs upon solemn occasions.

He looked at it, idly at first, and then with growing interest, as an idea was born in his brain. The dress must be almost sacred in character, or it would not be left here in the council house, and kind fortune had certainly put it on the poles for his particular use. Once more he was thoroughly convinced that he was watched over by the greater powers, not because of any especial merit of his, but for reasons of their own, and he clothed himself in the headdress and the strange, variegated robe that fell to his ankles. Then even Shif'less Sol would have had to take a third look to know him.

Henry's heart beat high and fast. He was thoroughly convinced that he had found a way. He had now only to use that rarest and greatest of qualities, patience, and, by a supreme exertion of the will, he managed to wait until it was far into the night.

Red Eagle had gone into one of the log cabins, and was probably asleep. Henry, from the crack, was not able to see what had become of the renegades, but he surmised that they, too, were sleeping somewhere. Two of the fires still burned in the open, but

123

nobody watched beside them, and he judged that the time was ripe for the trial.

He gave a final touch to the headdress and the buffalo robe. He would have been glad to have seen himself in a glass, but he was sure, nevertheless, that he looked his part of a great medicine man, a reincarnation of some ancient chief who had come back to spend a while within the sacred precincts of the council house. His rifle he managed to hide beneath the great painted coat, at the same time holding it convenient for his use, and, lifting the curtain of buffalo robe, he stepped out.

It was neither a dark nor a fair night, but much fleecy vapor was floating between earth and sky, imparting to the village and the forest a misty, unreal effect which was suited admirably to Henry's purpose, enlarging his figure and giving to it a fantastic and weird effect. Knowing it, and having the utmost confidence in himself, he chose a path directly through the center of the open, walking slowly, but taking strides of great length and stepping from tiptoe to tiptoe.

Two Indian sentinels, a Shawnee and a native of the village, were dozing by the wall of one of the log cabins, when they heard the step in the open. They lifted heavy eyelids and beheld a gigantic figure, attired in a garb that ordinary mortals do not wear, stalking toward the forest, caring nothing for the sentinels, the village or anything else. They were in the midway region between sleeping and waking, when images are printed upon the brain in confused or exaggerated shapes, and the mysterious visitor, who was even then taking his departure, seemed to them at least fifteen feet high, while, from under the headdress of twisted buffalo horns, two great eyes, hot and blazing like coals, stared at them. This terrifying figure, as they gazed upon it, raised a huge hand full of menace and shook it at them. They gave a yell of terror and darted into the forest.

Red Eagle, sleeping the sleep of the just and tired, heard the shout of alarm, and it impinged so heavily upon his unconscious brain that he was shocked at once into an awakening. He leaped to his feet and ran out of the cabin, just in time to meet the head chief of the village coming out of another one. The two stared at each other, and then they saw the great figure, in its mystic apparel, just where forest and open met. Each uttered a gasp, and, before they could gasp a second time, the apparition was gone among the trees, vanishing from their stupefied gaze like a wisp of smoke before the wind. Then Red Eagle and his host, great and wise chiefs though they were, looked at each other again and trembled.

Henry meanwhile was racing through the forest and toward

the north, always toward the north, and as he ran he shook with laughter. He had seen the look of dismay on the faces of the Indians and he rejoiced. He was sorry that he had not seen Braxton Wyatt and Blackstaffe too. Their minds were less subject to superstition than those of the red men, but no doubt in the first minute or two they were frightened also if they saw him.

Yet he believed that the renegades would arouse the Indians and perhaps would suspect that the terrific stranger, who had come and departed so mysteriously, was none other than the fugitive himself. He did not care if they did; in truth, he rather hoped they would. He could imagine their mortification and disappointment, and since they had gone to dwell with strangers and fight their own people, it was only a fraction of what they deserved.

The great headdress of twisted buffalo horns was heavy and the big painted buffalo coat flapped around him, but he would not discard them yet. Stray warriors might be in the forest near the village, and, if so, he wished to reserve for them his awful and threatening appearance. But he could not stand them more than a mile. Then he threw the headdress into a creek, hoping that it would float away with the current, but, thinking he would have further use for it, he kept the painted coat. Then he crossed the creek and resumed his northward flight at great speed.

He did not stop until dawn, when he felt that he was safe, for a day at least, from pursuit. He had brought with him what was left of the deer meat, and, sitting down by the bank of a small brook, he ate, drinking afterward of the clear stream and giving thanks. He had been saved again in a miraculous manner. When skill and strength themselves would have been of no avail, fortune had put the council house and the ceremonial robes in his way. He could not doubt that the greater powers were working in his behalf, and he felt all the elation that comes from the assurance of continued victory.

But it was a bleak dawn. A cold sun was rising in a cold, blue sky. There was no snow now, but the dry grass was white with frost, and whenever the wind stirred a little, the dead leaves fell with a dry rustle. He retreated deeper into the thicket, and he was glad that he had kept the great painted coat, as he wrapped himself in it from head to foot and lay down between two fallen logs, with the dense bushes over his head.

He must find another interval of rest and sleep, and feeling that his best chance lay here, he drew the coat very close. It kept him thoroughly warm, and, as soon as his nerves settled into their normal condition, he slept.

He awoke before noon, and the morning was still frosty and

125

cold. Yet the wilderness was more beautiful than ever. The frost had merely deepened its colors. While many dead leaves had fallen, myriads remained, and they had taken on more intense and glowing tints. The air had all the purity and tonic of an American autumn. The light winds were the breath of life itself.

He ate the last of the deer, and then he found bunches of wild grapes, small and bitter sweet, but refreshing. Later in the day he must secure game, though he still felt averse to shooting anything, since the creatures of the forest had saved him more than once. But in the end it would come to it.

It was a rolling country, and, walking to the crest of the highest ridge, he examined it in all directions. He saw only the great forest in its reds and yellows and browns, and he was alone in it, its uncrowned king, if he chose to call himself so.

Although the country was new to him, Henry believed that he was about two hundred and fifty miles north of the Ohio and in the region inhabited by the warlike northwestern tribes. Several of their great villages must lie not very far to the east of him, and he smiled at the thought that he was leading the pursuit back to the homes of the pursuers. He wondered what his comrades were doing, but he believed that they would remain in the swamp, or near it, until he came back.

Not knowing what else to do, he moved northward again, and presently heard a low, monotonous sound, which after a little listening he decided to be Indian squaws chanting. Further listening convinced him that there were only two voices, and he approached cautiously among the trees.

Two Indian women, one quite young and the other quite old, were cooking by the side of a small brook, in which they had evidently been washing deerskin clothing earlier in the day, as it now lay drying on the bank. Probably they were the wife and mother of some warrior preparing for his return from the hunt. Henry took little interest in the deerskins they had washed, but his attention was concentrated quickly upon their cooking.

They were broiling a fat, juicy wild turkey. He had an especially tender tooth for wild turkey, particularly when it was young and fat. It, more than anything else, was his staff of life, and now he set covetous eyes upon the one that was broiling over the coals. He did not like to rob women, but it must be done, and he bethought himself of his painted coat. Pulling it high over his head, concealing his rifle under it and uttering a tremendous woof, he stalked into the open in which the fire was burning.

The two Indian women, when they beheld the apparition,

126

uttered simultaneous screams and fled into the forest, while the hungry young robber, lifting their turkey from the fire, where it was already well broiled, disappeared among the trees in the opposite direction, happy to have secured his rations through the aid of fright only and without violence. He knew, however, that he could not afford to satisfy his hunger just then. Warriors, and perhaps a village, could not be far away, and the men, divining that the fright of the women was caused by a human being, would soon come in pursuit. So he went at least two or three miles before he sat down and ate a substantial dinner, reserving the remainder for future use. Truly the wild turkey was his best friend.

That night he lay again in the forest, and he was devoutly glad that he had saved the painted robe. The climate of the great valley is fickle, and it rapidly turned colder again. Raw winds whistled through the woods, and he had difficulty in finding a sheltered place where, even with the aid of the robe, he could keep warm. He selected at last a tiny glen, well grown with tall bushes on every side, heaped up parallel rows of dead leaves, and then, lying down between them, wrapped in the robe, fell asleep.

When he awoke his face felt cold, and opening his eyes, he found that it had good reason to be so. It was covered with snow, and upon the robe itself the snow lay deep. The whole forest was white, and, as he stood up, he heard branches cracking beneath the weight that had gathered on them in the night. It had come down in thick and great flakes, but so softly that it had failed to awaken him.

Henry, despite his courage and strength, was alarmed. It is one thing even for the best trained to live in the forest in summer, but quite another in winter. Nor was the aspect of the sky encouraging. It was somber with clouds, and, even as he looked at it, the snow began to fall again. It was not an ordinary snow, but the clouds just ripped their bottoms out and let their entire burden fall at once. A huge white cataract seemed to fill the whole air, and Henry's alarm deepened into dismay. The snow would soon be six inches deep, then a foot, and what was he to do?

He was thankful once more for the painted robe, and also for the wild turkey that he had pilfered, and knowing that he must keep warm, he started on a dreary walk toward the north. The snow was pouring so hard that he could scarcely see, but he heard a sound to his right, and presently he was able to discern an immense stag floundering in some undergrowth in which its hoofs seemed to be caught.

Henry could easily have shot the deer and it would have furnished an unlimited supply of food, at a time when he might be

127

snowed up for days. He always believed afterward, too, that the deer expected to be killed, as it ceased its struggles and looked at him with great, pathetic eyes. It was a magnificent stag, the largest he had ever seen, but he had no heart to shoot. His own eyes met the appealing gaze from those of the king of the woods and he felt sorry. Nothing could have induced him to shoot. He sincerely hoped that the stag would pull free, and as the thought came to him the wish was fulfilled.

The left forefoot, which was entangled, suddenly came loose and unhurt. Never did Henry see a transformation more rapid and complete. The stag, before pathetic and depressed, a beaten beast, expanded in the twinkling of an eye into a mighty monarch of the forest. He stood erect, threw back his great head in a gesture of triumph, looked once more at the human being whom nature had taught him instinctively to dread, but who had not harmed him when he was at his mercy, then stalked away, until he was lost behind the white veil of the snowy fall.

Henry felt gladness. He was glad that he had not shot, and he was glad that the stag had released his foot, or otherwise he would have perished under the teeth of wolves. Then he addressed himself to his own peril, which was great and increasing. He hunted the deepest portions of the woods, but the snow sought him there. He stood under the trees of the thickest boughs, but the white fall gradually poured through, heaping upon his head, his shoulders and the folds of his robe. He would brush it off and move on to another place, merely to find it gathering again, and, by and by, his great muscles began to feel weariness. He plodded for hours in the deepening snow, seeking a refuge from this persistent and deadly fall, but finding none. A sort of despair, almost unknown to him, oppressed him for a little while. He had fought off innumerable attacks of warlike and powerful savages, he had triumphed over hardships and dangers the very name of which would make the ordinary man shudder, and here he was about to be conquered by a mere shift of the wind that brought snow.

He could have shouted aloud in anger, but instead he summoned all his courage and strength anew and continued his hunt for a refuge.

CHAPTER XII
THE STAG'S COMING

The snow, famous in the annals of the tribes as one of the greatest that ever fell so early in the autumn, continued to pour down. Where Henry had sunk to his ankles, he now sank almost to his knees, and the wilderness stretched away, without offering the shelter of any covert or rocky hollow. His exertions made him very warm, but he was too wise to take off the painted coat, lest he cool too fast. To fall ill in the snowy forest, hunted by savages, was a thought to make the boldest shudder, and he took no chances.

He fought the storm for hours. Rightly it could be called no storm, as it was merely the placid fall of snow in huge quantities, but in the long run it contained more elements of danger than a hurricane. Night came and he was still struggling among the drifts, not walking now with firm, straight steps, but staggering. Nearly all of his tremendous strength was gone, exhausted, fighting against the impassive snowy depths that always held him back. Once or twice he fell, but his will brought him to his feet again, and he went on, his mind now directing wholly the almost inert mass that was his body.

Twilight came, adding a new gloom to the somber heavens. All the animals themselves seemed to have gone, and he strove alone for life amid the vast desolation. Then he recalled his courage once more. On this great expedition, when he was offering himself as a sacrifice for his people, the miracles were always happening. At the last moment, when it did not seem possible for him to be saved, he had always been saved, and surely the miracle would occur once more!

He came to a huge tree, blown down by the wind, but yet projecting above the snow, and sitting down on the trunk he leaned against an upthrust root. He closed his eyes, for a moment or two, and the desire to keep them shut, and sink into happy forgetfulness, was almost more than he could resist. He made a gigantic effort and pulled himself back to full consciousness, knowing that the easiest way, which in this case was the way of yielding, would be the fatal way. Drawing up the last ounces of his strength he staggered on, remembering to keep his rifle protected by the painted coat, and clinging also to the turkey.

He looked up at the heavens, but they gave no promise. They

were without a break in the massed clouds, and the snow poured down in an unceasing white fall. The range of vision was so short that he could not tell the character of country into which he was coming, and, presently, he struck marshy ground, into which his moccasined feet sank deep, coming forth wet and cold. It was a new danger, and he stamped his feet hard and walked faster in an endeavor to keep the circulation going and to keep them from freezing. It was a peril that he had not foreseen, and it would, in truth, be the very irony of fate if, after so many miracles had intervened to save him from pressing dangers, he should perish in a premature snow storm.

Usually, one could find shelter of a sort in the wilderness. The forest of the great valley had become in the course of ages so dense with thickets and matted tangles of fallen trees that one did not have to go far before coming to a lair into which he could creep. But now everything of the kind evaded Henry. His eyes, almost blinded by the snow, saw only the straight trunks of trees, and open ground that offered no protection at all. Moreover, the chill from his wet feet, in spite of all his efforts, was extending and he shivered.

But he would not despair. He might have had such moments, but they were moments only, and he fought on, as those, whose souls are made of courage, fight. Yet the wilderness became gloomier, more desolate and more menacing than ever. The fall of snow was less heavy, but a bitter wind rose and it came with an alternate shriek and moan. The air grew colder and the chill of the wind struck into Henry's bones. Nevertheless he struggled on in the darkening night, going he knew not where, nor to what.

Courage and will can triumph over most things, but not over all things. There comes a time when hour, place and circumstances seem to combine against the individual, and such an hour had come for Henry. He searched everywhere for some place in which he could lie until the storm had passed, but it was always nothing, nothing, just the open forest, and the driving wind, and the creeping chill which was steadily going into all his bones.

At last, scarcely able to raise a foot, he sank down on a fallen log and stared into the gloomy woods which gave back not a single ray of hope. Again he felt the dreamy desire to sink into rest and complete oblivion, and again he fought it off, knowing that it was the way of death. Then he looked up at the somber skies, and prayed for one more miracle.

Henry, despite his wild, rough life, had much reverence in his nature. The wilderness, too, with its varied manifestations, encouraged the belief in a supreme power, just as it had given birth among the Indians to a natural religion closely akin to the revealed religion of the white man. Now, he was hopeful that in the extreme moment help would be sent to him, and that the last of the miracles had not yet been performed. Closing his eyes he said his prayer over and over again to himself, and then opening them he stared as before at the desolate forest, empty of everything living save his own presence.

But was it empty? Straight ahead of him he seemed to see an outline through the falling snow, like a dim and dusky figure behind a veil. He rose, new strength flowing into his veins, and took a step or two forward, fearful that he had been deceived by one of the fancies or visions, supposed to float before the eyes of the dying. Then he saw. The dim outlines on the other side of the snowy veil grew clearer and he traced the figure of a stag, larger than any other stag that had ever trod the earth, gigantic and majestic.

The stag, too, was staring at him, and he knew it to be the same that he had seen earlier in the day, though it had grown wonderfully in size since then. It showed not the slightest trace of fear, but, instead, the great luminous eyes seemed to him to express pity.

A thrill of superstitious awe ran through him. But it was awe, not fear. The stag, gigantic and almost a phantom, did not threaten. It pitied, and as Henry gazed at it with the fascinated eyes of one in a dream or in an illusion so deep that it was a twin brother to reality, the deer turned and walked slowly among the trees. Twenty paces, and, stopping an instant, it looked back. The human figure was following and the deer walked on, its stride measured and magnificent.

Henry did not doubt that his prayers had been answered, and that another miracle had been ordered for his salvation. He became transformed as if by magic. His head, which had been so heavy that it sagged upon his shoulders, grew singularly light. The blood, stagnant before, leaped in his veins like quicksilver, and his steps were straight and firm. The size of the deer did not decrease for him. It loomed immense and powerful through the driving snow, and, as it led steadily on, never looking back now, he followed with equal steadiness.

The stag turned once, going sharply to the right, and, in a few more minutes, the ground grew quite rough. Then he saw through the veil of the snow high hills rising on either side, but the stag led into a deep and narrow valley between them. As they advanced, it narrowed yet further, and the trees and bushes on the crests above them were so dense that the snow was not deep there, and the bitter wind was cut off entirely. Either hope and confidence or some measure of returning warmth drove the chill from Henry's bones, as he forgot the wet and cold and pressed forward eagerly when the stag increased his pace.

Henry's mental state became one of exaltation. He did not know to what he was going, but he knew that life lay at the end of the stag's trail, and he was willing to follow as long as need be. Nor did he ever know how long he followed, but he did notice that the cleft was growing deeper and narrower. After an unknown time he emerged into a tiny valley that was more like a well, it was set so deep in the hills and its slopes were so steep, the cliffs in truth overhanging on two sides.

He uttered a cry of joy. This was to be his refuge, and here he would be saved. Stretches of ground under the hanging cliffs were bare of snow, and heaped high with dead leaves. Dead wood lay all about. The bitter wind, with its alternate shriek and whistle, swept overhead, but it did not touch the floor of the well. The air was still and it did not bite.

The stag turned and looked back for the second and last time, and Henry, either in reality or in an illusion so deep that it was as vivid as reality, saw an expression of kinship in the great luminous eyes. Once more, for him at least, the old golden age when men and animals were friends had come back to endure an hour or two. Then, lifting its head very high and seeming taller and more majestic than ever, it passed out of the valley at a narrow opening on the other side.

Henry, shaking himself violently to bring back his wandering faculties, concentrated them upon his present needs, which were still urgent. Crouching in the best shelter that the hanging cliff furnished, he rapidly whittled shavings from the dead wood, until he had formed a heap close to the stony wall. Then, with the flint and steel that every hunter carried and laboring desperately, he managed to extract from the flint enough sparks to set fire to the shavings, hanging over the tiny blaze and shielding it with his body lest it go out and leave him alone in the cold and the dark.

The flame persisted and grew, reached out, and bit into more shavings, and then into larger pieces of dead wood that Henry presented to its teeth. Dead leaves helped it along, and he fed to it larger and larger sticks, until he had a splendid leaping fire, the very finest fire that was ever built in this world, a fire that sent up many high flames, red in the center and yellow at the edges, a fire that made great, glowing coals in beds, capable of keeping their heat all night.

Then Henry knew that in very truth and fact he was saved. Let the wind whistle and shriek above his head! He cared nothing for it. He took off his wet leggings and moccasins, and dried them and his

132

feet and legs before the fire. The spirit of a youth returned to him. He tried to see how near he could hold his flesh to those wonderful coals and flames without burning it, and with the fire, which is a twin brother to life, he felt life itself flowing anew into his body.

His vitality was so great that his strength seemed to return all at once, and he built another fire as fine as the first, but a little distance from it. Then he lay between the two, and was warmed on both sides. Exposed to the double heat also, his moccasins and leggings soon dried and he put them on again. His feeling was now one of extraordinary comfort, and warming the turkey on the coals, he ate an abundant supper, while he listened to the wind overhead and saw snow drop in the valley, but not on him, where he lay well within the lee of the stone wall.

After resting awhile between the fires he began to gather wood, the whole valley being littered with it. He did not know how long the storm would hold him there, and he intended to have sufficient heat. He also heaped up the wood into a species of rude wall, until no drop of snow could blow into his cleft under the cliff, and then contemplated his work with satisfaction. He could stay here as long as the storm lasted, even for days, nor did he forget to give thanks once more for the wonderful manner in which the stag had saved him. It was first the buffaloes, then the bear and now the deer. What would it be next?

Henry let the two fires sink to glowing heaps of coals, and then, warming thoroughly before them the great painted buffalo coat, he retreated to the alcove behind his wooden wall and made his bed on the leaves. He felt for all the world like a bear gone into its snug den for the long winter sleep, and, as he drew the big coat about his body, he looked lazily at the fires, which were so placed that the heat from them warmed his corner despite the wooden barrier.

Then the usual relaxation, after a tremendous mental and physical struggle came over him, and he began to feel the extraordinary luxury of lying dry, warm, well fed and in safety. It was all the primitive man desired, the best he ever received, and Henry, who had been put in their position, rejoiced as one of those far, faraway men might have rejoiced, when he, too, attained all his wishes.

The feeling of luxurious ease kept him in a dreamy state a long time. Although he felt strong and active again, able to cope with any crisis, he had really been very near the end for the time being to the extraordinary powers with which nature had endowed him. Now, as his great vitality flowed back and he knew that he was safe, it was just a pleasure to lie still, to feel the warmth, and to see dreamily the

133

glow of the fires, in truth, to feel as his ancestors had felt in like comfort forty thousand years ago.

Meanwhile the air turned a little warmer, just enough to admit a return of the heavy snowfall and the big flakes began to pour down again. Some of them, blown by the wind, fell on the sheltered fires, and hissed as they melted. But Henry was not troubled. He knew they could not reach him.

At the same time, but many miles to the south, a great force of Indian warriors, led by the two wise and valiant chiefs, Red Eagle, the Shawnee, and Yellow Panther, the Miami, was going into camp. Yellow Panther had come up with a force also and they had struck again the trail of the fugitive, but the coming of the storm had hidden it, of course, and as the snow deepened they were compelled to abandon, until the next day at least, all thought of catching Henry Ware, taking instead measures for their own preservation. Among them were men who knew the country, and they soon found a deep valley, in which they built their fires and ate their venison.

Red Eagle and Yellow Panther sat with the renegades, Blackstaffe and Wyatt, by one of the fires, and talked earnestly of the pursuit. The chiefs did not like the white men who had gone with strangers to fight against their own, but they respected their knowledge and tenacity. The chase had been long and arduous, it had drawn off much strength from the tribes, but they were in unanimous agreement that it should be continued, no matter how long, until their object was achieved. The great snow itself, deep and premature though it was, should not turn them back.

Henry could not see this council through the miles of hills and driving snow, but had his thoughts been turned in that direction he would have made to himself a picture just like it, nor would he ever have doubted for an instant that the chiefs and the renegades would pursue him as long as pursuit was possible.

It was well into the night, when his eyes closed and the sleep that took hold of him was far deeper than usual, carrying him into an oblivion that lasted until far after the sun had risen over a world, still white and misty with the falling snow.

He was surprised to see that the storm had not yet stopped, but he was not alarmed. The two fires were still smouldering, and the dead wood that he had heaped up was sufficient to last many days. It was true that he had only the wild turkey for food, but he was sure, in time, to discover other resources. He had seen the proof over and over again, that, for the time at least, he was a favorite of the greater powers. He was too modest to think it due to any particular merit of his own, but it seemed to him that he had been chosen as an instrument, and, for that reason, he was being preserved through every hardship and danger.

Secure in his belief, which was more than a belief, a conviction rather, he began to make a home for himself in his tiny valley, which was not more than fifty feet across, and above which the hills, steep like the side of a house, rose three or four hundred feet. His first precaution was to build the fires anew, not with a high flame, but with a slow steady burning that would make great beds of coals, glowing with heat. Then he examined the pass by which he had come, to find it choked with seven or eight feet of snow, and he looked next at the one by which the deer had gone, to discover that it was much like the first, leading a distance that was yet indefinite to him, as he did not care to follow it through the deep snow to its end.

Shaking the snow from the painted robe he came back to the covert and waited with as much patience as he could summon. Now he missed greatly his four comrades, and their talk. With them the time would have passed easily, but since they were not there he must do the best he could without them. The problem of food which he had resolutely pushed away, forced itself back again. A big, powerful body such as his was like an active engine. It required much fuel. There would be no food but animal food, and he was in no mood for killing an animal now. But he could not hide from himself the fact that it must be done, sooner or later.

On the second day he went through the pass by which the deer had gone, beating down the snow under his feet, until it was hard enough to sustain him, and, after about two miles of such difficult traveling, came upon fairly level ground. Here, hunting about, he surprised several rabbits in their deep nests, and killed them with blows of his rifle muzzle.

The hunt took nearly all day, and, when he returned to the cove with his game, night was coming. He was surprised to find how welcome the place was to him and how much it looked like a home. There was his sheltered alcove, with the wall of dead wood in front of it, and there were two heaps of coals sending their friendly glow to him through the cold dusk.

It was a home, and it was more. It was a refuge and a fortress. He had been guided to it by the greater powers, and he should value it for all it had afforded him, warmth, shelter and protection from his foes. He was not one to be lacking in gratitude or appreciation, and he sent admiring glances about his well, for it was more like a well than a valley. Lonely it might be, but bodily comforts it offered in abundance to such as Henry.

He cleaned the rabbits and hung them up in the alcove, knowing that their bodies would freeze hard in the night, and thus would be preserved, giving him with the wild turkey a supply of food sufficient for two or three days.

He was awakened the second night by cries, faint but very fierce, and he knew they were made by wolves howling. The ferocity, however, was not for him, as during that singular period his feeling of kinship for the animals extended even to the wolf. He knew that they howled because of hunger. The deep snow was hard on the wolves, making it difficult to find or pursue their prey, and they sent forth the angry lament because they were famished.

Henry merely drew the painted robe more closely about his body, looked contentedly at the glow from the two fine beds of coals, closed his eyes once more and went to sleep. He did not look for wolves in his well, although he heard them howling again the next night, the note plaintive and fierce alike with the call of intense hunger. The fourth day, he went out through the pass and killed more rabbits, adding them to his store. He saw a deer floundering in the deep snow, but he would not shoot it. The time might come when he would slay a deer, but he could not do it that week.

Now he began to study the skies. He knew that the premature snow, deep as it was, could not last long, and, likely enough, it would be followed by heavy rain. Then the snow would certainly pour in a deluge down the hillsides, and the water might rage in a torrent in the ravine. His well would be flooded and he would have to take to flight, but it would be no harder on pursued than on pursuers.

Two more days passed and the warm weather did not come. The snow ceased to fall, but it lay gleaming and deep on the ground, and the sound of boughs, cracking beneath its weight, was almost incessant. Indifferent to the deep trail he left, he climbed again to the heights and ranged over a considerable area. A second time, a floundering deer presented itself to his rifle, and a second time he refused to fire. The deer seemed to expect no danger, as it gazed at him with fearless eyes, and, waving to it a friendly farewell, he passed on among the trees, every one of which stood up an individual cone of white.

Then he heard the howl of wolves and traveling on to a valley beyond he saw a pack running far ahead. Twenty they were, at least, and whether or not they chased a deer he could not tell, but the fierce note of hunger was in their voices, and whatever it was they pursued they followed it fast.

Then he turned back toward his home, weary with walking through snow so deep, too deep yet for his further flight northward, and the fires in the covert seemed fairly to shine with welcome for him. That night he broiled and ate an entire rabbit for supper, but felt that he must have a more varied diet soon, if he was to preserve his strength. He looked again for the clouds which were to bring the great rain, destroyer of great snows, but the skies were clear, frosty and starry, and his eager eyes did not find a single blur.

It was evident that he must use all his patience and keep on waiting. So he set himself to the task of putting his body in the best possible trim, until such time as he would have to subject it to severe tests. He exercised himself daily and he always saw that his bed under the ledge was dry and warm. He never permitted the fires to go out, and gradually, as the snow about them melted from the heat, the ground there became hard and dry.

He was still able to procure food without firing a shot, finding plenty of rabbits in the deep snow on the hills, but he grew intensely weary of such a diet, and he felt that if he had to linger much longer he would kill a deer, although he had been saved by one. Every hour he scanned the heavens looking for the clouds which he knew would come in time, since the cold could not endure at such an early period in the autumn.

He had been in his retreat a week when he felt a light and soft touch on his face, the breath of the west wind. It had almost a summer warmth, and, then he knew that one of the great changes in temperature, to which the valley is subject, was coming. Throughout the afternoon the wind blew, and water began to trickle in the ravine. The sound of soft snow sliding down the hill was almost constant in his ears. Toward dusk, the clouds that he had expected came floating up from the horizon's rim, but he did not believe rain would fall before the next day.

Nevertheless, he took precautions, building a rough floor of dead wood in the alcove, and arranging to protect himself from the downpour which he considered inevitable. He also put his stores in the place that would remain safest and dryest, and lying down, high upon the dead wood, he fell asleep. He was awakened in the night by a rushing sound. The great rain that was to destroy the great snow had come, several hours earlier than he had expected it, and it was a deluge.

The trickle in the ravine became a torrent, and he heard it roaring. The floor of his little valley was soon covered with six inches of water and he was devoutly glad that he had built his platform of dead wood, upon which he could remain untouched by the flood, at least for the present. That it would suffice permanently he was not sure, as the rain was coming down at a prodigious rate, and there was no sign that it would decrease in violence.

He did not sleep any more that night, but sat up, watching and listening. It was pitchy dark, but he heard the roar of distant and new streams, and the sliding avalanches of sodden snow. He felt an awe of the elements, but he was not lonely now, nor was he afraid. That which he wished was coming, though with more violence and suddenness than he liked, but one must take the gifts of the gods, as they gave them, and not complain.

Dawn arrived, thick with vapors and mists, and dark with the pouring rain. From his place under the cliff he could not see far, but he knew that the snow was dissolving in floods. The six inches of water in his valley grew to a foot, and he began to be apprehensive lest the whole place be deluged to such an extent that he be driven out, a fear that was soon confirmed, as he saw two or three hours after dawn that he must go.

It would be impossible to keep the lower half of his body dry, but he was thankful once more for the great painted coat, under which he was able to secure his rifle and powder against rain. He also fastened in his belt two of the rabbits that he had cooked, and then with the rest of his baggage in a pack, he made his start.

He was forced to wade in chilly water almost to his knees, and it was impossible to leave the valley by either end of the ravine, as it was filled with a roaring flood many feet deep; but with the aid of bushes and stony outcrop he climbed the lofty slope, a slow and painful task attended by danger, as now and then a bush would pull out with his weight. But, at last, his hands torn, and his face running with perspiration, he attained the summit, where he turned his face once more toward the north.

He decided that he would keep to the ridges as the snow would leave them first, and he could also find some protection in the dense, scrubby growth that covered them.

He never passed a more trying day. The actual danger of Indian presence even would have been a relief. The rain beat in an unceasing deluge, and he was hard put to it to keep his rifle and ammunition dry. The sliding snow made his foothold so treacherous that he was compelled to keep among the wet and flapping bushes, where he could grasp support on an instant's notice.

At noon, though there was no sun to tell him that it had come, he stopped in a dense thicket and ate one of the rabbits, reflecting rather grimly that though he had been anxious for the rain to come it was making him thoroughly uncomfortable. Yet even these clouds covering all the heavens had at least one strip of silver lining. The harder and more persistently the rain fell the quicker the snow would be gone, and once more the wilderness would be fit for travel and habitation.

When he had eaten the rabbit, although he longed for some other kind of food, he felt better. He had at least furnished fuel for the engine, and, bending his head to the storm, he left the thicket and continued his journey, a journey the end of which he could not foresee, as he never doubted for an instant that the Indian host was still pursuing. He left no trail, of course, in such a storm, but the rain could not last forever, and, when it ceased, some warrior would be sure to pick it up again.

When night came he was thoroughly soaked, save for his precious ammunition, around which he had wrapped his blanket also. Most of the snow was gone, but pools stood in every depression, and turbid streams raced in every gully and ravine. Where he had trodden in snow before he now trod in mud, and every bone in him ached with weariness. Many a man, making no further effort, would have lain down and died, but it was not the spirit of Henry. He continually sought shelter and far in the night crowded himself into the hollow of a huge decayed tree. He was compelled to stand in a leaning position, but with the aid of the buffalo coat he managed to protect himself from further inroads of the rain, and by and by he actually fell asleep.

The sun was high when he awoke, and he was very stiff and sore from the awkward manner in which his body had been placed, but the rain had stopped and for that he was devoutly thankful, although the earth was sodden from the vast amount of water that had fallen.

It took him three hours to light a fire, so difficult was it to procure dry shavings, but, in the end, the task was achieved and it was a glorious triumph. Once more fire was king and he basked in it, drying his body and his wet clothing thoroughly, and lingering beside it all the afternoon. But at night he put it out reluctantly, since the warriors were sure to be abroad now, and he could not risk the light or the smoke.

He slept under the bushes, but in the morning he saw in the south smoke answering to smoke, and he did not doubt that it was detachments of the Indian host signaling to one another. Perhaps they had come upon his trail, and it was sure, if they had not done so, that they would soon find it. Watching the signals a little while, he turned and fled once more into the north.

CHAPTER XIII
THE LEAPING WOLF

Henry came presently into lower ground, where he judged the snowfall had not been so great, as the amount of standing water was much less and the streams were not so swollen. The air, too, was decidedly warmer, and while the forest had been stripped of all its leaves, it did not look so gloomy. A brilliant sun came out, flooded trees and bushes with light, and gave to the earth an appearance of youth and vitality that it has so often and so peculiarly in autumn, although that is the period of decay. He felt its tonic thrill, and when he came to a clear creek he decided that he would put himself in tune with the purity and clearness of the world about him.

He had lain so long in his clothes that he felt he must have the touch of clean water upon him, and, daring everything, he put his arms aside, removed his clothing and plunged into the creek. It made him shiver and gasp at first, but he kicked and dived and swam so hard that presently warmth returned to his veins, and with it a wonderful increase of spirits.

When he came out he washed his clothing as well as deerskin could be washed, and, wrapped in the blanket and painted coat, ran up and down the bank, or otherwise exercised himself vigorously, while it dried in the bright sun. It was a matter of hours, but it pleased him to feel that he was purified again and that he could carry out the purification in the very face of Indian pursuit itself. When he put on his clothing again he felt remade and reinvigorated in both body and mind, and, resuming his weapons, he set out once more upon his northward way.

The day continued warm and most brilliant, as if atonement were being made to him for the storms of snow and rain. He came to a stretch of country in which it was obvious that very little snow, if any, had fallen, as the trees were still thick with leaves in the deep colors of autumn, and it was satisfying to the eye to look upon the red glow again.

Late in the afternoon he saw five smokes in a half curve to the south, and he knew well enough that they were made by his pursuers. They were much nearer than those he had seen earlier in the day, but it was due to the long delay made necessary by his swim and the drying of his clothes. The rapid gain did not make him feel any particular apprehension. The joy of the struggle came over him. He was matched against the whole power of the Shawnee, Miami and kindred nations, and if they thought they could catch him, well, let them keep on trying. They should bear in mind, too, that the hunted sometimes would turn and rend the hunter.

In order to gain once more upon the pursuit and give himself a chance to rest later on, he increased his speed greatly and also took precautions to hide his trail, which was not difficult where there were so many little streams. When he stopped about midnight he believed that he was at least ten or twelve miles ahead of the nearest warriors, who must have lost a great deal of time looking for his traces; and, secure in the belief, he crept into a thicket, drew about him the blanket and the buffalo robe, which were now sufficient, and slept soundly until he was awakened by the howling of wolves. He was quite able to tell the difference between the voices of real wolves and the imitation of the Indians, and he knew that these were real.

He raised up a little and listened. The long, whining yelp came again and again, and he was somewhat surprised. He concluded at last that the wolves, driven hard by hunger, were hunting assiduously in large packs. When mad for food they would attack man, but Henry anticipated no danger. He felt himself too good a friend of the animals just then to be molested by any of them, and he went back to sleep.

When he awoke again just before dawn he heard the wolves still howling, but much nearer, and he thought it possible that they had been driven ahead by the Indian forces. If so, it betokened a pursuit rather swifter than he had expected, and, girding himself afresh, he fled once more before the sun was fairly up.

It was the usual rolling country that lies immediately south of the Great Lakes, forested heavily then and cut by innumerable streams, great and small. The creeks and brooks were not swollen as much as those farther south, and Henry judged from the fact that here also the snowstorm had not passed. Nevertheless, he crossed many muddy reaches and he was compelled to ford two or three creeks the water of which reached to his knees. But his moccasins and leggings dried again as he ran on, and he was not troubled greatly by the cold.

It was a country that should abound in game, but no deer started up from his path, no wild turkeys gobbled among the boughs, and the little prairies that he crossed were bare of buffaloes. He assumed at once that it had been hunted over so thoroughly by the Indians that the surviving game had moved on. When the warriors found a new hunting ground it would come back and increase. He believed now that this accounted for the howling of the wolves deprived of their food supply and perhaps not yet finding where it had gone.

He maintained a rapid pace, and his wet leggings and moccasins dried gradually. The morning was frosty and cold, but wonderfully brilliant with sunlight, and here, where the forest had been free from snow, it glowed in autumnal colors.

He came to a deep river, but fortunately it flowed toward the northeast, the direction in which he was willing to go, and he was glad to find it, as he kept in the woods near its bank, thus protecting his left flank from any encircling movement. But a strong wind was blowing toward him and he not only heard the howling of the wolves, but the faint cry of the savages far behind them. It made him very thoughtful. Something unusual was going forward, since the wolves themselves were taking part in the pursuit or were pursued also. He could not understand it, but he resolved to dismiss it from his mind until it disclosed its own meaning.

He kept near the river, seeing it occasionally through the forest on his left, a fine sheet of clear water, over which wild ducks and wild geese flew, although the woods through which he ran seemed to be absolutely bare of game.

Then the river took a sudden curve farther east and he was compelled to turn with it. On his first impulse the thought of swimming the stream came to him, but he dismissed it, lest some swift warrior might come up and open fire while he was in the water, in which case, being practically helpless, he might become an easy victim. So he turned with the stream and, keeping its bank close on his left, he fled eastward. But he was fully aware that the change in the course of the river brought to him a new and great danger. The right wing of the pursuing host, traveling not much more than half the distance, would gain upon him very fast. Anxious not to be entrapped in such a manner he ran now at great speed for several miles, but was compelled then to slow down, owing to the nature of the country, which was growing very marshy.

Evidently heavy rains had fallen in this region recently, as he came to extensive flooded areas. It annoyed him, too, that the soft ground compelled him to leave so plain a trail, as often for considerable stretches he sank over his moccasins at every step. He walked on fallen timber whenever he could find it, making a break now and then in his trail, but he knew it would not delay the Indians long.

In order to save his breath and strength he was compelled to go yet slower, and finally he sat on a log for a rest of five minutes. Then the wind brought him a single Indian shout, not more than a quarter of a mile away, and he knew its meaning. The warriors on the right flank, coming up on a tangent of the curve, had seen his footsteps. They had not run more than half the distance he had and so must be comparatively fresh. His danger had increased greatly, but his command over himself was so complete that, instead of resting five minutes, he rested ten. He knew now that he would need all his strength, all the power of his lungs, because the chase had closed in and for a while it would be a test of speed. So he rested that every muscle might have its original strength, and he was willing for the Indians to come almost within rifle shot before he took to flight once more.

So strong was the command of his mind over his body that he saw two warriors appear among the trees about four hundred yards away before he rose. They saw him, too, and uttered the war whoop of triumph, but Henry was refreshed and he ran so fast that they sank out of sight behind him. Then he exulted, taunting them, not in words, but with his thoughts. They could never capture him, and once more he said to himself that he would keep on, even if his flight took him to the Great Lakes and beyond.

But the swampy ground intervened again, and his progress of necessity became slow. Then he heard the Indian yell once more, and he knew that the difficult country was enabling them to close up the gap anew. The wolves howled also, but more toward the south, a far, faint, ferocious sound that traveled on the wind like an echo. He did not understand it, and he had a premonition that something extraordinary was going to happen. It was curious, uncanny, and the hair on the back of his neck lifted a little.

He came through the swampy belt and to a considerable stretch of dry ground, but he heard the Indian yell for a third time, and again not more than a quarter of a mile away. The fact that this portion of the band had not run that day more than half as far as he was telling, and he recognized it. Perhaps the swamps had not been to his disadvantage, because on the dry ground they could use their reserves of strength and speed to much greater advantage.

Now he knew that his danger had become imminent and deadly and that every resource within him would be tested to the utmost. Out of the south came the Indian cry also, and it was answered triumphantly from the west. A shudder ran through Henry's blood. He was in the trap. The Indians knew it and they were signaling the truth to one another.

Now he made a great burst of speed, resolving to be well beyond their reach before the jaws of the vise closed in, and, as he ran, he longed to hear the howl of the wolves once more, a sound that he had used to hate always, but which would come now almost like the call of a friend. While he was wishing for it, the long whine rose, toward the south also, but a little ahead of the Indian cry. As before it was strange, uncanny, and a second time the hair on the back of his neck lifted a little. Evidently the wolves—instinct told him they were a great pack—were running parallel with the Indians, but for what purpose he could not surmise, unless it was the hope of food abandoned by the warriors.

His own feet grew heavy, and he heard the triumphant shouts of the Indians only a few hundred yards away. He was powerful, more powerful than any of them, but he could not run twice as long as these lean, wiry and trained children of the forest. His muscles began to complain. He had been putting them to the severest of tests, and the effect was now cumulative. A brown figure appeared among the bushes behind him and he heard the report of a shot. A bullet cut the dead leaves ten yards away, but he knew that the warriors would soon come nearer and then their aim would be better.

Now he called upon the last reserve of strength and tenacity, the portion that is left to the brave when to ordinary minds all seems exhausted, and made a final and splendid burst of speed, drawing away from the brown figures and once more opening the gap between hunted and hunters. But the shout came again from the south and on his right flank where fresh warriors were closing in, and despite himself his heart sank for a moment or two in despair. Was he to fall after so many escapes? How Braxton Wyatt and Blackstaffe would rejoice!

Despair could not last long with him. There was still another ounce of strength left, and now he used it, fairly springing through the thicket, while his heart beat hard and painfully and clouds of black motes danced before his eyes.

He saw a warrior appear among the bushes on the right, and, raising his own rifle, he fired. The stream of flame that leaped from the muzzle of his weapon was accompanied by the death cry of the savage, followed quickly by a long, fierce yell of rage from the fallen man's comrades.

Then the pursuit hung back a little, but it came on again soon, as terrible and as tenacious as ever. He reloaded his rifle as he ran, but he knew that unless some strange chance intervened soon he must turn and fight for his life. The ground dropped suddenly and he ran down a steep slope into a wide valley, the trend of which was from north to south. Here he gained a little, but he heard a shout on his right and saw three warriors coming up the valley, not thirty yards away. At the same time, the long, fierce whine of the wolves was registered somewhere on his brain, but he did not take definite note of it until afterward.

The foremost of the Indians fired and missed, to receive in return the bullet from Henry's reloaded rifle, but the other two came on, shouting. He hurled his hatchet and struck down the second, but the third paused twenty feet away and whirled his tomahawk about his head in glittering circles. Henry instinctively raised his rifle to ward off the blade in its flight, but he knew that the guard would not do. The tomahawk would leave the warrior's hand like a thunderbolt, and it would go straight to its destined mark. He saw the evil joy in the man's eyes, his anticipation of quick and savage victory, and then the cloud of motes before his own eyes increased to myriads. His heart, crying out against so much exertion, beat so painfully that he thought he could not stand it any longer, and a veil of thick mist was drawn down between him and the triumphant warrior. Then he suddenly stood erect and the hair upon his head lifted once more.

There was a horrible growl and a gigantic wolf, shooting out of the mist, launched himself straight at the warrior's throat. Henry heard the man's terrible cry and saw him go down, and then he saw the figures of other wolves, enlarged by the vapors, following their leader. But that was all he beheld then. Uttering a cry of his own, wrenched from him by the appalling sight, he snatched up his hatchet, turned and ran up the valley, with strength coming from new and unknown sources.

The heavy mists that were floating over the low ground enclosed Henry, but he did not look back. He knew instinctively that he was no longer followed. Once he thought he heard the horrible growling again, and shouts, but he was not sure. Too much had impinged upon his mind for him to distinguish between fancy and reality yet awhile, but a powerful feeling that another miracle had been wrought in his behalf seized upon him and would not let go. The wolves, whether it was chance or not so far as they were concerned, had come in time and their giant leader himself had cut down the warrior who was about to cleave the fugitive's head with his tomahawk.

The Indians would stop, appalled, and for a while would be

overwhelmed with superstition. But he knew that the paralyzing spell could not last long. Blackstaffe and Wyatt at least would urge them on, and it was for him to use the time that had been granted to him by miraculous chance.

When exhaustion came he had will enough to stop again and remain quite still until the fierce pains in his chest ceased and there was air for his lungs once more. He was sure of a quarter of an hour, and a forest runner such as he could do wonders in that space. A quarter of an hour meant for him the difference between life and death, and although his feet strove of their own accord to go on, his mind held them back at least two thirds of the time. Then he allowed his body to have its way, and he went down the valley not at a run, but a prudent walk, in order to give his lungs, heart and muscles a chance for further recovery.

The valley seemed to be about a quarter of a mile wide, heavily forested, and with a small creek flowing down the center. The hills that walled it in on either side were high and steep, and Henry thought it would be wiser to take to them, but, for the present, he did not feel like making the climb. He was not willing to put any check upon the new store of strength that was flooding his veins.

Ten minutes more and he heard a fierce whoop behind him. The Indians evidently had driven off the wolves, and, under the insistence of the renegades, would renew the pursuit. Another momentary sinking of his heart came. The numbers of the warriors, who could spread out in every direction, many of whom were yet comparatively fresh, were an obstacle that he could not overcome. The wolves had brought delay, but not escape.

Then his courage came back, not slowly or gradually, but like a leaping tide. He had seen only half of the new miracle. While he thought it finished, the other half was coming, was upon hunted and hunters even now. The veil of mist that had floated between him and the wolf and its victim was spreading up and down the valley, rising from the wet ground, dense and heavy, opaque like ink, despite its whiteness. Presently the great whitish cloud would enclose him and the warriors, hiding them from one another, and it would be strange if he could not escape them in the white gloom, where only ears served.

Turning his eyes upward to the skies that he could not now see, he gave thanks to the superior powers that were guarding him so well. Then he turned at a sharp angle, crossed the creek, and began to climb the hills on the east.

All the time the fog, thick and white, was pouring over the valley and the slopes. Half way up the hill Henry paused and looked back, seeing nothing but a vast white gulf. Then he heard the warriors in the gulf calling to one another, and now the spirit to laugh at them came back to him. They did not know that he was protected by a force greater than theirs that snatched him again and again from the savage band before it could close upon him.

He sat down among the bushes and continued to look at the valley, which reminded him now of a vast white river, all of it flowing northward, with the signals of the warriors still coming out of its depths, puzzled evidently, as they had a good right to be. Although they were only a few hundred yards away, Henry felt that there was little danger. The miracle was continuing. The great white flood poured steadily down the valley and rose higher and higher on the slopes. He went to the top of the hill, where it followed him and spread over the forest.

When he found a comfortable place in a thicket he lay down and drew around him the painted robe that had served him so often and so well. He knew the warriors would ascend the slopes, but the chances were a thousand to one against their finding him in so dense a mist, and the longer he rested the better fitted he would be for flight. Meanwhile the fog increased in thickness, rolling up continually in dense masses, and he inferred that he could not be far from some large stream or a lake or great flooded areas. Perhaps the creek that flowed down the valley emptied not far away into a river.

If he had not been so worn by the tremendous tests to which he had been put he would have gone on, despite everything, in the fog over the hills, but instead he lay close like an animal in its lair, adjusted anew about him the blanket and the painted coat and luxuriated. At intervals he heard the warriors calling in the valley, and once the sound of footsteps not more than twenty yards away reached him, but he was not disturbed. The chance that they would stumble upon him was still only one in a thousand.

He remained at least four hours in the bushes, and throughout that time he scarcely moved, having acquired the forest art of keeping perfectly still when there was nothing to be done. Then he saw the fog thinning somewhat, but he was completely restored. Youth had its way. His nerves and muscles were as strong as ever, and the great mental elation had returned. Why not? It was obvious that he was protected by the supreme powers. Miracle after miracle had occurred in his behalf. They had sent the wolves just in time, and then they had drawn the fog from the earth, hiding him from the warriors and giving him a covert in which he could lie until his strength was restored.

He rose now and began his cautious passage through the white veil over the hills. The fog was not lifting yet, but it was continuing to thin. He could see in it ten or fifteen feet, and he was not sorry, as the distance was enough for the choosing of a path, but not enough for the warriors to come within sight of him before they were heard.

Twice, the sounds of the searching warriors came to him, but each time he lay in the bush until they passed, when he would rise and continue his judicious flight.

Near the close of the day, and going toward the northeast, he was far from the valley, but obviously was coming to another, as the hills were sinking fast and he saw the tops of trees below him. The fog had been thinning until it was mere wisps and tatters, and now a smart wind seizing all these remnants whirled them off to the east, leaving a glorious clear sky, suffused in the west with the red and gold of the setting sun, a deep brilliant light that touched the whole horizon with fire.

Henry looked upon it and worshiped. He worshiped like a forest runner and a man of the old, old time, when nothing of heaven or of religion was revealed. He worshiped like an Indian to whom, as to many other races, the sun was a symbol of warmth, of light and life, almost the same as Manitou, that is to say, almost the same as God. Nor did he forget to be grateful once more. It was not for any merit of his that protection had been given to him so often, but because he was an instrument in a good purpose. So thinking, he was full of humility and meant to continue in the perilous path that he had chosen, the path of service for others.

The spiritual quality was strong in Henry's nature; in truth, it was rooted in the characters of all the five, although it differed in its manifestations, and he gazed long at the western heavens, where the splendid colors of the setting sun blazed in their deepest hues and then faded, leaving only a warm glow behind. The night, as the forecast already showed, would be clear and cold, and he descended into the new valley, which was much wider than the one he had left. It was comparatively free of undergrowth, and he saw through the trees the gleam of water which proved to be a river on his right, and of fair size.

He believed that the larger valley would receive the smaller one and its draining creek not far ahead, and a new problem was presented. Unless he swam the river and kept to the east the warriors would come on anew from the west and pin him against the stream.

Should he plunge into the cold waters? It was not a prospect that he liked; but, while he considered it, he became aware that the miracle created in his behalf was not yet finished. He had thought that it was done when the wolves intervened, and again that it was done when the great fog came, but there was yet another link in the lengthening chain of marvelous events.

A sound from the river and he stepped hastily to the shelter of a great tree trunk. It was the plash of a paddle, and as he looked, peeping from the side of the trunk, a warrior stepped from a canoe at the river's brink and took a long look at the forest. Henry judged that he was an outpost or sentinel of some kind, or perhaps a member of a provision fleet. The man tied his canoe with a willow withe to a sapling and strode away out of sight, doubtless intending to meet the band to which he belonged. Henry's heart leaped. He was always quick to perceive and to act, and he saw his opportunity.

Twenty swift steps and he was at the margin of the stream, one slash of his knife and the willow withe was cut, one sweep of the paddle and the stout canoe was far out in the stream, bearing with it the brave youth and his fortunes.

Henry exulted. Truly chance—or was it chance?—served him well! He had a singular feeling that the canoe had been put there especially for his use. No more running through the forest. He could call a new set of muscles into play, and there before him lay the stream, broad and deep and straight, a clear path for the good canoe that he had made his own.

He did not allow his exultation to steal away his caution, but after the first few sweeps of the paddle he sent the canoe close to the eastern bank, under the shadow of vast masses of overhanging willows. Here it blended with the dusk, and he handled the paddle so smoothly that he made no splash to betray his presence.

Now he examined his canoe, and he saw that, in truth, it bore supplies for a band, venison, buffalo meat, wild turkey, and, what he craved most of all, bread of Indian corn. The supplies were sufficient to last him two weeks at least, and he felt with all the power of conviction that the miracle was still working.

He sped down the stream with long, silent strokes, keeping always in the dusk of the overhanging foliage. The stars came out, and with them a full, bright moon, which he also worshiped as a sign and an emblem of the Supreme Will that had saved him. He fell into an intense mood of exaltation. The powers of earth and air and water had worked together in a singular manner. Never was his fancy more vivid. The flowing of the stream sang to him, and the willows over his head sang to him also. The light from the moon and stars grew. The dusk was shot with a silver glow. Apprehension, weariness went from him, and he shot down the river, mile after mile, apparently the only figure in the ancient wilderness.

He did not stop until two or three hours after midnight, when at a low place in the bank he thrust the canoe into a dense mass of water weeds and bushes, put the paddle beside him and ate freely of the captured supplies. The venison and buffalo meat were excellent, and while the water of the river was not as good as that of a spring, it was nevertheless cold and refreshing. Fresh warmth and vigor flowed into his body, and he declared to himself that he had never felt better and stronger in his life. He looked with satisfaction at his stores, which would last him so long, and he also saw in the canoe a folded green blanket, which its owner evidently had left there for future use. He would use it instead, since the cold was likely to increase and he meant to be comfortable.

Henry considered the canoe a godsend. It left no trail, and he had been careful to leave none when he came to the bank for its capture. Perhaps the Indian would think he had tied it carelessly and the current had pulled its fastenings loose. In any event, the fugitive was gone and his pathway was invisible, like that of a bird in the air. He looked up once more at the cold, blue sky, the brilliant full moon, and the hosts of shining stars. Cold the sky might be to others, but it was not so to him. It bent over him like a protecting blue veil, shot with the silver glow of moon and stars.

The thicket into which he had pushed his canoe was of weeds, reeds and willows, and very dense. The keenest eyes might search its very edge and fail to see the fugitive within. There was no view except overhead, and Henry resolved to remain there the whole of the next day. If the warriors came pursuing on the river he would be once again the needle in the haystack, and even if by some chance they should spy him out, he could escape, refreshed and invigorated, to the land.

Assured of his present safety, he spread his bed in the canoe, a somewhat difficult task, as everything had to be adjusted with nicety, but the close wall of reeds and bushes helped him to keep the balance, and at last he lay on the bottom with the Indian's blanket under him and his own and the painted robe above him. Then he went to sleep and did not awaken until the next day was hours old.

A bright sun was shining through the bushes over his head,

but he was glad that his body had been protected by an abundance of covers. The painted robe was white with frost, which even the hours of day had not yet melted, and near the edges there was a thin skin of ice on the river. His breath made little clouds of vapor in the cold morning. He was so warm and snug under the blankets that he felt the usual aversion in such cases to rising, and turning gently on his side, lest he tilt the canoe, he closed his eyes for that aftermath of sleep, a final and pleasant doze.

When he opened his eyes again he contemplated the sun through the veil of bushes and reeds. It was great and red, but it had a chilly effect, and he knew the day was quite cold. The willows began to shake and quiver and the wind that stirred them was nipping. He did not care. Cold stimulated him, and, making ready for new endeavors, he dipped for his breakfast into the captured stores.

Then he took note of the river, upon the surface of which much life was already passing. He saw a flock of wild ducks swimming strong and true against the current, and when they were gone a swarm of wild geese came with many honks out of the air and swam in the same direction. He knew that presently they would rise again and fly into the far south, escaping the fierce winter of the north.

The great fishing birds also wheeled and circled over the stream, and now and then one shot downward for its prey. On the opposite shore two deer pushed their bodies through the bushes and drank at the river's edge. On his own shore the puffing of a bear in the woods came to his ears. Evidently he had come from a region bare of game into a land of plenty.

The wild geese rose with a suddenness he had not anticipated and sped southward in a long arrow, outlined sharply against the sky. The great fishing birds silently disappeared, and Henry was alone on the river. He knew that the quick flight of his feathered friends was not due to chance. Undoubtedly man was coming, and he crouched low in his canoe, with his rifle ready.

CHAPTER XIV
THE WATCHFUL SQUIRREL

Henry saw about what he expected to see, two long canoes, containing a dozen or more warriors each, with the Shawnee chief, Red Eagle, and Braxton Wyatt in the first and Yellow Panther, the Miami chief, and Blackstaffe in the second. Chiefs and renegades and warriors alike swept the shore with questing eyes, but they did not see the one for whom they had looked so long lying so near, and yet hidden so well among the reeds.

He watched them without apprehension. He had full confidence in the veil about him, and he expected them to pass on in the relentless hunt. They, too, looked worn, and he fancied that the eyes of chiefs and renegades expressed disappointment and deep anger. Nobody in the long canoes spoke, and, silent save for the plashing of the paddles they went on and out of sight.

Henry might have taken to the woods now, but he was too wary. He wished to remain on the element that left no trail, and he felt also that he had walked and run long enough. He intended to travel now chiefly with the strength of his arms, and the longer he stayed in the canoe the better he liked it. Its store of provisions was fine, and it was easier to carry them in it than on his back. So he waited with the patience that every true forest runner has, and saw the morning merge into the afternoon.

It was almost evening when the long canoes came back, passing his covert. They had found the quest vain, and concluding, doubtless, that they had gone too far, were returning to look elsewhere. But the paddlers were weary, and the chiefs and renegades, too, drooped somewhat. They did not show their usual alertness of eye as they came back against the stream, and Henry judged that the pursuit would lapse in energy, while they went ashore in search of warmth and food.

A half hour after they were out of sight he came from the weeds, and, with great sweeps of the paddle, sent the canoe shooting down the river. He was so fresh and strong now that he felt as if he could go on forever, and all through the night his powerful arms drove him toward his unknown goal. He noticed that the river was broadening and the banks were low, sometimes sandy, and he fancied that he was approaching its outlet in one of the Great Lakes. And the chase had led so far! Nor was it yet finished! The chiefs and the renegades, not finding him farther back, would reorganize the pursuit and follow again.

Day came bright and warm, much warmer than it had been farther south, and Henry paddled until evening although he found the heat oppressive. Paddling a full day and part of a night was a great task for anybody and he grew weary again. When the night came, seeing no reeds and bushes in which he could hide the canoe, he resolved to sleep on land. So he lifted it from the river and carried it a short distance inland, where he put it down in a thicket, choosing a resting place for himself not far away.

He spread one of the blankets as usual on dead leaves, and put the other and the painted coat over himself. Then, knowing that he would be warm and snug for the night, he relaxed and looked idly at the dusky woods, feeling perfectly safe as the warriors must be far to the south.

The only living being he saw was a gray squirrel on the trunk of a tree about twenty feet away. But he was a friend of the squirrel, and he regarded it with friendly eyes, noting the sharpness of its claws, the bushiness of its tail, and the alertness of its keen little nose. It was an uncommon squirrel, endowed with great curiosity, and perception, a leader in its tribe, and it was intensely interested in the large, still body lying on the leaves below.

The squirrel came farther down the tree, and stared intently at Henry, uncertain whether he was a friend or a foe. Yet he had all the aspect of a friend. There was no hostile movement, and the bold and inquiring fellow ventured another foot closer. Then he scuttled in alarm ten feet back up the trunk, as the figure raised a hand, and threw something small that fell at the foot of the tree.

But as the human being did not move again, the courage and curiosity of this uncommonly bold and inquiring squirrel returned, and, gradually creeping down the tree, he inspected the small object that had fallen there. It smelled good, and when he nibbled at it it tasted good. Then he ate it all, went back up the bark a little distance and waited gratefully for more of the same. Presently it came, and he ate that bit, too, and after a while a third. Then the human figure threw him no more such fine food, but went to sleep.

The squirrel knew he was asleep, because he left the tree, walked cautiously over the ground, and stood with his ears cocked up, scarcely a yard from the vast, still figure that breathed so deeply and with such regularity. He had seen gigantic beings before. From the safety of his boughs he had looked upon those mountains, the buffaloes, and he had often seen the stag in the forest. Mere size did not terrify him, and now he did not feel in the least afraid. On the

153

contrary, this was his friend who had fed him, and he regarded him with benevolence.

The squirrel went back up the tree, his claws pattering lightly on the bark. He had a fine knot hole high up the trunk, and his family were sound asleep in it, surrounded by a great store of nuts. There was a warm place for him, the head of the family, but he could not stay in it. After a while he was compelled to go out again, and look at the unconscious human figure.

Emboldened by his first experience which had been so free from ill result, he descended upon the ground a second time and went toward Henry. But in an instant he turned back again. His keen little ears had heard something moving in the forest and it was not any small animal like himself, but a large body, several of them in fact. He ran up the tree, and then far out on a bough where he could see.

Five Indian warriors walking in single file were approaching. They were part of an outlying band, not perhaps looking for Henry, but, if they continued on their course, they would be sure to see him. The squirrel regarded them for a moment with little red eyes, and then ran back to the trunk of the tree.

Henry, meanwhile, slept soundly. There was nothing to disturb him. The wind did not blow and so the dry branches of the forest did not rustle. The footsteps of the approaching Indians made no noise, yet in a few more moments he ceased to sleep so well. A sound penetrated at last to his ear and he sat up. It was the chattering of the gray squirrel, and the rattling of his claws on the dry bark of the tree, his bushy tail curving far over his back, and his whole body seeming to be shaken by violent convulsions. Henry stared at him, thinking at first that he was threatened by some carnivorous prowler of the air, but, as he looked away, he caught a glimpse through the bushes of a moving brown figure and then of another and more.

Henry Ware never struck camp with more smoothness and celerity. One hand swept up his blankets and the painted robe, another grasped his rifle, and, as silent as a night bird itself, he vanished into the deeper thicket where the canoe lay. There, crouched beside it, he watched while the warriors passed. They would certainly have seen his body had it been lying where it had been, but they were not near enough to notice his traces, and they had no cause to suspect his presence. So, the silent file passed on, and disappeared in the deep woods.

Henry stood up, and once more he felt a great access of wonder and gratitude. The superior powers were surely protecting him, and were even watching over him while he slept. He walked back a little and looked at the tree, on which the gray squirrel had chattered and rattled his claws. He thought he caught a glimpse of a bushy tail among the boughs, but he was not sure. In any event, he bore in mind that while great animals had served him, the little ones, too, had given help as good. Then he bore the canoe back to the river, put in it all his precious possessions, and continued his flight by water.

There was a chance that warriors might see him from the banks, since he had proof of their presence in the woods, but relying upon his skill and the favors of fortune, he was willing to take the risk. He had an idea, too, that he would soon come to the lake, and he meant to hide among the dense thickets and forests, sure to line its low shores.

His surmise was right, as some time before noon the river widened abruptly, and a half hour later he came out on the border of a vast lake, stretching blue to the horizon and beyond. A strong wind blowing over the great expanse of water came sharp and cold, but to Henry, naturally so strong and warmed by his exertions, it furnished only exhilaration. He felt that now the great flight and chase had come to an end. He could not cross this mighty inland sea in his light canoe, and doubtless the chiefs and the renegades, unable to follow his trail by water, where he left no trail at all, would give up at last, and hope for more success another time.

So believing, and confident in his belief, he looked around for a temporary home, and marked a low island lying out about five miles from the shore. The five had found good refuge on an island once before, and he alone might do it again, and lie hidden there, until all danger from the great hunt had passed.

He acted with his usual boldness and decision, and paddled with a strong arm toward the island which seemed to be about a mile each way and was a mass of dense forest. His canoe rocked on the waves, which were running high before the wind, but he came without mishap to the island, and, pushing his canoe through thickets of reeds and willows, landed.

Leaving the canoe well hidden, he examined the island and was well pleased with it, as it seemed to be suited admirably to his purpose. The forest was unbroken and very dense. Probably human beings never came there, as the game seemed very tame. Two or three deer looked at him with mild, inquiring eyes before they moved slowly away, and he saw where wild turkey roosted in numbers at night.

In the center of the island was a small dip, where only bushes grew, and he decided that he would make his camp there, as the great height of the trees surrounding it would hide the smoke that might arise from his subdued campfire. But he did no work that day, as he wished to be sure that his passage to the island had not been observed by any wandering warriors on the mainland. There was no sign of pursuit, and he knew now that fortune had favored him again.

He slept the night through in the canoe, and the next morning he set to work with his hatchet to make a bush shelter for himself, a task that took two days and which he finished just in time, as a fierce wind with hail swept over the island and the lake. He had removed all his supplies from the canoe to the hut, and, wrapped in the painted robe, he watched hail and wind beat upon the surface of the lake, until it drove in high waves like the sea. There was no danger of warriors trying the passage to the island in such weather, and his look was that of a spectator not that of a sentinel. The great nervous strain of the long flight, and its many and deadly perils, had passed, and he found a pleasure in watching the turmoil of the elements.

The old feeling that he belonged for the time to a far, far distant past returned. He was alone on his island, as many a remote ancestor of his must have been alone in the forest in his day, and yet he felt not the least trace of loneliness or fear. Everything was wild, primeval and grand to the last degree. The huge lake, curving up from the horizon, had turned from blue to lead, save where the swift waves were crested with white. The hail beat on the trees and bushes like myriads of bullets, and the wind came with a high, shrill scream. The mainland was lost in the mist and clouds, and he was not only alone on his island, but alone in his world, and separated from his foes by tumbling and impassable waters.

Henry's mind was in tune with the storm. He looked upon it as a celebration of his triumph, the end of the flight and the chase, a flight that had been successful for him, a chase that had been unsuccessful for the chiefs and the renegades, and the blood merely flowed more swiftly in his veins, as the hail beat upon him. He did not care how long wind and hail lasted; the longer the better for him, and, flinging out his hands, he waved a salute to the storm god.

He remained for hours looking upon the great spectacle, that pleased him so much, and then kept dry by the huge painted coat, he went back to the brush hut. But night only and the necessity to sleep could have sent him there. He did not yet light a fire, contenting himself with the cold food from the canoe, nor did he do so the next day, as the storm was still raging. When it ceased on the third day all the trees and bushes were coated with ice, and he was a dweller in the midst of a silver forest. Then, with much difficulty he lighted a small fire before the hut, warmed over some venison and a little of the precious bread. He would not have to kill any game for a week or ten days and he was glad that it was so, since he was still averse to slaying any member of the kingdom of the animals that had befriended him so much.

The peace of the elements lasted only a few hours. Then they were in a more terrible turmoil than ever. The wind whistled and shrieked, and the snow came down, driven here and there in whirling gusts, while the lake roared and thundered beneath the drive of the hurricane. Although there were lulls at times, yet as a whole the storm lasted a whole week, and it was remembered long by the Indians living in those northern regions as the week of the great storm, unexampled in its length and ferocity.

But Henry found nothing in it to frighten him. Rather, the greater powers were still watching over him, and it was sent for his protection. His own bold and wild spirit remained in tune with it at all times. The brush hut was warm and snug and it held fast against wind, hail and snow. Now and then he lighted the fire anew to warm over his food or merely to see the bright blaze.

At the end of the week he shot a deer among a herd that had found shelter in extremely deep woods at the north end of the island, and never did he do a deed more reluctantly. But it gave an abundance of fresh food, which he now needed badly, and he added to his stores two wild turkeys.

When the storm ceased entirely a very deep snow fell, and he put off his intention to leave. He expected to use the canoe, but he might be forced to leave it, and, traveling in the woods with the snow above a man's knees, would be too hard. So he waited patiently, and made his little home as comfortable as he could.

In another week the snow began to melt fast, and he set forth on his great return journey. The canoe was well supplied with provisions and the lake was quiet. He paddled for the mouth of the river, and, when he passed within the stream, the whole country looked so wintry that he believed the Indians must have gone to their villages for warmth and shelter. Firm in his opinion he paddled boldly against the current and took his course southward, though he did not relax his caution, as the Indians often sent out parties of hunters, despite cold or storm. They were not a forehanded people, and the plenty of summer was no guard against the scarcity of winter. They must find game or die, and Henry had very little real fear of anything except these questing bands.

But he paddled on all the day without interruption. The dense forest on either shore was white and silent, and, when night came, he drew the canoe into the bushes, making his camp on land. The temperature had taken a great fall in the afternoon, and with the dark intense cold had come. The mercury went far below zero and the bitter wind that blew bit through the painted coat and all his clothing clean into the bone. It was so intense that he resolved to risk everything and build a fire.

He managed to set a heap of dead wood burning in the lee of a hill, and he fed the fire for a long time, at last letting it die down into a great mass of coals that threw out heat like a furnace. Over this he hovered and felt the cold which had clutched him like a paralysis leaving his body. Then he wrapped the two blankets around the painted coat and slept in fair comfort till morning, sure that the intense cold would prevent any movement of the Indians in the forest.

But the dawn disclosed a river frozen over to the depth of four inches, and his canoe, which he had taken the precaution to put on land, would be useless, at least for several days, as the ice could not melt sooner. Most forest runners, in such a case, would have abandoned the canoe, and would have gone on through the forest as best they could, but Henry had learned illimitable patience from the Indians. If the cold put a paralysis on his movements it did as much for those of the warriors. So he looked to the preservation of the canoe, and boldly built his fire anew, eating abundantly of the deer and wild turkey and a little of the bread, which he husbanded with such care. At night he slept in the canoe and occasionally he scouted in the country around, although the traveling was very hard, as the deep snow was covered with a sheet of ice, and he was compelled to break his way. He saw no Indian trails and he concluded that the hunting parties even had taken to their tepees, and would wait until the thaw came.

His task for the next seven or eight days was to keep warm, and to preserve his canoe in such manner that it would be water tight when he set it afloat once more on the river. He built another brush shelter, very rude, but in a manner serviceable for himself, and with a fire burning always before it he was able to fend off the fierce chill. The mercury was fully thirty degrees below zero, but fortunately the wind did not blow, or it would have been almost unbearable.

Henry chafed greatly at the long delay, but he endured it as best he could, and, when the huge thaw came and all the earth ran water, he put his canoe in the river once more and began to paddle

158

against the flooded current. It was a delicate task even for one as strong and skillful as he, as great blocks of ice came floating down and he was compelled to watch continually lest his light craft be crushed by them. His perpetual vigilance and incessant struggle against the stream made him so weary that at the end of the day he lifted the canoe out of the water, crept into it and slept the sleep of exhaustion.

The next day was quite warm, and the floating ice in the river having diminished greatly he resumed his journey without so much apprehension of dangers from the stream, but with a keen watch for the hunting parties of warriors which he was sure would be out. Now that the great snow was gone, Miamis and Shawnees, Wyandots and Ottawas would be roaming the forest to make up for the lack of food caused by their customary improvidence. Moreover, it was barely possible that on his return journey he might run into the host led by Yellow Panther and Red Eagle.

He kept close to the bank in the unbroken shadow of the thickets and forests, and as he paddled with deliberation, saving his strength, a warm wind began to blow from the south. The last ice disappeared from the river and late in the afternoon he saw distant smoke which he was sure came from an Indian camp, most likely hunters.

It was to the east of the river, and hence he slept that night in the dense forest to the west, the canoe reposing among the bushes by his side. The following day was still warmer and seeing several smokes, some to the east and some to the west, he became convinced that the forest was now full of warriors. After being shut up a long time in their villages by the great snow and great cold they would come forth not only for game, but for the exercise and freedom that the wilderness afforded. The air of the woods would be very pleasant to them after the close and smoky lodges.

Now Henry, who had been living, in a measure an idyll of lake and forest, became Henry the warrior again, keen, watchful, ready to slay those who would slay him. He never paddled far before he would turn in to the bank, and examine the woods and thickets carefully to see whether an enemy lay there in ambush. If he came to a curve he rounded it slowly and cautiously, and, at last, when he saw remains from some camp farther up floating in the stream he seriously considered the question of abandoning the canoe altogether and of taking to the forest. But his present mode of traveling was so smooth and easy that he did not like to go on a winter trail through the woods again.

The mouth of a smaller and tributary river about a mile

farther on solved the problem for him. The new stream seemed to lead in the general direction in which he wished to go, and, as it was deep enough for a canoe, he turned into it and paddled toward the southwest, going about twenty miles in a narrow and rather deep channel. He stopped then for the night, and, before dark came, saw several more smokes, but had the satisfaction to note that they were all to the eastward, seeming to indicate that he had flanked the bands.

As usual, he took his canoe out of the water and laid it among the bushes, finding a similar covert for himself near by, where he ate his food and rested his arms and shoulders, wearied by their long labors with the paddle. It was the warmest night since the big freeze, but he was not very sleepy and after finishing his supper he went somewhat farther than usual into the woods, not looking for anything in particular, but partly to exercise his legs which had become somewhat cramped by his long day in the canoe. But he became very much alive when he heard a crash which he knew to be that of a falling tree. He leaped instantly to the shelter of a great trunk and his hand sprang to his gunlock, but no other sound followed, and he wondered. At first, he had thought it indicated the presence of warriors, but Indians did not cut down trees and doubtless it was due to some other cause, perhaps an old, decayed trunk that had been weighted down by snow, falling through sheer weariness. In any event he was going to see, and, emerging from his shelter, he moved forward silently.

He came to a thicket, and saw just beyond it a wide pool or backwater formed by a tributary of the creek. In the water, stood a beaver colony, the round domes of their houses showing like a happy village. It was evident, however, that they were doing much delayed work for the winter, as a half dozen stalwart fellows were busy with the tree, the falling crash of which Henry had just heard, and which they had cut through with their sharp teeth.

He crouched in the thicket and, all unsuspected by the industrious members of the colony, watched them a little while. He did not know just what building operation they intended, but it must be an after thought. The beaver was always industrious and full of foresight, and, if they were adding now to the construction of their town carried out earlier in the year, it must be due to a prevision that it was going to be a very cold, long and hard winter.

Henry watched them at work quite a while, and they furnished him both amusement and interest. It was a sort of forest idyll. Their energy was marvelous, and they worked always with method. One huge, gray old fellow seemed to direct their

160

movements, and Henry soon saw that he was an able master who tolerated neither impudence nor trifling. In his town everybody had not only to work, but to work when, where and how the leader directed. It gave the hidden forest runner keen pleasure to watch the village with its ordered life, industry and happiness.

He felt once more his sense of kinship with the animals. He was a thoughtful youth, and it often occurred to him that the world might be made for them as well as for man.

The beaver was an animal of uncommon intelligence and he could learn from him. The big gray fellow was a general of ability, perhaps with a touch of genius. All his soldiers were working according to his directions with uncommon skill and dispatch. Henry concentrated his attention upon him, and presently he had a feeling that the leader saw him, had known all the time that he was lying there in the thicket, and was not afraid of him, convinced that he would do no harm. It added to his pleasure to think that it was so. The old fellow looked directly at him at least a half dozen times, and presently Henry was compelled to laugh to himself. As sure as he was living that big old beaver had raised his head a little higher out of the water than usual, and glancing his way had winked at him.

He forgot everything else in the play between himself and the beaver king, and a king he surely was, as he had time to direct, and to direct ably, all the activities of his village, and also to carry on a kind of wireless talk with the forest runner. Henry watched him to see if he would give him the wink again, and as sure as day was day he dived presently, came up at the near edge of the pool, wiped the dripping water from his head and face and winked gravely with his left eye, his expression being for the moment uncommonly like that of a human being.

Henry was startled. It certainly seemed to be real. But then his fancy was vivid and he knew it. The circumstances, too, were unusual and the influences of certain remarkable instances was strong upon him. Moreover, if the king of the beavers wanted to wink at him there was nothing to keep him from winking back. So he winked and to his great astonishment and delight the old king winked again. Then the beaver, feeling as if he had condescended enough for the time, dived and came up now on the far side of the pool, where he infused new energy into his subject with a series of rapid commands, and hurried forward the work.

Henry's delight remained with him. The old king had been willing to put the forest runner on an equality with himself by winking at him. They two were superior to all the others and the king alone was aware of his presence. Since the monarch had distinctly winked at him several times it was likely that he would wink once or twice more, when enough was done for dignity's sake. So he waited with great patience.

But for a little while the king seemed to have forgotten his existence or to have repented of his condescension, as apparently he gave himself up wholly to the tasks of kingship, telling how the work should be done, and urging it on, as if apprehensive that another freeze might occur before it could be finished. He was a fine old fellow, full of wisdom, experience and decision, and Henry began to fear that he had been forgotten in the crush of duties pertaining to the throne.

In about ten minutes, the gray king dived and came up a second time on the near side of the pool. It was quite evident, too, that he was winking once more, and Henry winked back with vigor. Then the beaver began to swim slowly back and forth in a doubtful fashion, as if he had something on his mind. The humorous look which Henry persuaded himself he had seen in his eye faded. His glance expressed indecision, apprehension even, and Henry, with the feeling of kinship strong upon him, strove to divine what his cousin, the beaver, was thinking. That he was not thinking now what he had been thinking ten minutes before was quite evident, and the youth wondered what could be the cause of a change so abrupt and radical.

He caught the beaver's eye and surely the old king was troubled. That look said as plain as day to Henry that there was danger, and that he must beware. Then the beaver suddenly raised up and struck the water three powerful blows with his broad flat tail. The reports sounded like rifle shots, and, before the echo of the last one died, the great and wise king of his people sank like a stone beneath the water and did not come into view again, disappearing into his royal palace, otherwise his domed hut of stone-hard mud. All of his subjects shot from sight at the same time and Henry saw only the domes of the beaver houses and the silent pool.

He never doubted for an instant that the royal warning was intended for him as well as the beaver people, and he instantly slid back deeper into the thicket, just as a dozen Shawnee warriors, their footsteps making no noise, came through the woods on the other side, and looked at the beaver pool.

CHAPTER XV
THE LETTER

Henry was quite sure that the beaver king had given him a direct warning, and he never liked afterward to disturb or impair the belief, and, moreover, he was so alive with gratitude that it was bound to be so. Lying perfectly still in the depths of the thicket he watched the Indians, powerful warriors, who, nevertheless, showed signs of strain and travel. Doubtless they had come from the edge of the lake itself, and he believed suddenly, but with all the certainty of conviction, that they were following him. They were on the back trail, which, in some unexplained manner, they had struck merely to lose again. Chance had brought them to opposite sides of the pond, but he alone had received the warning.

They stood at the water's edge three or four minutes, looking at the beaver houses and talking, although Henry was too far away to understand what they said. He knew they would not remain long, but what they did next was of vital moment to him. If they should chance to come his way he would have to spring up and run for it, but if they went by another he might lie still and think out his problem.

The leader gave a word of command, and, dropping into the usual single file, they marched silently into the south. Henry lay on the north side of the pool, and when the last of the warriors was out of sight, he rose and walked back to his canoe, which he must now reluctantly abandon. He could not think of continuing on the water when he had proof of the eye that many warriors were in the woods about the creek.

The canoe had served him well. It had saved him often from weariness, and sometimes from exhaustion, but dire need barred it now. He put on the painted coat, made the blankets and provisions into a pack which he fastened on his back, hid the light craft among weeds and bushes at the creek's margin, and then struck off at a swift pace toward the west and south.

While bands would surely follow him, he did not believe the Indian hosts could be got together again for his pursuit and capture. After their great failure in the flight and pursuit northward they would melt away largely, and winter would thin the new chase yet more. His thought now was less of the danger from them than of his four brave comrades from whom he had been separated so long and

163

whom he was anxious to rejoin. It was more than likely that they had left the oasis and had come a long distance to the north, but where they were now was another of the serious problems that confronted him from day to day. In a wilderness so vast four men were like the proverbial needle in the haystack.

But Henry trusted to luck, which in his mind was no luck at all, rather the favor of the greater powers which had watched over him in his flight and which had not withdrawn their protection on his return, as the king of the beavers had shown. All the following day he fled southward, despite the heavy pack he carried, and made great speed. Here, he judged, the winter had not been severe, since the melting of the great snow that he had encountered on his way toward the lake, and he slept the next night in the lee of a hill, his blankets and the painted coat still being sufficient for his comfort.

At noon of the next day, coming into low ground, mostly a wilderness of bushes and reeds, he heard shots and soon discovered that they came from the rifles and muskets of Indians hunting buffalo and deer, which could not easily escape them in the marshes. For fear of leaving a trail, sure to be seen in such soft ground, he lay very close in a dense thicket of bushes until night, which was fortunately very dark, came. Then he made off under cover of the darkness, and saw Indian fires both to the right and to the left of him. He passed so close to the one on his right that he heard the warriors singing the song of plenty, indicating that the day had yielded them rich store of deer and buffalo. Most of the Indians were not delicate feeders and they would probably eat until they could eat no more, then, lying in a stupor by the fire, they would sleep until morning.

He did not stop until after midnight, and slept again in the protection of a steep hill, advancing the next day through a country that seemed to swarm with warriors evidently taking advantage of the weather to refill the wigwams, which must have become bare of food. Henry, knowing that his danger had been tripled, advanced very slowly now, traveling usually by night and lying in some close covert by day. His own supplies of food fell very low, but at night, at the edge of a stream, he shot a deer that came down to drink, and carried away the best portions of the body. He took the risk because he believed that if the Indians heard the shot they would think it was fired by one of their own number, or at least would think so long enough for him to escape with his new and precious supplies.

He was correct in his calculations, as he was not able to detect any trace of immediate pursuit, and, building a low fire between two hills, he cooked and ate a tender piece of the deer meat.

That night he saw a faint light on the horizon, and believing that it came from an Indian camp, he decided to stalk it. Placing all his supplies inside the blankets and the painted robe, he fastened the whole pack to the high bough of a tree in such a manner that no roving wild animal could get them, and then advanced toward the light, which grew larger as he approached. It also became evident very soon that it was a camp, as he had inferred, but a much larger one than his original supposition. It had been pitched in a valley for the sake of shelter from cold winds, and on the western side was a dense thicket, through which Henry advanced.

The Indians were keeping no watch, as they had nothing to guard against, and he was able to come so near that he could see into the whole bowl, where fully two hundred warriors sat about a great fire, eating all kinds of game and enjoying to the full the warmth and food of savage life. Henry, although they were his natural foes, felt a certain sympathy with them. He understood their feelings. They had gone long in their villages, half starved, while the great snow and the great cold lasted, but now they were in the midst of plenty that they had obtained by their skill and tenacity in hunting. So they rejoiced as they supplied the wants of the primeval man.

The scene was wild and savage to the last degree. Most of the warriors, in the heat of the fires, had thrown off their blankets, and they were bare to the waist, their brown bodies heavily painted and gleaming in the firelight. Every man roasted or broiled for himself huge pieces of buffalo, deer or wild turkey over the coals, and then sat down on the ground, Turkish fashion, and ate.

At intervals a warrior would spring to his feet and, waving aloft a great buffalo bone, would dance back and forth, chanting meanwhile some fierce song of war or the chase. Others would join him, and a dozen, perhaps twenty, would be leaping and contorting their bodies and singing as if they had been seized by a madness. The remainder went on with the feast, which seemed to have no ending.

The wind rose a little and blew, chill, through the forest. The dry boughs rustled against one another, and the flames wavered, but roared the louder as the drafts of air fanned them to greater strength. The warriors, heated by the heaps of coals and the vast quantities of food they were devouring, felt the cold not at all. Instead, the remaining few who wore their blankets threw them off, and there was a solid array of naked brown bodies, glistening with paint and heat. Innumerable sparks rose from the fires and floated high overhead, to die there against the clear, cold skies. When a group of singers and dancers ceased, another took its place, and the fierce, weird chant never stopped, the wintry forest continually giving back its echoes.

The wilderness spectacle had a remarkable fascination for Henry, who understood it so well, and, knowing that there was little danger from men who were spending their time in what to them was a festival, he crept closer, but was still well hidden in the dense thicket. Then his pulses gave a great leap, as four figures which had been on the other side of the fire came distinctly into his view. They were Red Eagle, head chief of the Shawnees; Yellow Panther, head chief of the Miamis; and the renegades, Braxton Wyatt and Moses Blackstaffe, who had pursued him so long and with such tenacity. They were talking earnestly, and he crept to the very edge of the thicket, where scarcely three feet divided him from the open.

He knew that only a chance would bring the four near enough for him to understand their words, but after a half hour's waiting the chance came. Blackstaffe, who took precedence over Wyatt because of his superior years and experience, was doing most of the talking, and the subject, chance or coincidence bringing it about, was Henry himself.

"The warriors discovered a white trail, the trail of one," said the renegade, "but we don't know it was Ware's. He may have perished in the great freeze, and if so we are well rid of a dangerous foe, an eye that has always watched over our movements, and a bold spirit that always takes the alarm to the settlements below. I give him full credit for all his skill and courage, but I'd rather his bones were lying in the forest, picked clean by the wolves."

Henry felt a little thrill of satisfaction. "Picked clean by the wolves?" Why, the wolves themselves had saved him once!

"I don't think he's dead," said Braxton Wyatt. "I don't know why, but I believe I understand him better than any of you do. I tell you he's even stronger and more resourceful than you suppose! Look how often he has escaped us, when we were sure we held him fast! He'd find a way to live in the big freeze, or anywhere. I've an idea that he's back up there by the lake somewhere, and that the trail the warriors found was that of another of the five, perhaps the traces of the fellow Shif'less Sol."

Henry's pulse leaped again, now with joy. The shiftless one had not been taken nor slain, and doubtless none of the others either, or they would have referred to it. But he waited to hear more, and not a dead leaf nor a twig stirred in the thicket, he was so still.

"It seems strange," said Blackstaffe, thoughtfully, "that we have not been able to take him, when more than a thousand warriors were in the hunt, carried on without stopping, except during the big snow and the big freeze. And the warriors are the best in the west, men who can come pretty near seeing a trail through the air, men without fear. It almost seems to me that there's been something miraculous about it."

Then one of the chiefs spoke for the first time, and it was Yellow Panther, the Miami.

"Blackstaffe has spoken the truth," he said. "Ware is helped by evil spirits, spirits evil to us, else he could not have slipped from our traps so often. He has powerful medicine that calls them to his aid when danger surrounds him."

Yellow Panther spoke with all the gravity and earnestness that became a great Miami chief, and, as he finished, he looked up at the skies from which the fugitive had summoned spirits to his help. The great Shawnee chief, Red Eagle, standing by his side, nodded in emphatic confirmation. Henry felt a peculiar quiver run through his blood. Had he really received miraculous help, as the two chiefs thought? Lying there in such a place at such a time there was much to make him think as they did.

"We've spread a mighty net, and we've caught nothing," said Braxton Wyatt, deep disappointment showing in his tone. "We've not only failed to get the leader of the five, but we've failed to take a single one of them."

Now Henry's heart gave a great leap. He had inferred that all of his comrades were yet safe, but here was positive proof in the words of Wyatt. Why had he ever feared? He might have known that when he drew off the Indian power they would be able to take care of themselves.

"I think," said Blackstaffe, "that we'd better continue our march to the south, and also keep a large force in the north. If we don't stumble upon him in a week or two our chance will be gone, at least until next spring. All the wild fowl flew south very early and the old men and women of the tribes have foretold the longest and hardest winter in two generations. Is it not so, Yellow Panther?"

"The cold will be so great that all the warriors will have to seek their wigwams," replied the Miami chief, "and they will stay there many days and nights, hanging over the fires. The war trail will be deserted and the Ice King will rule over the forest."

"I've no doubt the old men and old women are right," said Braxton Wyatt, "and you make me shiver now when you tell me what they say. Perhaps the spirits will turn over to our side and give all the five into our hands."

They moved on out of hearing, but Henry now knew enough.

167

His comrades were untaken and he understood their plan of campaign. If he and the four could evade it a little longer, a mighty winter would shut in, and that would be the end. He was glad he had come to spy upon the host. He had been rewarded more richly than he had hoped. Now he crept silently away, but for a long time, whenever he looked back, he still saw the luminous glow of the great fires on the dusky horizon.

He was so sure that no warriors would come, or, if they did come, that his trained faculties would give him warning in time, that he slept in a thicket within two miles of the camp. He was up before dawn and on the southern trail, knowing that the Indian host would soon be on the same course, though going more slowly. His trail lay to the east of that which had led him north, but the country was of the same general character. Everywhere, save for the little prairies, it was wooded densely, and the countless streams, whether creeks or brooks, were swollen by the winter thaw.

The desire to rejoin his comrades was very strong upon Henry, and he began to look for proofs that they had been in that region. He knew their confidence in him, their absolute faith that he would elude the pursuit and return in time. Therefore they would be waiting for him, and wherever they had passed they would leave signs in the hope that he might see them. So, as he fled, he watched not only for his enemies, but for the trail of his friends.

He was compelled to swim a large river, and the cold was so great that he risked everything and built a fire, before which he warmed and dried himself, staying there nearly two hours. A half hour before he left, he saw distant smoke on his right and then smoke equally distant on his left. Each smoke was ascending in spiral rings, and he knew that they were talking together. He knew also that their engrossing topic was his own smoke rising directly between. A fantastic mood seized him, and he decided to take a part in the conversation. Passing one of his blankets back and forth over his own fire, he, too, sent up a series of rings, sometimes at regular intervals, and again with long breaks between.

It was a weird and drunken chain of signals and he knew that it would set the Indians on the right and the Indians on the left to wondering. They would try their best to read his signals, which he could not read himself; they would strive to put in them meaning, where there was no meaning at all; and he worked with the blanket and the smoke with as much zest and zeal as he had shown at any time in his flight for life.

No such complicated signals had ever before been sent up in the wilderness, and he enjoyed the perplexity of the warriors to the utmost as he saw them talking to one another and also trying frantically to talk to him. The more they said, the more he said and the more complicated was the way in which he said it, until the smoke on his right and the smoke on his left began to sweep around in gusts of indignation and disappointment.

His fantastic humor deepened. He sincerely hoped that Blackstaffe was at the foot of one smoke and that Braxton Wyatt was at the foot of the other, and the more they were puzzled and vexed the better it suited his temper. He sent up the most extraordinary spirals of smoke. Sometimes they rose straight up in the heavens, now they started off to the right, and then they started off to the left. Although they meant nothing, one could imagine that they meant anything or everything. They were a frantic call for help or an insistent message that the trail of the fugitive had been discovered, or merely a wild statement that the night was not going to be cold, nor the next day either, or an exchange of compliments, or whatever those who saw the things chose to imagine.

After hoping for a while so intensely that Braxton Wyatt and Blackstaffe were on either side of him, Henry felt sure it was true, so ready is eager hope to turn its belief into a fact, and he rejoiced anew at their vexation, laughing silently and long. Then he abruptly kicked the coals apart, smothered the smoke, and taking up his pack fled again, much amused and much heartened, for further efforts. He could not remember when he had spent a more enjoyable half hour.

He maintained his flight until far after midnight, when, coming into stony ground, he found excellent shelter under a great ledge, one projecting so widely that when he awoke in the morning and found it raining, he was quite dry. It poured heavily until the afternoon, and he did not stir from his covert, but, wrapped in the painted coat and blankets, and taking occasional strips of the deer meat, he enjoyed the period of rest.

It rained so hard that he could not see more than fifty yards away, and in the ravine before his ledge the water ran in a cold stream. The forest looked desolate and mournful, and he would have been desolate and mournful himself if it had not been for the single fact that he was able to keep dry. That made all the difference in the world, and the contrast between his own warm and sheltered lair and the chill and dripping woods and thickets merely heightened his sense of comfort.

When the rain stopped it was followed by an extremely cold night that froze everything tight. Every tree, bush and the earth itself was covered with glittering ice, a vast and intricate network, a wilderness in white and silver. It was alike beautiful and majestic, and it made its full appeal to Henry, but at the same time he knew that his difficulties had been increased. He would have to walk over ice, and, as he passed through the thickets, fragments of ice brushed from the twigs would fall about him. For a while, at least, the Ice Age had returned. It was sure, too, to make game very scarce, as all the animals would stay in their coverts as long as they could at such a time, and he must replenish his supplies of food soon. But that was a difficulty to which he gave only a passing thought. Others pressed upon him with more immediate force.

His moccasins had become worn from long use and they slipped on the ice as if it were glass. He met this difficulty by cutting pieces from one of the blankets and tying them tightly over his feet with thin strips from his buckskin garments. He was then able to walk without slipping, and he made good progress again through the forest, the exertion of travel keeping him warm. Meanwhile he watched everywhere for a sign, a sign from the four, keeping an especial eye for the trees, for it was upon them that the forest runners wrote their letters to one another. In his soul he craved such a letter and he did not really know how intensely he craved it. The bonds of friendship that united the five were the ties of countless hardships and dangers shared, and not one of them would have hesitated an instant to risk his life for any one of the others.

It was characteristic of Henry's patience and thoroughness that, though he found nothing, he kept on looking. He wanted a letter, and he wanted it so long and with so much concentration that he began to believe he would find it. It was only a short letter that he wished, merely a word from his friends saying they had passed that way. A straight, tall figure, with eager, questing eyes, he went on through the silver forest. When the light wind blew, fragments of the ice that sheathed every bough and twig fell about him and rattled like silver coins as they struck the ice below, but mostly the air was quiet, and the glow from a mighty setting sun began to shoot such deep tints through the silver that it was luminous with red gold. Thinking little now of its beauty and majesty, the hunter pressed on, not the hunter of men nor even a hunter of game, but a hunter for a word.

The mighty sun sank farther. Most of the gold in its rays was gone, and it burned with an intense red fire, lighting up the icy forest with the glow of an old, old world. Henry still looked. The dark would come soon, when he must abandon the search for the word and seek shelter instead. But his hope was still high that he would find it before night closed down.

When the red glow was at its deepest he saw in the very core and heart of it that for which he was looking. Eye-high on the stalwart trunk of an oak were four parallel slashes from the keen blade of a tomahawk. They could not have been put there by chance. A powerful hand had wielded the weapon and the four cuts were precisely horizontal and close together. He had found his word. It was as plain as day. The four had passed there and they had left for him a letter telling him all about it. This was only the first paragraph in the letter, and he would find others farther on, but he devoted a little time to the examination of the first.

He studied minutely the cuts and the cloven edges of the bark, and he decided that they were at least two weeks old. So the letter had been posted some time since, and doubtless its writers had gone on to another region. But if they posted one letter they would post others, and he felt now that communication had been established. True, the chain connecting them was long, but it could be shortened inch by inch.

He made a series of widening circles about the tree, looking for the second paragraph of the letter, and he found it about a hundred yards to the eastward, exactly like the first, four parallel slashes of a tomahawk, eye-high, deep into the trunk of a stalwart oak. He found a third paragraph precisely like the first and the second, a hundred yards farther on, and then no more. But three were enough. They indicated clearly the course of the four which was into the northeast. In the morning he would change his own direction to conform with theirs.

The letter gave him a great surge of the heart, but the night came down quickly, dark and cold, the bitter wind blew again, and the ice fell about him in a rain of chill crystals. He knew that the temperature was falling fast, and that it would be his hardest night so far. He must have a fire, risk or no risk, and it was a full three hours before he was able to coax one from dead wood that he dragged from sheltered recesses. Then it felt so good that he built a second, intending to sleep between them. His supply of food was low, but knowing how needful it was to preserve his strength and the full fresh flow of his blood, he ate of it heartily, and, then when the ground, wet between the fires from the melted ice, had been dried by the heat, he made his bed and slept well, although he awoke once in the night and finding the cold intense put fresh wood on the fires.

The next morning was one of the coldest he had felt, and he was reluctant to leave the beds of coals, but his comrades had given him a sign, and he would not dream of ignoring it. He threw ice upon the fires, and with a sigh felt their heat disappear. Then he followed the trail to the northeast, hunting at intervals for a renewal of the sign lest he go wrong. Three times he found it, always the four cuts, eye-high, always in the trunk of a stalwart oak, and always they led in the direction in which he was going. The cuts were very deep, and he was quite sure that they had been made by Shif'less Sol, who added to remarkable strength wonderful cunning and mastery in the use of a tomahawk.

About noon, he came to a vast, shallow, flooded area, a third of a mile or more across, but extending farther to north and south than he could see either way. Doubtless the four had crossed there before the heavy rains made the flood, and as he was unwilling to take the long circuit to north or south he decided to make the passage on the ice which was thick and strong.

He had been so free from danger for some time that he took little thought of it now, but when it was absent from his mind it came. When he was well out upon the ice he heard the crack of a rifle behind him and a bullet whizzed by his ear. He ran forward at great speed before he looked back, and then he saw a dozen warriors standing at the edge of the ice, but making no motion to pursue. As he was now out of range, he stopped and examined them, wondering why they did not follow him. The solution came quickly.

The band suddenly united in a tremendous war whoop and from the woods on the other side of the ice came an answering whoop. He was trapped between them, and they could afford to be deliberate. His heart sank, but as usual his courage came back in an instant, stronger than ever. Alert, resourceful, the best marksman in all the West, he did not mean to be taken or slain, and he looked about for the means of defense. As it was not a lake, upon the frozen surface of which he stood, merely a great shallow flooded area, there were clumps of bushes and little islands of earth here and there, and he ran to one not twenty feet away, a tiny place, well covered with big bushes. The Indians, seeing him take refuge, set up a yell from both shores, and Henry, settling down in his covert, waited for them to make the first move.

He knew that the warriors would be deliberate. Considering their victim secure in the trap, they would reckon time of no value, and would take no unnecessary risk. He believed they were hunting bands, not those that had trailed him directly, and that his encounter with them was chance, a piece of bad fortune, nothing more than he should expect after such a long run of good fortune.

Warriors of the different bands sent far signals to one another across the ice, and then slowly and with care each party built a large fire, around which the men sat basking in the heat, and now and then, with a cry or two, taunting the fugitive whom they considered so tight in the trap. The red gleam of the flames upon the ice, contrasting with his own situation, struck a chill into Henry. The wind had a clear sweep over the frozen lagoon, and the rustling of the icy bushes above him was like a whisper from the cold. He wrapped himself thoroughly in the painted coat and the two blankets, put the rifle in front of him, where he could snatch it up instantly, and beat his hands together at times to keep them warm, and at other times held them under the blankets.

He understood human nature, and he knew that they were rejoicing in their own comfort, while he might be freezing. They felt that way because it was their way, and he did not blame them. It was merely his business to thwart their plans, so far as they concerned himself. He recognized that it was a contest in which only superior skill could defeat superior numbers, and he summoned to his aid every faculty he possessed.

The Indians did not move for an hour, luxuriating by their fires, and occasionally taunting him with cries. Then four warriors from either shore went upon the ice at the same time, and began to advance slowly toward his island, making use of the clumps of bushes that thrust here and there through the frozen surface of the lagoon.

Henry slipped his hands from the blankets and watched both advancing parties with swift glances, right and to left. They were using shelter and advancing very slowly, but beyond a certain point both were bound to come in range. He smiled a little. Much of his forest life recently had been in the nature of an idyll, but now the wild man in him was uppermost. They came to kill and they would find a killer.

He knelt among the bushes, which were thin enough to allow him a clear view in every direction, and put his powder horn and bullet pouch on the snow in front of him. He could reload with amazing rapidity. They did not know that. Nor did they know that they were advancing upon the king of riflemen. Naturally, they would suppose him to be a wandering hunter lost in a dangerous region.

The party on the west presently began to pass from the shelter of one tuft of bushes to another, twenty yards away, and in doing so the four were wholly exposed. It was a long shot, much too long for any of the Indians, but not too long for Henry. He fired at the leading warrior, and, before he had time to see him crashing on the

173

ice, he was reloading his rifle with all the speed of dexterous fingers. He heard a yell of rage from the Indians, and, glancing up, saw the three dragging away the body of the fallen man. But the party on the other side, knowing that his rifle had been emptied, but not knowing with what speed he could reload, came running.

His weapon flashed a second time, and with the same deadly aim. The leading warrior in the second party fell also, dead, when his body touched the ice, and his comrades gave back in fear. They had not known such terrible sharpshooting before, and the man whom they had thought so securely in the trap must have two rifles at least. Both parties, carrying their dead with them, retreated swiftly to shore, and gathered about the fires again.

Henry reloaded a second time, patted affectionately the rifle that had served him so well, put it once more in front of him, and sheltered his hands as before under the blankets. The bands had received a dreadful lesson. The loss of two good warriors was not to be passed over lightly, and he knew they would delay some time before taking further action. Meanwhile, the night was coming fast and the cold was increasing so greatly that it alarmed him, despite the blankets and the painted robe. The wind sweeping over the frozen surface of the lagoon had an edge that cut like steel. The very blood in his veins seemed to grow chill, and he felt alarm lest his hands grow too stiff with cold to handle the rifle. The bushes, although they hid him from a distant enemy, did not afford much protection. Instead, they were like so many icicles.

The two bands built their fires higher, until the flames threw a glow far out on the ice, and Henry saw their hovering figures outlined in black against the red. They filled him with anger, because they could maintain the siege in comfort, while he had to fight not only a human foe, but the paralyzing cold as well. He stood up now, stretched his arms, stamped his feet and exercised himself in every manner of which he could think, until a certain amount of warmth came to his body. But he knew it would not last long. Presently the cold would settle back fiercer and more intense than ever.

The night advanced, the dusk deepened and the siege of Henry by the warriors and the cold grew more formidable. He was anxious for the Indians to make another attack, but he knew now they would not do it. They would wait patiently for the fugitive in the trap to fall inert into their hands. After all he was in the trap! And it was a trap worse than any other he had ever met. Then he said fiercely to himself that he might be in the trap, but he would break out of it.

174

For the second time, he took violent physical exercise to drive away the creeping and paralyzing cold, and then he resolved upon his plan to burst the trap. The night was fairly dark with streamers of cloud floating across the heavens, and it might grow darker. Far to north and south stretched the glimmering white ice, with dark spots here and there, where the clumps of bushes or trees thrust themselves above the frozen surface.

Wrapping himself as thoroughly as he could, and yet in the best way to leave freedom of action, he crept from the bushes and bending low on the ice ran to a clump about thirty yards to the south, where he crouched a while, watching the warriors at the two fires. He could still see very clearly their figures outlined in a black tracery against the flames, and they might have sentinels posted nearer, but evidently his own change of base had not been suspected. Perhaps the fear of his deadly rifle kept them from coming so near that they could see his movements, and they relied upon the great cold to hold him within the original clump of bushes. The blood in his veins that had grown chill seemed suddenly to turn warm again. Even a passage of a few yards from one little island to another was enough to create hope. There was no trap so tight in which he could not find a crevice, or make one, and he prepared for the second stage in his journey, a cluster of trees a full hundred yards to the south.

He would have dropped to his hands and knees if it had not been for the fear of freezing his fingers, a risk that he could not afford to take for a moment, alone in the desolate wilderness and surrounded by deadly perils. So he merely stooped low and ran for the trees, the wrappings of blanket on his feet saving him from slipping.

But he gained them and there was yet no alarm. The black tracery of the Indian figures still showed before the fires, where they were hovering for the sake of the grateful heat, and, as well as he could judge, his flight was unsuspected.

The third island was much better than the first two. Although it was only eight or ten yards across, it supported a cluster of large trees, and had a little dip in the center, in which he lay, while the cruel wind was broken off by the trees or passed over his head. There was an access of warmth, and he had a tremendous temptation to lie there, but he fought it. It was hard to distinguish warmth from numbness, and, if he remained without motion, he would surely freeze to death, despite the trees and the dip.

Reluctantly he began the fourth stage in his flight, and his reluctance was all the greater because the island for which he was making was at least three hundred yards away, and the wind, cold as the Pole and cruel as death, was rising to a hurricane. It made him waver as he ran, and his fingers almost froze to his rifle. But he reached the fourth island, where he sank down exhausted, the fierce wind having taken his breath for the time. The fires now were far away and he could not distinguish the Indians from the flames, but he did not believe any of them had come upon the ice to attack him or to spy him out. While the tremendous cold almost paralyzed him, it would also withhold their advance upon him for a while.

He rose from his covert and started again, although he felt that he was growing weaker. Such intense exertion, under such conditions, was bound to tell even upon a frame like his, but he would not let himself falter, passing from island to island, resting a little at every one, bearing toward the southeast, and intending to enter the forest about a mile from the fire on that side. Meanwhile, the chill of the deadly cold and elation over his escape fought for the mastery of him. He reached the last little island, scarcely ten yards from the shore, and as he stepped upon it, two dusky figures threw themselves upon him.

Henry was thrown back upon the ice, but though the blow was like a lightning flash, he realized, in an instant, what it meant. The warriors had not been wholly paralyzed by the cold, and they had stationed guards at other points along the lagoon to prevent his escape, but these two were seeking so hard to protect themselves from the cruel wind that they had not seen him until he was upon them. Knowing that the question of his life or death would be decided within the next half minute, he put forth every ounce of his mighty strength, and swept the two warriors together in his arms.

His rifle clattered upon the ice, and with the two men clinging to him, struggling vainly to reach tomahawk or knife, he rose to his feet, still clutching the warriors. But the feet of all three slipped from under them, and down they went again with a tremendous impact. The warriors were on the underside, and Henry fell upon them. There was a rending crash, as the ice, thinner at that point, owing to the protection of the island, broke beneath the blow.

Henry felt the grappling fingers slip from him, and he sprang back just in time to see the two warriors sink into a narrow but icy gulf, from which they never rose again. Uttering a cry of horror, he picked up his rifle and ran for the forest. He knew that chance, or perhaps the will of the greater powers, had saved him again, but, as he ran, he shuddered many times, not from the cold, but at the ghastly fate that had overtaken the warriors. The impression faded by and by. When one is in a bitter struggle for life he does not have time to think long of the fate of others, and the savage wilderness through which he fled was too bitter of aspect then to breed a long pity.

He was quite sure that he had shaken off the Indians, for the time, anyhow, and again the vital question with him was warmth. The running was bringing a measure of it, but he could not run forever, and he soon sank to a walk in order to save himself. But he maintained this gait for a long time, in truth, until dawn was only three or four hours away, and then he decided that he would build a fire. It was a risk, but he chose to take the smaller risk in order to drive off the greater.

It never before took him so long to kindle his blaze. He found a place sheltered from the wind, whittled many shavings from dead wood, and used his flint and steel until his hands ached, coaxing forth the elusive sparks and trying to make them ignite the wood. They died by hundreds, but, after infinite industry and patience, they took hold, and he sheltered the tiny and timid blaze with his body, lest it change its mind and go away after all. Though it sank several times, it concluded finally to stay and grow, and, having decided, it showed vigor, burning fast while Henry fed it.

As the fire threw out abundant heat he reveled in it. Now he knew better than ever before that fire was life. He could feel the blood which had seemed to be ice in his veins thawing and flowing in a full warm flood again. The beat of his heart grew stronger and the stiff hands acquired their old flexibility. His face stung at first, but he rubbed ice over it, and presently it too responded to the grateful heat. An immense comfort seized him and he felt drowsy. Comfort would become luxury if he could lie down and sleep, but he knew too much to yield to the demands of his body. After spending two hours by the fire and becoming thoroughly soaked in heat, he put out the coals and went on again. As he walked, he ate the last of his food, and now he must soon find more. The problem of his escape from the Indians had been solved, but the problem of finding his comrades was upon his mind, though it must be put off while he solved that of food.

He considered it a miracle that his rifle had not gone into the water with the two warriors. But was it a miracle? Was it not rather another intercession of the greater powers in his favor? Alone in the wilderness at such a time a rifle was at least half of life, even more, it was the very staff of it. Without it he would surely perish. He patted the rifle with the genuine affection one must feel for so true a weapon. It was a fine rifle, beautiful in his eyes, with a long, slender barrel of blued steel, and a polished and carved stock. It had never failed him, and he knew that it would not fail him now.

He thought of the rabbits which had been such an abundant resource once. Many of them must be in their nests under the ice and snow, and he searched for hours but found none. Yet he could go two or three days without food, and he did not despair, showing all his usual pertinacity, never ceasing to look. The hunt led him into rocky ground, and, between the ledges, he noticed an opening that caused him to take a second look. Several coarse hairs were on the stone at the entrance, and when he saw them he knew. It was his animal brother at home, and he did not forget his gratitude, but he must live.

He seized a long stick and thrust it savagely inside. The bear, awakened from the winter sleep which he had begun luxuriously not long ago, growled fiercely and rushed out. Then Henry snatched up his rifle and shot him. The bear had lost much of his fat, but he was a perfect treasure house of supplies, nevertheless, and steaks from his body were soon broiling over the coals. Henry, remembering how much food he needed in such intense cold, and, while he was undergoing physical exertions so great, ate heavily. As much more as he could conveniently carry he added to his pack, knowing that he could freeze it at night, and that it would keep indefinitely. He would have liked the bearskin too, but he did not care to add so much to his burden, and so he left it reluctantly.

He was a new man now, made over completely. The wilderness, so far from being desolate and hostile, took on its old comfortable aspects. It was a provider of food and shelter to one who knew how to find them, and certainly none knew better than he. The wants of the body being satisfied, he began to plan anew for the junction with his comrades. The great cold would not last much longer. A temperature twenty or thirty degrees below zero never endured more than a few days. Like as not, it would break up in a warm rain, to be followed by moderate weather, and then he could hunt the trail of the four in comfort.

His pack was much heavier when he started and the icy coating of the earth was still slippery, but he made excellent progress, and he was able to fix in his mind the direction in which the marks on the trees had pointed. He knew that he must turn back somewhat toward the north in order to reach that line, and such a change in his course would increase the danger from the Indians, but he did not hesitate. He made the angle at once, and then he began to observe the trees with all the patience and minuteness of which a forest runner in such a crisis was capable.

It was almost dusk when he found the sign, four slashes of a tomahawk, eye-high on the stalwart trunk of an oak, and a hundred

178

yards farther on a similar sign. He traced them fully a mile, and then as the night shut down, dark and impenetrable, he was compelled to stop. He dared another fire, the cold was so intense, and began his journey again the next morning over the ice.

The rise in the temperature that he had expected did not occur, nor were there any signs of a change. Evidently the great cold had come to stay much longer than usual, and, while it hindered his own journey, it also hindered possible pursuit by the Indians, of whom he saw no traces anywhere until the third day after he had killed the bear. Then he observed a great smoke in the south, and he approached near enough to discover that it was an Indian village, probably Shawnees. It seemed to be snowed up for the winter, holed up like a bear, and, anticipating no danger from it, he continued his leisurely hunt eastward.

He lost the traces for a whole day, but recovered them the next morning, and now they were much fresher. Sap, not yet dead in some of the trees, had oozed but lately into the cuts, and his heart beat very hard. His comrades could not be far away. He might reach them the next day or the day after, and now he was actuated by a curious motive, and yet it was not curious, when his character is considered.

He built a fire by the side of one of the pools, with which the forest was filled. Breaking the ice and daring the fierce chill of the water, he took a quick bath. Then, while he was wrapped in the blankets and the painted coat, he washed all his clothing thoroughly, as he had done once before, and dried it by the fire. When he was able to put it on again, he washed the blankets in their turn and dried them. He would have served the painted coat in a similar manner, but, as that was impossible, he rubbed and pounded it thoroughly.

His forest toilet complete, Henry felt himself a new man once more, inwardly and outwardly, freshened up, made presentable to the eye. He knew that he was haggard and worn. Hercules himself would have been, after such a flight and pursuit, but at least he was dressed as a forest runner, neat by nature and careful in his attire, should be.

Now he followed the traces with renewed strength and speed, and he found that they came more closely together, a fact indicating the absence of Indians from the immediate region, as the four would not leave so broad a trail, unless they knew it would not bring a strong force of Indians upon them. Straight now it led, and he crossed numerous frozen streams and pools or lagoons, and then the night that he felt sure was to be the last one came, as bitterly cold as ever.

The next morning he did not put out his fire as usual, instead he built it up higher, and, passing one of the blankets rapidly back and forth over it, sent up ring after ring of smoke. They did not thin away and vanish until they were high in the clear, intensely cold blue sky.

When his eyes had followed the rings a little while he turned them toward the eastern horizon and watched there closely. Despite all the efforts of his will his heart throbbed hard. Would the answer come? He waited a full half hour, and then his pulses gave a great leap. Rings of smoke began to rise there under the sky's rim a full mile away, ascending like his own into the cold air, where, high up, they thinned away and vanished. Then his pulses gave another great leap as a second series of rings rose close beside the first, to be followed quickly by a third and a fourth. Four fires and four groups of smoke rings rising into the air! The last doubt disappeared. Paul, the shiftless one, the silent one, and Long Jim were there. Doubtless they had signaled before, and now at last he had called to them.

In his wild exultation he kicked the coals of his own fire apart and started swiftly toward the four groups of smoke rings. On his way he sent forth a long thrilling cry that pierced and echoed far through the wintry forest, and like the distant song of a bugle a similar cry came back. As he broke into a run, four human figures appeared upon the crest of a low hill and burst into a simultaneous shout. Then they exclaimed, also together:

"Henry!"

After that, although their emotion was deep, they made no great show of it. The border was always terse.

"I knowed you'd shake 'em off, Henry," said the shiftless one.

"But it must have been a long chase," said Paul.

"Wish I'd been with you," said Long Jim.

"Big work," said Tom Ross.

"I didn't do it all my myself," said Henry. "I was helped by the people of the forest. They came to my aid again and again."

Paul looked at him wondering, and Henry told them how he had been warned by the animals one after another, and he could not believe it was mere chance.

"The woods are full o' strange things," said Shif'less Sol, thoughtfully. "An' I never try to explain 'em all to myse'f. I let 'em go fur what they are."

"How has it been with all of you?" asked Henry.

"We stayed a long time on the oasis in the swamp," replied Paul, "and then we started toward the north, hanging on to the rear of the pursuit, and trying for a chance to help you, though we never found it. At last the great cold made us seek shelter, but we were sure it would compel the warriors to abandon the chase and drive them into their villages."

"After all, it was King Winter that intervened finally in my behalf."

"That's true. And while we were hovering about, hoping to help you, we left the long trail which I suppose you saw."

"Yes, I came upon it, and it led me to you."

"An' now," said Shif'less Sol, "sence all the warriors hev been drove into winter quarters, an' none o' us hez been killed or took, s'pose we go into them kind a' quarters ourselves, an' keep warm."

"Whar?" asked Silent Tom.

"Why, our old hollow in the cliff!" exclaimed Paul. "The warriors would not think of marching against it again before next spring, if at all, and it's the warmest, safest and finest place in all the wilderness."

"A good choice," said Henry.

"Right thar we'll go," said Shif'less Sol.

"Ez soon ez we kin make tracks fur it," said Long Jim.

"Shore," said Tom Ross.

They started at once, and all things turned in their favor. The wilderness remained frozen and bitter cold, but there was no pursuit. By all rules, game should have been scarce at such a time, but they found plenty of it. Day after day they traveled through the woods, crossing the Ohio on the ice, and at last they drew near the rocky home they had defended so valiantly, and which once more extended to them a silent welcome.

Now they built their fires anew, killed game and obtained abundant supplies of food and furs, though for two weeks Henry was not allowed to join the others in the chase, resting like Hercules after his mighty labors. Then, while the great cold lasted, they, the eyes of the woods, built up their strength and spirit for new labors and dangers in the spring.